EARLY DEPARTURES

EARLY
DEPARTURES

justin a. reynolds

KATHERINE TEGEN BOOKS
An Imprint of HarperCollins Publishers

Katherine Tegen Books is an imprint of HarperCollins Publishers.

ISBN 978-0-06-274840-9

Typography by David DeWitt
20 21 22 23 24 PC/LSCH 10 9 8 7 6 5 4 3 2 1

First Edition

To all those no longer with us, who are still with us

I hope the leaving is joyful—and I hope never to return.

—Frida Kahlo

facts

In 1785, French chemist Antoine Lavoisier discovers that matter can neither be created nor destroyed.

Fifty-five years later, German physician Julius Robert Mayer concludes the same is true of energy.

Sixty more years later, Albert Einstein gives us $E=mc^2$.

Which means mass and energy are exchangeable, and therefore, the total amount of mass and energy in the Universe is constant.

There will always be the same amount of energy and matter.

I say this because if matter doesn't die, if energy can't die, then no one really dies.

Five years.

Five thousand.

Five billion.

You will still be here.

So, before they close their eyes for the last time, when they promise you—

I'll always be with you, I'm everywhere you are.

They will.

They are.

When tragedy strikes—and no, I don't mean the barbarism of watching someone pour milk *before* cereal, or laboring to make that last square of toilet paper, the one superglued to the cardboard, be enough.

I mean, *actual* tragedy.

Like, when no one wants to tell you your parents are dead.

Like, when your stupid brain can't decide which outfit—if the dress, the suit you chose, is what they'd want to wear forever.

Like, when your best friend really needs you, but you're gone, baby, gone.

See, actual tragedy monsters your heart.

Actual tragedy saws you in half.

Before and After.

Like cheesy weight-loss commercials where on one side you're chubby, bald, bad posture, bacne—and then you swallow a magic capsule and *voilà!*, you're eighteen-pack abs, more hair than five woolly mammoths, and astonishingly clear skin.

Look, they're saying, this is you then, but this is you now.

That's tragedy: a hard pill you swallow that changes everything.

And one day, you look in the mirror, and a stranger is there where you used to be.

You'll interrogate yourself endlessly.

If only you'd done this slower, that faster.

Now you know the true cost of a split second.

You never stop paying.

This is what no one tells you—

100

—the worst day of your life begins like any other.

The sun shows up before you want.

You left the fan on all night, your throat's scratchy, nose itchy.

You claw sleep from your eyes.

Press your feet into carpet, curl your toes.

The kitchen tile's freezing.

It's June in Ohio so it's eighty degrees, or thirty-five inches of rain, or snowflakes.

You rifle through cabinets, the pantry. Pillage two Pop-Tarts, eat them raw.

You dash back upstairs, bang on the bathroom door, yell at your sister for hogging the hot water.

Dad materializes in the hallway, says if you want he'll boil water on the stove, pour it over your head, *same as a shower*, he claims.

Only with third-degree burns, you fire back.

His laugh's a breathy hiss, like a snake gasping.

You cannonball into your parents' bed, pillows scattering in your wake, but Mom doesn't look away from her book, says your breath stinks even though you're nowhere near her nose. So you logroll over to her, blow all that hot pastiness into her face, and she pushes your head away, says *boy, if you don't quit*, but she's trying not to laugh, and your lips aim for her cheek but she bobs and you glance her eyebrow.

The bathroom door bursts open, your sister shouts *happy now?* from the hallway, then slams her bedroom door shut.

So yeah.

A day you couldn't pick out of a lineup.

A day like most before it.

Except on June eighth, at 11:43 in the morning, your life, your entire world, snaps in two. Forevermore, there is only before 11:43 and after 11:43.

No one tells you this. That your life is always a few shitty seconds from absolute devastation. From irredeemable destruction.

Because in the end, all it takes is twelve seconds, and two otherwise innocent, seemingly disconnected things merge to obliterate my life.

1. Dad continued his I-suck-at-technology ways.

2. My best friend wished my parents a happy anniversary.

23 MONTHS AFTER THE FUNERAL

also known as now

Everyone shows up to a Hills party—cool for people-watching, not cool for personal space. Tonight's party-thrower is among the more popular kids at Elytown High, meaning you gotta walk sideways to get anywhere.

"Umm, what the hell are they playing?" Autumn asks.

I shrug. "Trap-rock-bluegrass?"

"Mmm, I'm thinking alternative-emo-backpack rap."

Autumn and I slot music three ways: good, listenable, kill the DJ.

"Listenable," she says.

And I agree. Besides, expecting good music at a Hills party is like swimming in Scotland thinking you'll spot the Loch Ness Monster.

Autumn's brow slides up. "Beer?"

"I'm good," I tell her. "Gonna check out the pool."

She squeezes my hand and I'm not sure if this means *be right back* or *see you later*. She picks her way toward the keg until a couple of girls stop her to chat.

I dispense a week's worth of *hey, what up*s in the ninety seconds it takes to reach the sliding patio panels.

This view dropkicks my jaw, every time.

Standing here, the lake gobbling the horizon, black waves colliding like monster trucks, you could convince me we're at the edge of the world.

I nearly forget I'm not alone.

My chest vibrates. I pinch my phone from my shirt pocket.

I've ignored her last three calls.

"Hey, you're already at the party," Whit says, like an accusation.

"Yeah, I told you I—"

She cuts me off. "When were you gonna tell me?"

For a moment, I pretend that what follows is good, happy.

When were you gonna tell me you're really taking pride in your lawn-mowing?

When were you gonna tell me you can actually sing?

But this isn't that. This is the setup to an ongoing series I call *What's Wrong with Jamal*, starring Jamal Anderson as himself and costarring Everyone Else.

She asks again, so I bite. "Tell you *what*, Whit?"

"You're skipping class again? Really? I thought we . . ."

I hold the phone away from my ear until she stops talking. "I'm not skipping," I say into the receiver.

12

"Then how come Mrs. Sweat wants a meeting Monday?"

"Okay, I got to school the other day and I didn't feel well and..."

Whit sighs. "Dammit, Jamal. This is serious."

How long before she says *your future*?

"This is your future we're talking..."

Kids dot the lawn like pushpins. Kids in the infinity pool guzzle from red Solos, play flip-cup on the edge. This pool's a mood ring, the cool cerulean water now purpling.

When Whit finishes outlining my current path toward oblivion, I tell her:

I'm sorry.

It won't happen again.

Not to worry.

"They *will* remove you from my custody, Jamal. Is that what you want?"

This is the part where I reaffirm my commitment, where she questions if she's failing me. "I want to stay where I am," I tell her. And I mean it.

"We gotta figure this out," Whit says.

This being me.

But before I can reply, Autumn's tugging on my arm.

"I gotta go," I tell Whit, ending the call. "What's going o—" But I don't finish.

I follow Autumn's eyes across the patio just before the detonation.

His laughter trips a blast of memories, each a land mine that shrapnels through me. That goofy grin, slumped shoulders, his knees bent like he can hide his Goliath ass.

"Maybe the Universe wants you to make good," Autumn says, in a way that makes the Universe sound like some benevolent god, or at the very least, your *I'm just trying to help* mom.

Except that's not the Universe I know.

And it's definitely not the Universe that knows me.

98

Nutshelled: last time I spoke to Quincy Barrantes, I was an asshole.

I own it.

And okay, sure, we've had conversations since then, like:

'Scuse me.

Nooope.

Yeah, *lots* of those exchanges.

But mostly, I take minor precautions to ensure our paths don't intersect. Like when I flung my bike into prickly shrubs, then dived in after it. And yeah, Q ended up walking the opposite direction, but whatever.

In the interest of zero unhealthy confrontations, avoidance is the best policy.

Which, trust me, Q also appreciates; only thing he hates more than me is confrontation. Q, a magnet for bullies—how many times had I stepped in front of him? Taken blows meant for him?

"You gotta stand up for yourself, otherwise this is how it's always gonna be, Q. You wanna spend your life a human punching bag?"

But he'd push out a silly smile—I couldn't tell if he was oblivious or really that good inside. "I'd rather spread love, you know? Imagine if that's how everyone responded? With love? You'd rather live in that world, right?"

"But we don't," I'd answer, impatience boiling.

"Gotta start somewhere, right?"

To be honest, that's one of the things that irritated me most—how he'd add *right* at the end of something you wanted to disagree with.

I debate whether I should go say something.

Hey, man, some party, huh?

Hey, man, how 'bout those nachos?

Hey, man, how's life these last two years?

But when I look back, Q's gone.

And then Autumn's all—"Oh snap, my soooong!"—as she drags me to the epicenter of the human ocean.

I finally spy him leaning against the far wall, a human kick-stand.

I push through the crowd, but I'm too late, kid's already Houdini'd.

*　　*　　*

16

Autumn sets her drink down, guides her *Mighty Moat* T-shirt up and off. Unbuttons her shorts, nudges them down her hips.

And, well—

I try not to stare, but her canary-yellow two-piece is accentuating all of her accentuations, complementing her dark-brown skin like it was commissioned for her.

"You're getting in the water, J. Even if I have to harpoon your ass."

But I'm steady shaking my head. "Don't think I'm swimming tonight."

She points to my legs. "You're wearing trunks under your jeans, J."

"Yeah. Just like to be prepared for . . . different . . . scenarios."

"Like swimming?"

"I suppose swimming's a scenario, yeah."

She leads me poolward. She dives in, swims ten yards beneath the water, a black-and-yellow blur, before breaking surface, her body seesawing in the slanting-sloping waves.

"It feels great," she promises.

"Hold up. Something's happening," I say.

Everyone's rushing to the far end of the pool. Autumn's long strokes get her there ahead of me.

Most of the kids outside have formed a huddle.

Someone asks, What's your name?

"Quincy," he answers. " You can just call me Q."

I stand on tiptoes. Q's front and center, beaming.

17

Which is odd. Dude avoided attention like you avoid skunks—wide berth.

Everyone's chanting: "Q! Q! Q!" And Q gulps three cups back-to-back-to-back, each empty falling at his feet. Everyone's clapping, high-fiving, egging him on. He downs another with ease, swipes the foam from his mouth, and tosses his head back in a laughing howl.

"Q's a beast," somebody shouts.

A new chant starts: "In the pool! In the pool! In the pool!"

Q takes a tentative step forward, his posture wobbly.

"In the pool! In the pool! In the pool!"

He's at the edge now, staring into the deep end. He rocks his arms back and forth, like he's building momentum for an Olympic dive, bends at the waist like there's treasure at the bottom and he means to find it.

"In the pool! In the pool!"

But then someone yells: "Q! No! No, Q!"

The chanting stops; everyone pivoting to see the culprit.

"Booooo," a few kids shout. "You killing the vibe, man!"

And they're looking at me. I'm the vibe killer.

"We're not gonna let him drown," someone says hella casually, the way you'd say *we're not gonna let him eat another taco.*

I hustle around, grab Q's arm. "Hey, man, maybe sit this one out?"

And no, I'm not expecting gratitude—it's not like I saved

18

his life; he might've been fine in the pool—but I'm definitely not prepared for rage.

I've never seen Q angry—not like this—not even when he should've been.

"Oh snap, we've got a Jauncy sighting, guys," someone yells from the back of the yard.

A shiver moves down my spine. When's the last time someone shouted Jauncy? When's the last time someone *said* Jauncy?

And now a few more kids are yelling it.

The party host suddenly materializes beside us. "Guys, ohmigod, you gotta do a Jauncy at my party. Seriously, we need a Jauncy reunion!"

And now a new chant. "Jauncy, Jauncy, Jauncy . . ."

I ignore them, turn back to Q. "You're okay?"

But Q's boiling. "Yo, why'd you do that, man?"

"Why I'd do *what*?"

"*That*." His voice cracks the slightest. His eyes are pink and watery, but it doesn't mean tears; he could have beer in his eyes. Or sweat.

The Jauncy fervor's dying rapidly behind us.

Which, good.

Jauncy's the last thing I want to revive.

"Serious? C'mon, bro, you were dizzy. You could've cracked your head on the pool floor."

"That was mine."

"What was yours, Q?"

"Quincy."

"What?"

"Friends call me Q," he says. "Call me Quincy."

And as he walks away, I'm a civil war: brain proud he's standing up for himself. Heart wanting to run after him, ask *what the hell's wrong with you?*

Pool at my back, I look out at the lake, all that water dyed in denim moonlight.

"Harpoon readied, our world-class marine biologist zeroes in on her target," a voice narrates behind me. I turn around and I can't help but laugh. Autumn, floating in the middle of the pool, arms posed as if aiming a speargun.

I shake my head. "I don't think marine biologists use deadly weapons. Especially on animals."

"Yeah, well." She raises her arms, her right eye squinting as if peering through a scope. "This is a peaceful harpoon, designed to politely subdue, so we can tag and track water life."

"Ah. A *peaceful* harpoon. Those must be hard to find."

She shrugs. "I just hope it's strong enough. Jamals are a particularly hairy species, you see."

"Oh, really," I say, cracking up. I ball up my shirt, toss it into the grass.

"Keep it steady now," Autumn calls out. "Steady. Steady. Fire!"

Her arms recoil, and I wait a beat, then clutch my chest.

"You're right, no pain," I say, grinning. "In fact, this spear kinda tickles."

Because why worry about your former friend when your person is right in front of you?

"Get over here," Autumn says, tugging her pretend rope.

And I fall in.

97

Jamal: So, guys, you already know what time it is.

Q: So, we're just gonna get right to it. Stay tuned for another episode of . . .

Jamal & Q: JAUNCY IN THE STREETS!

CUT TO: a queue outside a movie theater

Q: What movie are you seeing?

Girl with Dreads: *Challenger's Crossing*

Q: Oh, nice. So, you like Carla Thomas?

Girl with Dreads: Love her. She's the best.

Q: Between *Yolanda's Choice, Paper or Plastic* . . .

NOT A REAL MOVIE flashes on the screen

Q: And *Carwash Cliff Gets Down in Idaho* . . .

NOT A REAL MOVIE flashes on the screen

Q: Which one was your favorite Carla Thomas performance?

Girl with Dreads: Oh, definitely *Paper or Plastic.*

Q: Yeah, what was it about that one you liked?

Girl with Dreads: She's so versatile and, like, she just made you feel every scene.

CUT TO: inside a small coffee shop

Jamal: So, this is a segment called "Tables Turned," where you get to ask us any question you want.

Barista: Hmm. I don't know.

Jamal: Literally, anything.

Barista: Are you gonna buy coffee?

CUT TO: standing outside a bookstore, with books prominently displayed in the window

J: Name one book.

Middle-Aged Man in Windbreaker: What kind of book?

J: Any book ever written.

Windbreaker: Umm . . . let me think.

J: Could've been a book you read as a kid.

Windbreaker (laughing): I was too busy having girlfriends, man. Books are for people who can't get dates.

Zoom in on Jamal's confused face

J: Okay, but just any book, doesn't have to be one you read. Literally, any book.

Windbreaker: I don't know, the Bible?

J: You're going with the Bible?

Windbreaker: Is that a book? That's not a book. It's one of those scroll things, dammit. This is making me look bad.

A chime plays and CORRECT flashes on the screen

By rule, all Hills parties migrate to the beach.

This party's easier than normal. At the back of the yard, buttressing the hillside, wind-worn stairs spiral toward the sand.

I dry off inside, small-talking, as kids descend to the shore and squirt too much lighter fluid into a woodpile—a mega bonfire is also a Hills party requirement.

The house clears fast; a few stragglers hug their goodbyes before hiking to their parked cars, but mostly everyone flocks beachward.

Autumn, flanked by her girlfriends, asks if I'm ready to head down. She's still in her yellow two-piece, except she's slipped back on her shorts; a thin yellow band peeks out over her denim waist. I tell her I'll meet her, that I wanna enjoy the view a bit longer. She kisses my cheek, whispers in my ear: "Are you okay?"

I nod, kiss her back.

But the truth is, I'm not.

Because despite my best efforts, my brain's abuzz with *what to do about Q.*

So, naturally, a moment later, I plow right into him, knocking him to the ground.

"Yo, Q, my bad, man." I extend a hand, which he ignores. "I mean, Quincy. Sorry."

He brushes himself off without a word.

"Look, I'm sorry for barreling into you. And for interfering earlier. I was just trying to . . ." I think about what Dr. Ocean's always saying at therapy, that *I can only control what I say and do, but not the response. I can't force someone to see it my way, to feel as I do.* I shake my head. "Actually, you know what? It's not important. Have a good night, Quincy."

I start for the beach, but I don't get far before spinning around. "You're not hitting the beach?" I call back.

Q tilts his head. "Nah."

"You should," I reply too quickly, triggering an awkward silence as we both contemplate how to proceed. I pretend to wring my mostly dry shorts.

Q clears his throat. "It was ginger ale."

"Huh?"

"I wasn't chugging beer, man."

I laugh. "For real?"

26

"I'm not an idiot. Or did you forget that, too?"

And I stop laughing.

Because yes, I deserve that.

But also, the thing I *didn't* forget is this: Q's refusal to accept his share of the blame.

To own his mistakes.

He swivels back to me. "Actually, I *am* gonna hit up the beach."

And I nod, as the moonlight pushes Q's shadow into the rocks below.

95

For seven years, we were the Best Kind of Brothers.

We'd lie in our blanket forts, or in my backyard, sleeping bags zipped to our chins, staring at stars. Each time, the sky felt new.

We watched 757s punch into clouds, and we'd brag about how special this was.

We were better than blood because we'd chosen our brotherhood.

Because we kept choosing, time and again.

We started three tree houses that never got further than sketches on notebook paper and a few boards nailed into trees.

We were built to last.

We stretched our jokes for days, years.

We wrestled everywhere—in our living rooms, our moms

yelling *take that upstairs, take that to the basement*, in our yards until our jeans were grass-scuffed, until our T-shirts were torn. We ambushed each other—sneaking up behind the other person when they were carrying milk or a plate of spaghetti, laughing our asses off even as we mopped or peeled noodles from the wall. We lied for each other.

He gave me shit when my mom insisted on cutting my hair— *your head looks like a globe, bro. You've got patches of islands and a big continent over here, what is that, South America?* But then he convinced his cousin Alonzo to come through and shape me up. *You think I'm gonna let my boy go to school like that*, he said when I'd thanked him. *Only person who gets to take shots at you is me*, he'd said, thumbing his chest.

We were long-haul friends.

We were old before our time.

We were going to apply to the same colleges.

We'd be roommates, in college and after.

We'd backpack across Africa; we'd laugh at ourselves as we pretended to be clueless adventurers—*we're going on holiday, see*, he'd say. And I'd say, *yes, yes, mate, on safari, if you will.*

There were some things we didn't have to say.

Some things we just knew, the way you know the sun is out there, the way your body knows to breathe without your help.

We knew we'd always be there for each other. And not the way you usually say it, easy come, like you're picking lint from a sweater.

We would be *there*.

Beside.

Next to.

Behind.

We were built for this.

This, forever.

But no one told us nothing lasts.

That forever is just something they print on greeting cards.

Not that we would've believed them.

No one warned us everything crashes.

And that what didn't break always burned bright, fast.

No, we learned this alone, and hard.

94

I take a long sip to stall.

We'd snared soda from a cooler.

"Someplace quiet," Q'd said and I followed him past the bonfire, up the ridge.

This was quiet. The party hushed like a closed door.

And somehow, just by sitting here, we'd made it quieter.

This, one of those *what would you say if you ever got the chance* moments.

I swallow hard, the ginger ale sizzling down my throat, like it's alive.

"Sooooo," I say, stall-extending.

We're barely five feet apart, but if you measured from Point Jamal to Point Q, there are light-years between us.

Q pulls his knees into his chest but they immediately slide back. I'd forgotten this: how it's like he has zero body control. Like if you got close enough, you'd see strings flailing his arms and jerking his sneakers.

So random, what we remember, and when.

Third grade someone yelled at him, *man, yo' neck so long, your mama's a swan.* A corny crack that would easily roll off Q's tail feathers today—but back then it sent him spiraling; dude wore turtlenecks for like forty school days straight.

Seventh grade I convinced Q to choreograph a hip-hop dance for winter formal; *everyone's gonna join in, trust me,* I'd promised, as we practiced in my basement. *Our lives are about to change,* I'd assured him, as we stood in the center of the dance floor, waiting for the DJ to play our track.

It's hard: sifting the past without dredging it up.

Fighting the urge to say how things used to be.

Because what you're really asking when you say I miss the old days, when you say the old you would've done this, or said that, is: Why did you change?

You're saying *this* isn't the *you* I want.

"I watched a few of our videos the other day," I say.

Q's face scrunches like he has no clue what I'm talking about. I get it, though; he's not gonna make this easy.

"Jauncy? That thing we spent most of our waking hours creating?"

"Oh," he says in a way that sounds like *so what.*

"We were pretty funny."

Q shrugs. "One of us, anyway."

I laugh. "Don't be so hard on yourself, man."

And I see it. The faintest smile. Then nothing. But it's enough of a flare to keep me searching for the things we lost.

"See what I did there? Number-one rule in comedy . . ."

"The truer a joke, the funnier it is. Surprised you remember that."

"I know it didn't always seem like it, but I was listening."

He shrugs.

"You still tryna be Kendrick Fallon?" I ask.

Q shoots back. "You still rudderless as hell?"

I could return fire, but instead I absorb the blow, quietly.

The moon dips behind a cloud.

I try again. You want vulnerability, you gotta be vulnerable, right? "So, I'm watching our videos and I suddenly realize, man, I haven't felt funny in a while."

"If seventeen years is a while, I guess I agree."

"Damn, Q lands another haymaker. He keeps this up, Jamal's not gonna last two rounds," I say in my best boxing-commentator voice. "Any other jabs you wanna throw?"

Q nods. "Oh, trust, I got hella uppercuts I could throw."

And I should defuse things, but. "Well, let's get to 'em then. What you waiting for?"

Q, eyes still tracking the moon, snarls, "Dude, I've never thrown an actual punch in my life, but don't push me."

A few kids run along the edge of the waves, tossing a Frisbee down the shoreline.

"You didn't have to throw a punch because *I* was there to throw them for you. I was always th—"

Q tornadoes around. "You were *always what*? There for me? Is *that* what you were about to say to me?"

"Oh, so unless I was there for you the way *you* wanted me to be, then dead everything I did? None of what I did matters, I guess."

Q throws his hand up. "You *still* don't get it. The only way you're actually there for someone is to be there the way *they* need, not on *your* terms."

I tap my chest. "Oh, *I* don't get it? Me? So, what, I guess you're the expert on showing up for your friends?"

He's practically spitting now. "Compared to you? Hell yeah."

"When did you *ever* ask me what *I* needed, Q?"

"Hmm." Q strokes his chin. "Was I supposed to ask you before or after you decided to completely shut me out? I guess before, right, when I was only ninety-seven percent shut out."

And somehow, I'm standing now, which only infuriates me more, because damn, this dude is nearly my height sitting. "*I* shut *you* out? You mean because I didn't play computer games or make corny videos after my parents died? I'm sooo sorry *my* pain hurt *your* feelings, Q. My bad, bro."

Q shakes his head. "Wait, hold up, was this the pain of your parents dying or the pain of having your whole head jammed up your ass?"

And now I'm staring him down, fists tighter than chromosomes.

"You wanna hit me, J? I wish you would. Man, I wish."

And my blood's all fire now, my palms prickling, fingers tingling, teeth grinding, pulse thumping outta my throat.

This is it.

Time slows, the lake blurs.

I cock my arm.

There are moments so inexplicable we call them fate.

Label them destiny.

Hindsight tells us we were always hurtling here.

Whatever forces yoked Q and me together tonight, they've decided how it ends.

The waves lunge at us.

Bile churns in my stomach, any minute and it'll geyser from my lips.

"I *should* hit you," I say to Q. I say to myself.

It's dumb how fast the Universe flips, how happy's never a tight grip.

"Do it," he barks. "What are you waiting for?"

And I don't know what's more disrespectful: that he's shit-talking while sitting or grinning like he just won a twenty-dollar scratch-off.

And this is not the Q I know.

But this isn't the Jamal I know, either.

And the truth is, I don't know much of anything, except the one thing that matters: He killed them.

Q killed my parents.

My arm fires. My fist cuts through the air, a spaceship

35

navigating the meteorites of historical bullshit between us.

I close my eyes. Brace for impact.

And I don't know if it's my eyes clenched too tight, or if my brain's so hot my vision shorts, but suddenly all's black, everything heavy.

This moment like an anvil dropped from the sky.

93

"What the hell are you doing?" Autumn says.

She practically tackles me, propelling me into Q, all of us crashing into the sand.

I struggle for breath, stumble to my feet. "No, what are *you* doing?"

Autumn shakes her head. "I told you, J. I won't be with a caveman. You wanna be an *actual* tough guy, try apologizing."

"Apologizing?" I spit out a tongueful of sand. "For what?"

She makes her *you know what I mean* face. But I wave her off. "Nah. This dude needs to apologize to *me*."

Q brushes off his shorts and laughs. "That ain't happening."

Autumn, a human traffic light, steps between us, holds up a palm at Q, a palm at me.

"This is stupid. You both are right and you both are wrong and . . ."

But Q shakes his head, points at Autumn. "Yo, this your bodyguard?"

"Don't point at her." I step closer to knock his hand away, but Autumn bumps me back.

Q laughs, holds up his hands in surrender. "Autumn, you seem cool. Maybe in another life, we'd be friends. But I feel bad for you because you don't see what's coming."

Autumn shakes her head. "What are you talking about?"

Q smiles. "You think Jamal actually likes you? You're a placeholder, Autumn."

"Q, I'm warning you, that's enough." I try to step in front of Autumn, but she stands her ground.

"People like you and me don't matter to people like him. We're just seat fillers. The second someone he likes more comes around, he'll ball you up."

"That's not true," she says. "I know you think that's what happened to you but it's not true."

"That's *exactly* what happened."

A few kids hear our commotion and post up along the perimeter to watch.

"Q, just stop," I say.

"Be smart, Autumn. He'll toss you and not think twice. My advice? Leave him first."

"Is that what you think? That he tossed you? How can you

toss something you never had?"

Q looks confused. "What are you talking about?"

I touch Autumn's shoulder. "Autumn, please, just . . ."

But she pats my hand, like *it's okay, I got you,* her voice already softening. "Look, I honestly don't want to hurt your feelings, Q. But you were *barely* friends. Jamal felt sorry for you. Tried to be nice to you. But you . . . you were smothering him, man. He couldn't breathe. And he had so much going on—"

Q looks incredulous. "Smothering? I was trying to be there!" His voice hot, sharp. "Is that what he told you? That I was some pitiful kid he rescued like Captain Save-a-Loser?" He turns to me. "*Barely* friends? Really, dude?"

I don't need to see Autumn's face to know she's hurt, but she swivels to show me, anyway. And for a second, they've joined forces. A temporary alliance against their common enemy.

"Jamal . . . ," Autumn says, my name like a hair caught in her throat.

I shrug. "I don't see how the terminology I used matters . . ."

But Q's a runaway train. "Everything matters! J, you were my *best* friend and you were in the worst pain, what was I supposed to do?"

And it's like, for a moment, the anger isn't as red, the resentment not so bitter. Because his question is valid. *What was he supposed to do?*

"No, answer me, Jamal. What would you have me do?"

And I don't know.

I don't know.

I don't know.

More kids trickle over, a circle slowly forming around us.

"I don't know," I hear myself say.

"That's what I thought," Q says, his words wet with venom. "The truth is you sacrificed me. I was your scapegoat."

And now I'm shaking.

And I want to say because you killed them.

You killed them.

And I would sacrifice you a thousand times over if it would bring them back.

"Just say the words," Q's insisting. "You needed a villain. Someone to be mad at, and you chose me, the only person outside of Whit who would've stuck around no matter what. I told myself over and over it wasn't personal. But there's only so many times you can tell yourself that before you sound stupid even to yourself."

"You wanna know the real reason I was so angry? Why I'm still angry?"

"I'm right here, aren't I?"

"I'm so angry because you . . ."

Now Autumn grasps my shoulder. "J, don't."

But I move beyond her grip, closer to Q. "Because you . . . because you . . ."

But I can't do it. I just can't.

Quincy laughs. "Didn't think so." He nods toward Autumn.

"See. You're in love with a coward."

Autumn scoffs. "You know, for someone so concerned with me interjecting myself, you sure love including me."

"Honestly, Q? I don't get it. Like, what's your problem? Why are *you* so mad?" I ask.

"You know what the funny thing is?" Q shakes his head, claps his hands. "I'm *not* mad at you. Even though you punked out when I needed you most. Despite the fact that during the worst days of my life, you couldn't even text an *o* and *k*." Q laughs. "Nah. I'm more pissed at me. That *I* was stupid enough to waste all those years with you. That even when it was beyond clear to everyone else in the world that you weren't gonna show up, I was still dumb enough to believe you were on your way." Q takes a step toward us. "So, you wanna know what my problem is? It *was* you, Jamal," he says, jabbing his finger into my chest. "But you *aren't* my problem now. Not anymore. Not ever again."

And I'm stunned.

And I'm so angry my chest hurts.

And I can't form a single, solid word, everything in me transformed, evaporated into steam and heat. I don't register the crowd of kids watching from the embankment, their faces in various states of *what the*—

I know that Autumn's gripping my wrist.

I know her friends have materialized behind her.

I reach for Q, without even knowing why.

Without knowing what I'd do if he stopped.

Knowing that if Q really wanted, he could javelin me to the moon.

But he pushes through me, his fingers flicking me away like I'm fuzz.

Like I'm nothing, and less.

92

And I'm sliding my hands up Autumn's arms, asking her if she's okay, telling her how sorry I am, does she want a drink, does she want to leave, is she cold, and I wonder if she feels me trembling.

She answers three or four times before I actually hear her.

A rogue raindrop bull's-eyes my forehead, the sky a purple-black bruise.

"Do *you* wanna go?" she asks, dangling her keys.

"Yeah," I say. "Maybe."

She slaps them into my palm.

My eyebrows raise. "You're not coming?"

"I'll get a ride."

"I can wait. If you wanna stay longer, it's cool."

I lean in for a hug, but it's like embracing an armchair.

"You okay?" I ask again.

"Of course she's not okay," one of her friends says. "She was just embarrassed in front of the whole school, and you just let it happen."

I tilt my jaw. "What was I supposed to do?"

"Defend your girl's honor," she shoots back.

I turn back to Autumn. Waiting for *her* to defend *my* honor. But she won't even hold my gaze. I try to lead her to privacy a few feet away, but she's not budging. "Autumn," I say softly. "Can we please talk?"

Normally, she'd take my face between her palms, kiss my forehead, my nose. Our eyes locked, she'd say, *me and you no matter what.*

But now, her body's speaking a language I can't even place.

"I'm sorry for . . . Nothing he said is true. You know that."

"Yeah, I know," she says, in a voice I haven't heard.

"Look, can we please just . . ."

Her friends close ranks, slingshotting themselves from her rear to a flanking position at either hip. "I'll catch up with you later," she says. "Just park in your driveway, toss the keys under the seat."

And she knows what happens when I get behind the wheel.

"What if I keep them in my room and you come through whenever you're ready?"

And I see this idea floating through her brain, and for a sec, she's climbing the ladder, stepping through the window into my bedroom—

But what's a bubble if not for bursting?

"Just leave them under the seat, okay," she says, knowing that in all likelihood I won't be able to leave this party.

This house.

This neighborhood.

That it's possible I won't even open the driver's side door.

Yet she's doing this anyway.

Which, maybe that's her point.

That I need her in ways she doesn't need me back.

That maybe I need her more:

Than she needs me.

Than I know.

"Autumn, I've told you things that I—"

"Apparently, you didn't tell me everything."

"What didn't I tell you?"

Her eyes looking through me. "You said Quincy was just a dude. An acquaintance. But that, all that history between you two, that's way more."

Which, okay, is it possible I'd edited the narrative a bit— given Autumn the much-abridged version? Maybe.

But the Jamal–Quincy story arc's still the same.

Ahem. Once upon a time, we were cool. Then he killed my parents. The end.

"Okay, so we used to be friends. Who cares?"

She points to herself. "Me, Jamal. Your girlfriend. I care."

"Wait, so you're getting vexed by semantics?"

"No, Jamal, I'm getting vexed by the fact that if you lied about that, which is a dumb-ass thing to lie about, then what else are you lying about?"

"You don't get it."

"Because you never wanted me to. What, you thought if I found out how you'd done Quincy, I'd think you were a shitty human, right?"

I roll my tongue around my cheeks. "Autumn. Please. Don't do this. Let's just . . . let's just go somewhere and talk and I'll tell you everything you wanna—"

But her voice pushes me away. "You should go, Jamal."

And maybe it's the full moon that's got hearts twisted.

"For real?"

"Yeah. For real." Somehow her friends press in even tighter.

"You gonna be that way off the strength of some salty-ass dude I used to know? Like, word? Wow, I thought you and me rocked differently."

"I thought so too, Jamal," she says, folding her arms. "Guess we're both learning a lot tonight."

"That, Autumn." I point to the area of sand we'd vacated. "That wasn't about you."

"How was that *not* about me?"

"How *was* it?"

"See, this is the part you don't get. The lesson you won't let yourself learn." She shakes her head. "When someone loves you, Jamal, they love all of you. *I* love all of you. Your pain is my pain. Your anger is my anger. So, when you're in the thick of it, I'm in the thick of it. But you? It's like the more people wanna love you, the harder you wanna push them away."

"That's not true."

"No?"

"Not at all."

"Jamal, how long have we been together?"

I squint in confusion. "What's that got to do with . . ."

But she's not finished. "Do you love me, Jamal?"

"Wait, what?"

"Do. You. Love. Me."

"You know what? I'm not playing this game with you."

"Who's playing, Jamal? Huh? You or me?"

"Man, this full moon got everybody out their mind tonight."

"Or finally in their right mind. Tell me you love me. Say the words."

"Yo, you buggin'. Like for real."

"It's easy, right? Four words. You love to talk, right? So, talk. *I love you, Autumn.*"

"Why are you trying to embarrass me right now?"

"Oh, I'm embarrassing you, Jamal? *I'm* embarrassing *you*? My friends are standing here not listening to you tell me *you love* me. I think I'm the one embarrassed."

"Like, you saw what just happened. You know my head's all over the place and now you wanna have a full-on state of the union."

And I know I'm dumb as hell.

And I do love her.

Other than my sister, I love Autumn more than anyone on this planet.

Which is exactly why I *can't* tell her.

Because the Universe is a trained assassin.

And as soon as it's out there, the second you verify your weaknesses, expose your soft spots, the Universe starts counting down, and then it's only a matter of time before it stalks and destroys everything and everyone you love.

I know, because I've already seen it happen.

The only thing worse than loving someone so much?

Telling them.

"We've been together for two years and you've never, not once, told me you loved me. Two years. And I never, not once, complained. I never pushed. I never even nudged you, Jamal. I knew you were afraid. I understood why. And I knew, eventually, you'd get there. But . . . it's like Q said, eventually you sound stupid even to yourself."

I feel it in my throat. The burn. The next words I speak, my voice will crack in two. "Autumn. Baby. Please, just . . ."

And for a second, the look she's giving me, her frustration's kinda melty. But then I see it, that this isn't a thing she can let go. I see it, a transformation, her hardening right in front of me. I'm losing her.

It's like having Friend Finder on—you know exactly where your friends are, but still you weren't actually with them.

I know where Autumn is, but I can't be there with her.

She shakes her head. "Maybe I'll catch you later."

And I should let myself be hurt, but I shrug. I double down. "Yeah, well, maybe I won't be around later."

She nods. "Like I said, leave the keys under the seat."

I break our gaze, glance at her friends. Tip my head like I'm wearing a top hat, like I'm leaving a drawing room. "You ladies have a good night." Then I'm weaving solo through the entire Elytown High student body, most of whom, thankfully, have resumed partying.

I say a few goodbyes.

Thank the host for having me.

Smile like it's all good.

Laugh like never better.

Shake the keys in my palm like dice, tell myself, *you got this, Jamal. It's no big deal.*

I trudge up the long sloping dune, thoughts stuttering across my brain like ticker tape.

How could Q not even acknowledge what he'd done?

How could he compare his actions to mine?

Yeah, I missed something important in his life—I admit it.

But he was the cause of the tragedy in mine.

And what does it mean that in barely two minutes, I'd lost Autumn?

The absence of four words didn't mean the absence of love.

Love could be fully present even if the words weren't.

Didn't she feel it? Hasn't she felt loved?

49

Wasn't the feeling, the knowing, better than any words?
And also, less importantly:
How am I going to get home?
Whit, the only person in the world I can call.
Whit, my only person.

I'm halfway up the weathered stairs, thinking how, on a dime, a tide could completely turn and level you.

I'm nearly to the top when I hear the screams.

I pause.

    Because maybe it was a kid playing.

    Maybe it was my imagination.

    Maybe it was the music.

    The wind and lake and waves.

    But then I hear it again.

    Another scream.

    Away from the party.

    On the other side of the dunes.

    None of the bonfire kids seem to notice.

    I scan for Autumn, but she's nowhere I can see.

    I tear back down the stairs.

    My hands won't stop shaking, and then I realize it's because my entire body's shaking. I race up the sandy hill, causing a mini sandvalanche, and I lose my footing. I roll halfway down the other side before I catch myself.

I hear another scream, closer but also somehow quieter.

But I see no one.

My eyes sweep the horizon, and that's when I see it.

An arm or a leg volcanoing, breaching the water's surface, then slamming violently back beneath the waves.

And now I'm sprinting across the beach, my chest on fire, legs, arms, pumping, firing. I imagine myself a blue flame spiraling toward the water, and I am faster than I've ever been.

But still not fast enough.

I attack the crooked, cracking stairs two at a time—slipping halfway from the top but catching myself and pogoing back up—until I'm on the long concrete dock.

Lightning splits the sky into jagged halves, thunder claps, and now rain sluices down my face.

My shirt's drenched. I pry it loose, let it drop behind me.

I don't break stride. I run harder.

The loose pebbles and jagged divots punish my feet, but I don't slow, I can't slow.

When I reach the end, I can't tell water from sky, both black and angry.

And were I smart, I'd make sure the water's clear, that it's deep enough.

Too shallow and I splinter my neck, snap my spine.

Too rocky and I piñata all over the shoal.

But there's no look-before-leap time.

And it's too late to alter my trajectory—the waves already reaching for me, the surface approaching fast and hard—this could be it.

I steal another breath and knife through the waves.

I'm not dead.

I swim like mad, arms spiked, legs kicked; I have to be close.

Only every wave looks the same.

I stop swimming. I bob in the water, turning slowly, scanning the darkness, small fish glancing my toes.

I spin 'round and 'round, tell my heart to please shut the fuck up, stop yelling, stop panicking, just let me—just give me a sec to—

And then maybe fifteen yards toward the moon, movement, something jerks.

It takes everything I have to fight the current.

But when I make it, there's more nothingness.

I take the deepest breath, inhaling summer air and midges, and plunge into the water. For a moment it's so dark I can't tell if my eyes are open.

I drop lower.

Lower.

And there, below me in the murkiness, a body limp and drifting.

I surge deeper, my fingers narrowly missing their arm.

I need air.

But retreat for the surface and they're lost forever.

I slowly exhale, exhausting every molecule I can scrape from my lungs, a thousand tiny bubbles roaring from my lips; I kick, I thrust, with all my might, diving deeper and deeper.

This far down, I can't see anything.

I throw my fingers out, groping for the smallest piece of anything.

And then I feel it.

Fabric.

I pull upward, snag more of the shirt, press them to my chest, and with my free arm paddle like mad for the surface.

They knock into my head and I swallow several mouthfuls of water. I grit my teeth, keep paddling, but I'm discombobulated and I'm not entirely sure if I'm swimming up or down. But I keep battling until I see the faintest glimmer of moonlight.

We puncture the surface, and that's when I realize who:

Q's choking and retching, and he's thrashing, dunking our heads, his fear dragging us back under the tow.

"Q, stop fighting me. You're gonna drown us both."

But he keeps fighting and I can't tell you how much water I've inhaled.

I smack him hard across his face, and he stops.

Hearing my own ragged breaths scares me.

I study the horizon.

Q slumps forward, his face striking the water. I snap him back to me, like I'm performing the Heimlich.

I slap him again.

"Q, wake up, man."

Another slap, harder.

"Q! Wake your ass up, man. I'm not playing with you."

He stirs, just barely.

That has to be enough for now. I can't do anything for him in this water. Q's only chance is if I make it to shore.

If I can get us most of the way, the current might do the rest, cough us onto the beach.

Not for the first time I wish I was taller, bigger.

The four inches and sixty pounds Q has on me feels like a dump truck.

I flip us both onto our backs, hook my forearms under Q's shoulders, and do my best to kick on either side of Q's body, but I can't get enough clearance, our progress half what it should be, my strength all but gone.

I can't do this.

We're not gonna make it.

Above us a small plane hums through the clouds.

I look back toward the shore.

And somehow it's closer.

I keep flailing.

And it's closer.

Moving toward me in painful inches.

I see the bonfire down the beach, orange flames dancing.

More inches.

Now I hear the low rattle of bass from the party speakers.

We're still too far to hear voices.

I let myself smile. We're going to make it.

Because fuck the odds, man.

There's something to be said for the human spirit, and I'm almost laughing when—

An agonizing pain tears through my lower body.

My knee, calf, feet crash into something sharp and jagged; I feel blood leaving me.

C'mon, Jamal. Focus. Keep going, man. You can't stop.

I say this to myself.

I imagine Q saying this to me.

I try to regain my form, recapture my rhythm, but it's gone.

We're barely moving.

No. No. C'mon, J. Not today. Not like this.

I kick, I pump, I paddle.

I thrash. I thrust. I flail.

But we're sinking now.

And I can't tell what I feel more: excruciating pain, or paralyzing dread.

I fight to keep Q's head above water, even letting my own head submerge.

I cough and I tread until Q shifts, even heavier now, and his weight grapples me under the waves. Eyes wide, I lunge for the surface, but every second pushes it farther away.

I can't breathe.

I try to push Q's stomach upward, hoping to throw him into

the current. But he barely budges, just falls down harder on me.

And I know this is the end, we're sinking faster than I can paddle.

The moon shrinks to nothing.

And this is how it feels to exhale your last breath.

90

Eyes open or closed when I die?

Which would be better, when they find me?

If they find me.

Would they say, this guy fought to the end?

Does closing my eyes mean I give up?

Would it mean anything to Whit?

To Autumn?

Are her keys still in my pocket?

It's her only set—I know because she'd recently locked them in the car.

Her locksmith cousin to the rescue, made her promise she'd make a spare, and I'd reminded her, but . . .

Isn't that life?

You think there's always tomorrow?

But then a column of lights injects into the water; there's something rushing toward us. And my waist is lassoed, Q's, too, and like a collapsing dream, we're ripped from the deep.

89

I don't realize it's me screaming.

That when they say please, stop fighting us.

It's me they're talking to.

And I'm guessing PTSD isn't a thing that happens literal seconds post-trauma, but.

I mean, who knows, maybe it's all the water I inhaled—

I'm afraid to open my eyes because this doesn't feel right.

I don't feel right.

As if my head and body have parted ways.

And what if this is how you feel when you're newly dead?

Someone's repeating my name—"Jamal. Jamal."—their voice drippy and hollow, like there's a fishbowl over their head.

A hand touches my cheek like it knows me, and the voice is saying *open your eyes, Jamal. Please, open your eyes.*

And when I finally do, Autumn's leaning over me, a terror in her face I hope she never feels again.

I try to smile but instead I throw up on the sand. Several minutes and I can't stop throwing up, my body exorcising Lake Erie in violent heaves that feel like a giant's kicking my kidneys.

Were this a cartoon, you'd pounce on my stomach and a fountain would spout from my lips, a distressed fish swimming atop.

"W-w-where's Q?" I sputter. Every breath, a struggle. Like suddenly if I want my lungs and nose to work, I have to consciously tell them to.

"Where's Q? Is Q okay? Where is he?"

Autumn's disappeared, and no one else answers.

But then I see him. Q's not five yards away, lying faceup atop a blanket, the large quilt barely long enough to keep half his body off the sand.

I start to stand but they pull me back.

"Just relax," they say.

Except no one else is relaxed.

Kids I've known all my life semicircle around Q, hands covering their horror, hands gripping other hands, hands wringing, praying.

I jerk from their grasp, but I'm moving too fast, too soon.

And I nearly topple onto Q, crashing beside the woman now pumping Q's chest.

And this isn't TV CPR.

This is bones cracking, wrists popping.

This is watching life empty from someone you thought you'd know forever.

Watching them drain so fast, it's like there's a pump attached to their feet, sucking the life with such efficiency that you can actually see it receding, dropping from their head to their waist to their ankles, dipping lower and lower.

He's still not breathing, she says to the man forcing air into Q's lungs.

As if just now Q's made a choice.

But they keep rotating—from his head to his chest, chest to his head—as if it might go on forever. And if it did, if they never stopped, then in a way, it would be like Q was still here.

I beg Q to wake up. I yell at him. I make him promises I can't keep.

Why's it so easy to die?

Each of us is a stupid fuse waiting to trip, with no one to flip us back on.

Moments ago, Q's breaths were jagged and shallow, but they were breaths.

But now—I raise my hand to Q's nose—and, nearly nothing.

I feel next to nothing.

88

There was this resuscitation scene in, I forget the movie, where the near-victim's eyes spring open and she's coughing, and all of the onlookers' faces go from panicked to relieved because she's gonna make it, and she even tries to sit up as if waking from a dream.

And I remember Q's mom, Ms. Barrantes, shaking her head, rolling her eyes. *It rarely happens that way*, she said. *Most of the time, you can't save them.*

So, when Q suddenly gasps for air, I'm happy but stunned.

Not that it should surprise me. Q, he's always been the type of person who defies all odds.

"Hey, man," I say to him. But he doesn't talk back. He just stares at me a beat, before his eyes snap shut again. "He's okay, right?" I tap his shoulder. "He's just resting, right?" I ask.

But if anyone knows the answer, they're not saying.

And by the time they slide Q into the ambulance, he's fading again.

I pull myself up, curse when my newly bandaged leg bangs into the rear bumper.

"Whoa." The tall paramedic's face scrunches. "You family?"

"We're brothers," I lie.

"Call your parents. Tell them to meet us at . . ."

Autumn approaches and I'm distracted.

She makes a gesture with her hand that I don't understand.

"My keys," she says. "Sorry. Just . . . if you have them . . ."

I fish them from my pocket, surprised they're still there.

"Thanks," she says.

And it's possible her fingers linger in mine a second longer than necessary.

It's confusing—how your heart holds your love and your hurt in the same chamber.

"I'm glad he has you right now," she says.

I am, too, but I don't want to leave her here, even though an hour ago I'd done just that.

And the way she's looking at me before turning to look back at her friends, like she can't hold my eyes for too long, she feels it, too.

A few days after my parents died, I struggled to see out of my right eye. There'd been warning signs that I'd ignored: floaters and everything blurred, like the world was suddenly covered in plastic. I had a detached retina, from the accident. *You were a day or two away from permanently losing your vision,* the surgeon chided me.

That's how things feel with Autumn.

Like we're being pulled apart in ways that appear small.

We could ignore it. Convince ourselves we could go on like this.

Except if we don't fix it, today or tomorrow, we'll lose it forever.

"Do you want me to—"

"No," she interrupts. "You're where you should be."

I nod, promise to text when I know something.

I look out both small windows, each round like a porthole, and it's like that machine the eye doctor pulls down in front of you—*do you see better here or here?* And it's like we're standing still, the beach pulling away from us. Autumn steadily gliding away from me, like she's on a conveyor belt.

Ahead: our sirens scream *movemovemove.*

Behind: our flashing lights illuminating two dozen terrified faces, like jack-o'-lanterns.

I try to calculate how far we are from the hospital, but my brain's mush.

The paramedic radios the ER—*we've got a sixteen-year-old male with*—she rattles off Q's stats like he's a baseball card. I catch pieces.

His lungs sound wet.

Pulse ox's shit.

"Don't worry, he's still in there," the tall paramedic assures me. "He's a fighter."

I resist asking how many times she's said that and been wrong.

An hour ago, our hands were fists.

And now, I grip his fingers in mine.

His eyes flicker.

He tries to pull the oxygen from his mouth, but the paramedic holds it in place.

"Quincy, I need you to control your breathing, okay?"

But Q's squirming now, trying to wiggle himself free.

His eyes bulge as he squeezes my hand.

"I think he's trying to say something," I tell the paramedic. She moves the mask aside and I lean toward Q's face.

"You should save your strength, man."

But Q's shaking. "J, is . . ."—his voice drops a word— ". . . okay?"

"Is who okay, Q?"

"The girl . . . is she okay?"

The paramedic and I exchange glances. I have no idea who he's talking about but now's not the time for bad news.

"Everyone's okay. Everything's fine," I say.

"She made it," he whispers, shutting his eyes. "She made it," he repeats. Tears roll down both cheeks.

87

The sirens snap off.

Then they're pulling Q out, racing him inside, gurney wheels twitching on concrete, then linoleum. I run behind them.

In stride, the tall paramedic points to a counter enclosed in thick glass, like at a bank. "Here," she yells. "Check in."

And maybe it's the ER docs' superintense faces, or how fast they're pushing Q through the foyer, down the hall, but I am suddenly back in that water.

All of me submerged.

Dread crashing into me, spinning me every way but up.

Because what if this is it? The last time I see Q.

What if the way things are now is the way things are left forever?

"Wait," I hear myself say. "Just wait."

And the tall paramedic glances over her shoulder, but they don't slow.

"There's something . . . I need to tell him . . ."

But they're exploding through the double doors.

"He needs to know that I'm . . ."

But they're already shrinking down the dim corridor.

I start after them, my palms pressed against either Authorized Personnel Only door just before they close, but the receptionist, a smiling lady with purple highlights, reads my mind. Waves me over.

"That your brother?"

"No." I don't say: *he used to be.* "He's my friend." I don't say: *best.* I don't caveat: *former.*

"Well, he's in good hands."

She presses a restaurant-style pager into my palm, says, "It'll buzz when there's an update," says, "sit anywhere you'd like." As if she's the hostess and I'm here for an ice cream float.

And being out here, in this waiting area the size of my living room, with its balding blue carpet and plastic chairs the curve and color of orange peels, feels as far away as I've ever been from Q.

I find the least vandalized chair, de-pocket my phone.

To Autumn: **We made it to the hospital. They say he's fighting. They took him to the back. Just waiting. More when I know.**

I scroll a couple threads down.

To Whit: **Hey, don't freak out, but there's been a . . .**

A what?

An accident? But had it been?

An incident? No. Too weak.

What will freak her out the least? I picture Whit's OB, Dr. Stokes, studying me from the swivel stool, then turning back to Whit. "No unnecessary stress," he'd made us promise.

I type **hey just checking in**, but I leave it unsent. I call her instead, but it rings until her voice mail picks up. Somehow, I manage to leave her a short—yet rambling—message.

In my limited hospital waiting room experience, one of two channels is always playing on the mounted TV: a cooking show, probably because they're hoping it makes you hungry enough to risk the hospital cafeteria.

Or, it's the local news.

Right now, there's a tightrope-walking squirrel—*OMG, look at Solomon Squirrel gooooo. Wow, he's really moving!*—which, I'm definitely not a nature expert, but squirrels scurrying across wires is pretty normal, no? But then, *boom*, the big reveal: this squirrel actually walks the rope STANDING UP.

The man beside me has been chuckling the entire segment, but now he nudges me, still chuckling. "A tightroping squirrel. Now I done seen everything."

I nod, but truthfully, I'm worried for this nice man, because if this—a squirrel on a rope—is the final feather in your *what crazy thing will they come up with next* cap, I don't know, it just seems like a pretty thin feather.

But I force a smile, muster a laugh, because like I said, he's nice.

Also, I believe in karma, or at least that whatever energy you fling into the Universe boomerangs back, and I don't know, since energy's transferable, maybe if I cast out enough good vibes, they might find Q, find the doctors and nurses trying to save him.

"Jamal! Jamal, where is he? Where's Q?" I know Q's mom's voice the way I still know my mom's. I pop up without thinking as she bursts into the room.

What was I expecting? A hug?

This isn't a reunion.

"He's in the trauma center. I think. They rushed him back." I hold up the pager. "She said this will buzz when we can talk t—"

But she's already rocketing toward the desk.

That's when it dawns on me: not only is Ms. Barrantes a nurse, she works *here*. She probably has special access, can find out things you normally couldn't.

Except the purple-haired lady is suddenly standing, motioning for Ms. Barrantes to lower her voice. "Simone, please. Simone, listen to me. I understand you're upset. I do. But just because you work here doesn't mean you can . . . look, I promise you, I promise you, that as soon as I know something

70

about Q, anything, I will walk right over to you personally and I will—"

My lap vibrates.

I call out, "Ms. Barrantes!"

I hold up the pager, a beacon of quivering red light.

86

The walk to conference room C is the longest, but Ms. B's on a mission to break the world record for arrival time. I jog to keep up.

The hallway walls are lined with charts of our body systems—the skin cross-sectioned and layered. And it hits me—I'm just skin draped over bones.

I mean, I knew that, but.

It's weird because when our bodies, our organs, are working, we think about them nearly never percent of the time.

Ms. B sets down her phone, turns to me.

"I'm happy you're here," she says while we wait for the doctor. "Surprised. But happy. He misses you, Jamal. When you two stopped hanging out, he wouldn't talk about it, but he took it hard. And then his dad decided to be an asshole and get cancer . . ."

I frown. "Huh?"

A small smile. "Just a dumb joke Mr. B used to make." She shrugs. "I don't know what I'm doing, Jamal. Figured we could use some levity, you know?"

"Levity's cool," I say. Because I want Ms. Barrantes to have everything she needs: her son, levity, not-so-funny jokes, peace.

Ms. Barrantes nods. "I didn't know you two were hanging out again."

"Yeah," I say, because correcting her right now seems stupid, selfish.

"No wonder he was so excited for this party. I know . . . I know my son isn't the most social. I try not to push him, but . . . I just want him to be a kid. To have fun. And he tries . . . he tries . . . *so* hard."

"He's an awesome kid. An awesome human."

She swipes at her tears. "He really is."

And then footsteps louder, louder, until they stop outside the door.

Someone just standing there, waiting.

Which makes me think it's bad.

Because you don't wait for good news, right?

You race in, you explode in, because there's almost no bad way to deliver good news.

Ms. Barrantes doesn't seem to notice. "You sure you feel

73

okay, Jamal? You call your sister?"

"I left her a message."

"Try her again."

"Okay, I will."

"You don't have to wait here with me. You can go. I can call you with news."

I shake my head. "Thanks, but if it's okay with you, I wanna stick around."

She squeezes my hand. "Yeah, well, I appreciate the company."

Ms. B's standing, stretching, when the conference room door swings open.

And before the doctor says one word, Ms. B's wagging her head.

"Dr. Rodriguez, no. No," she says, firmly. "Nuh-uh. Not my son."

"Simone..."

"Not my Quincy. You better go somewhere else with that. You hear me?"

"Simone, I'm so..."

"You take that somewhere else, Kevin! I don't want it! Please! Please. I don't want it."

I want to reach for her, comfort her, but I'm cement.

Dr. Rodriguez clears his throat, busies himself with his hands, staring down at them, wringing them, poking his cuticles, sliding the silver wedding band up and down his finger.

I wonder when he decided to be a doctor, to devote his life to saving lives, if he thought about these moments.

Stepping into a room that's anxious for good news, even mediocre news, except there's neither. There's only worse and worser.

But his voice, unlike his hands, is steady and calm, a series of soft *I'm so sorry we did all we can I'm so sorry we did all we can I'm so sorry I'm so sorry I'm so sorry* fluttering around the room, flying over our heads.

And I'm waiting for my alarm to sound.

I'm waiting to sit up in my bed.

Blink this nightmare away.

I keep waiting and waiting but.

Ms. B slumps over like her bones have liquefied, crashes to her knees, the doctor barely stopping her from spilling all over conference room C, her screams loud enough that people rush in: *Is everything okay? Is everything okay?*

But how could it be?

Everything's never gonna be okay again.

85

one week before the funeral

The doctor snatched the surgical cap from his head. "Is there someone I—I . . . can call for you?"

"No." Whit glanced at me, then the door. "It's just . . . us."

"What about grandparents?" the doctor asked.

"None left," Whit said.

"Aunts, uncles, cousins?"

"We have a great-aunt in Cali, I think. Or Arizona. Look, Doctor, I'm sorry if this is rude, but when can we see them? We just want to see our parents."

"I'm so sorry," he said. "But your parents are . . . they, umm . . . they d—"

But I erupted from my seat, sprinted down the hallway to the ER. There were heavy curtains on one side of the wide corridor, and regular rooms with walls and doors on the other.

Most of the rooms were empty, filled with beige machines and platters of shiny instruments. I was halfway down the hall when I arrived at the first closed door.

My hand turned the knob when a voice said her name.

I turned around to see Trauma 2's door propped open, a man mopping, a woman spraying a mist onto a metal table.

"Did you say Jada?" I asked the man.

He glanced at the woman.

She sucked her teeth. "Told you you can't whisper."

He waved her off. "Who you, little man?"

"I'm looking for Jada Anderson."

He scratched his cheek. "You gotta ask the front desk. They'll help you."

But I could feel it, the things he wasn't saying. "Was she here?"

His face fell.

The woman cleared her throat. "Don't do it," she warned. "They'll fire you for that."

He stood up straight, soaked the mop head into the bucket. "I'm sorry, but just go back down this hall and . . . c'mon, little brother, don't cry, man. C'mon." He scratched his chin, like he was thinking. "Look," he said softly. "Who you say you looking for?"

"Jada Anderson. She's . . . she's my mom. And my dad, he's Andre Anderson. I'm looking for him, too. If you can show me where either one of them is, I'd . . ."

And that was when I saw them. Just behind him. In a second

room *inside* trauma room two marked TR-2B.

I pushed past him, and he tried to grab me, but I was too quick. The woman didn't even try to stop me. I had to stand on tiptoe to see.

And there they were.

Mom and Dad were flat on their backs atop two metal tables, their eyes pointed toward the ceiling lights. Two nurses moved between the tables, fastening a gown onto Mom, wiping Dad's face.

I palmed the metal door plate and pushed, just as I was grabbed from behind.

"Noooo," I screamed.

I punched his arms, but he wouldn't let me go.

"No matter what happens, little man, you gon' be okay." His voice was damp as he carried me out of the room. "You gon' be okay," he said, over and over.

I flailed and screamed but I couldn't escape his hold. And we were nearly at the front desk when Whit came flying down the hall, yelling *you can't do that don't ever do that again it's just you and me now okay you can't just take off Jamal you can't just you can't just—*

84

They tell her: Simone, please, you have to wait. Please, Simone. Just another minute.

They're cleaning up.

They're almost finished.

If she could just be—

They'll take her to him as soon as they—

"I'm not going anywhere or listening to anyone until I see my son. You will take me to my son *now*."

She doesn't raise her voice. And her screams, her wails, are now a periodic burst of s-s-sobs, her face afflicted with a soundless pain, like when the hurt is lodged in the back of your throat, still chambered in your heart.

I never again want to see someone hurt so badly.

See someone suffer.

This is your face, helpless.

This is hope, smithereened.

This is *good things happen to good people*, solid as a soap bubble.

There's no divine hand reaching down to save the person you love.

Today's all out of miracles.

83

"I can't fathom how you must feel, Ms. Barrantes."

The woman in the gray dress sits as if she's auditioning for Human with Extraordinary Posture, her hands folded, face even. Her only embellishment a silver bracelet that rattled as she shook our hands.

A grief specialist, Dr. Rodriguez called her, as he'd led us through a section of the hospital straight out of a horror flick.

Our only light a rope of low-wattage bulbs in metal cages strung the length of the cinder-block walls. Most of the ceiling missing too, bundles of cables dangling, some hanging low enough we had to move around them, some of them hissing.

We hurried right by the Authorized Personnel Only signs.

"Where are we going, Doctor?" Ms. Barrantes asked.

"They'll explain better than I can," he said. Before I could point out that she'd asked *where*, not whom or what, he added: "Please, hear them out, Simone."

When we came to the mouth of the final hallway, it was so aggressively dark and quiet, I hesitated, searched Ms. Barrantes's face for affirmation this was okay, that we were safe—but all I saw was pain.

Without knowing our destination—or what awaited us—our commitment solidified with each step. Somehow, we both knew that no matter what lay on the other end of this dark rainbow, we'd say yes. What was there to lose?

In the conference room, when he'd finally calmed her down enough to hear him, Dr. Rodriguez had said what was at best a rather peculiar thing: "There is tremendous opportunity here, Simone. Don't let it slip through your fingers."

I first assumed he wanted her to donate Q's organs—waited for him to say: *this is how Q lives on.*

But this isn't that. This is several galaxies removed.

When the labyrinth ended, we were in front of a single elevator, its door open, a dingy orange light shining from its ceiling. We're barely inside the car when Dr. Rodriguez's finger mashes SB. The door closes, and the elevator hiccups as we descend.

"What's SB?" I asked.

Ms. Barrantes made a face. "Subbasement."

"What's in the subbasement?"

"Nothing," she whispered.

"This is as far as I go," Dr. Rodriguez said, holding the elevator door. "It's the third door on your left."

But Ms. Barrantes didn't move, and I followed her lead. "Why am I here? What are we doing?" She wagged her head. "You can't just ... just ... drop me off into some creepy hallway, Kevin."

"I'm sorry, but it has to be this way, Simone. Listen to what they have to say. I think ... I think you'll find solace."

We stepped out of the elevator and watched the doors close. And suddenly, it was so dark I could see just as much with my eyes closed. Ms. Barrantes felt for my hand, and together we took a few small steps forward. Then a few more, until we heard a click, and a buzzy halogen bulb flickered on, giving us enough light to continue moving forward .

We walked.

Past one door.

Quietly, carefully, we walked past another.

We saw it at the same time, the third door on the left, light escaping from the gap beneath it.

Ms. Barrantes looked at me, then turned the knob.

Now here we are.

"Losing a child," the woman continues. "No one should ever bear that cross."

"You've lost a child?" Ms. Barrantes asks.

The grief specialist shakes her head. "I don't have children," she says with a pause that sounds like *I can't*. "But I've lost people I've loved. My husband last year."

"I'm so sorry," Ms. Barrantes says.

"He'd never been sick before. Not even a cold. All his coworkers gave him a hard time, said he made them look bad. *Just take one sick day, Ross*, they'd say. Everything Ross did, he did faithfully. That was his way. One night he woke up with severe abdominal pain. The doctors said they needed to remove his appendix, there was no time to waste . . ." The woman's face neutral. "When they cut him open, they found mets in his pancreas. He was already stage three. He died four months later."

And I want to say something comforting, but what?

"When the Center came to us, I was skeptical, as I'm sure you are now. Ross was their second case. What they did for him, for us . . . I left my practice of twenty-three years to sit in this chair to talk to people like you. To offer you that same gift."

Ms. Barrantes takes a sharp breath, wipes her eyes. "I just want to see my son. I don't care if I have to climb onto that hospital table to be with him . . . I have to see him."

"Ms. Barrantes, what if he sat up on that table? What if the two of you walked out of that room together?"

Ms. Barrantes opens her mouth but says nothing. Her face perspiring. I hop from my chair.

"Ms. B, are you okay?" I ask.

Ms. Barrantes cuffs her ears like she's blocking out a painful frequency only she hears, her face color draining rapidly, as if some internal plug's been pulled.

"Ms. Barrantes, talk to us. What's happening?" the specialist says. "Ms. Barrantes!"

But Ms. Barrantes slumps forward, eyes glazed, sweat racing down every part of her face like rain on an umbrella.

The woman mashes a button hidden behind the desk, and a buzz fills the room. Two black-clad men rush in like there's a suspect to subdue, a woman in a lab coat trailing.

One of the men points to me, then at the wall. "We need you over there now."

The lab coat woman seems unfazed. "Wanda," she says to the specialist. "Please, escort Jamal next door."

But I move toward Ms. Barrantes. "I'm not leaving her."

Wanda reaches for my arm, but I pull away. "I'm staying."

The lab coat woman nods. "It's okay, Wanda."

One man supports Ms. Barrantes's head while the other snaps the head off a Q-tip-sized stick, fans it beneath her nose.

The lab coat woman removes a tablet from her pocket, slides her finger across the screen, points an edge toward Ms. B, prompting two rapid beeps.

She tilts the screen my direction: a series of colliding green and blue clusters, like a weather map.

I have no idea what I'm looking at.

And finally, the woman, realizing this, smiles. "She's fine. Understandably a little anxious."

On cue, Ms. B's eyes flit open.

"I fainted," Ms. B says, rubbing her temples.

"You did." The lab coat woman smiles, extends her hand.

85

"I'm Dr. Maya Iverson, Ms. Barrantes. And while I certainly wish you didn't need our services, I'm happy you've accepted our offer."

Ms. B kneads her neck. "I haven't accepted anything. I'm not certain I even understand the offer."

Dr. Iverson returns the tablet to her coat pocket. "We want to reunite you with your son, Ms. Barrantes."

Ms. B laughs. "Reunite us. Just like that, huh? Like we got separated at the mall."

Dr. Iverson smiles. "You're a nurse. You know doctors love to gloss over the details. But yes, we're supremely confident."

"I've heard rumors for years. We all have . . . but you never think something like this is truly possible . . ." Ms. B's face like she's just left a dream.

"I appreciate your position. Trust me, I understand *how* it works, yet when I consider what we've done, what we're doing, I can barely fathom any of it."

"As a parent . . ." Ms. B grips her mouth, her hand shaking. "As a parent, you think about what'll happen to them when *you* die, but . . . not this. You're not supposed to outlive your child."

And what do you say to that?

Nothing.

Silence hitting the room hard enough to rattle walls.

So quiet you hear halogen crackling in the overhead lights.

Dr. Iverson's smile gone. "I know. I know . . . it's a lot to process, and . . . nothing, no one, can change what's happened. But if we can soften the blow even just a bit, isn't that something?"

And it's not my place to speak, but. "This is real? This isn't some scam?"

Dr. Iverson's smile returns. "It's a hundred percent real." She meets Ms. B's gaze. "If you accept our offer, Quincy *will* live again."

Ms. B sits up straight, pulls the skin beneath her red eyes taut. "For how long, doctor?"

Dr. Iverson's brow furrows. "How long?"

"How long until my son would die again?"

Dr. Iverson nods faintly.

"Wait," I say. "What do you mean, die again?"

Dr. Iverson's eyes stay on Ms. B. "We won't know until Quincy's completed the fifth phase of the reanimation."

"So we're talking, what? Five years? Ten years?"

Ms. B wags her head. "No, Jamal. That's not what they're offering. Is it, Doctor?"

"We're offering you the chance to say goodbye to your son."

"For how long, though?" I press.

The first bubbles of impatience finally break through the surface of the doctor's face. "As I said, we won't know until . . ."

I cut her off. "Okay, but what's the longest you've brought any of the others back?"

"We make amazing strides every day. The technology is improving all the time. What we're accomplishing is nothing short of mirac—"

"Please, answer the question, Doctor," Ms. B interjects.

Dr. Iverson folds her arms. "What we've done in the past

is not an indication of . . ."

"*Doctor*," Ms. B says firmly.

Dr. Iverson shakes her head. "Nineteen days, seven hours."

My face drops. "I know this sounds crazy, but I thought, at minimum, we were talking months, but . . . but this is . . ."

"One day, soon, we'll be able to safely extend the reawakening. But for now . . ."

Ms. B nods. "So, even if it's successful, and I imagine it's a big if, Quincy would live for a couple more weeks?"

"The good news is we have reason to believe Quincy will exceed our initial estimate."

"How much longer?" I ask.

"I'd rather not speculate, but so far the diagnostics point to several more days. Which may not seem like an astronomical difference, but when you're talking about bringing a person back to life, every minute matters."

And that's fair. Why had I been so shocked about the time frame? They were undying a human being. *Any* amount of time would be amazing.

"I'm sorry, Doctor," I say. "I guess I just heard you could bring Q back and I just assumed it was . . . forever. But obviously, even if it's just for a few weeks, it's still . . ."

"No," Ms. B says, her wobbly voice stretching *no* to two syllables. "No," she says again, more firmly. "No," she repeats.

And it's like you can feel the fight happening in her brain—inside her heart.

Dr. Iverson shakes her head. "No, what?"

The uncertainty gone from Ms. B's voice. "My answer is no. We're going to let Quincy pass in peace."

Dr. Iverson raps her knuckles atop the desk. "Ms. Barrantes, I don't think you understand what we're offering you. This is a once-in-a-lifetime . . ." The doctor looks at me for backup.

"Ms. B, are you sure?" I ask.

She nods. "Many moons ago, my first nursing job was on an oncology unit, and I was terrified to make a mistake. What if I hurt someone? I quadruple-checked everything. Even their lunch orders. But then, a few weeks into the job, I watched a patient who'd been in my care die. There were other options the patient could've tried. Another surgery. More chemo. But she declined. And her family was so sad and angry. They took it personally. Why didn't she want to keep trying? Keep fighting? And I'll never forget what another nurse told them. 'Sometimes it's not *can* we, but *should* we?'" Ms. B shakes her head. "No one wants my son back more than me. But this. This feels selfish, bringing him back just so *I* get to say goodbye. Waking him up just so he can die again."

But Dr. Iverson isn't giving up. "It's like we dropped a dinosaur into your lap, Ms. Barrantes. I get it. It's a lot. But time *is* of the essence here. The reanimation window is incredibly narrow, and . . ."

Ms. B interrupts. "You know, this entire time, all I thought about was what *I* wanted. But who's asking what Quincy would want?"

And who could argue with that?

"I'm sorry, Ms. Barrantes," Dr. Iverson says. "But I think you're making a mistake you'll lament for the rest of your life."

But Ms. B's standing now. "Maybe," she concedes, already opening the door. "But if there's anything I was reminded of today, it's how brief the rest of our lives can be."

82

Ms. B hustles back down the hall, and once again I double my efforts to keep up.

But then the office door flies open. Dr. Iverson rushing after us, her eyes wild.

"Ms. Barrantes, the difference in your story is," Dr. Iverson shouts down the hall. "That person got to decide."

I look at Ms. B. She presses the elevator button.

Dr. Iverson's voice still booming. "She had time to come to terms. To say her last words."

The elevator chimes, the door opens. Ms. B steps inside and I follow, Dr. Iverson right behind us now.

"Quincy didn't get that tonight. But doesn't he deserve it?"

I tilt my head to catch Ms. B's eyes. "Are you sure?" I ask softly, so only she can hear.

The door now sliding.

"Ms. B," I say quietly.

Dr. Iverson one step outside the threshold. "Ms. Barrantes, doesn't your son deserve the same chance?"

"Ms. B," I say again. "Ms. Barrantes? Ms. Barrantes?"

The doors nearly closed.

But then Ms. B throws her arm in between.

"Why my son? Why my Quincy?"

Dr. Iverson frowns. "I'm afraid that I can't tell you."

"And why not?"

"I'm sorry, I'm not being cute. I can't tell you because I don't know. I qualify our reanimation candidates, but I don't select them."

The elevator alarm sounds. It wants to close, but Ms. B's arm is there.

She nods at me, and we step back into the hall. "Who does the selecting?"

"Usually? A board."

"You said usually. Not this time?"

"I'll be honest, we haven't reanimated anyone under these circumstances."

I jump in. "Circumstances?"

Dr. Iverson glances my way. "We've performed nine reanimations. All were already being prepped prior to their deaths, because their deaths were expected."

"But my son's death was decidedly not expected."

Dr. Iverson nods.

"So, this would be your first spontaneous reanimation?"

Another nod.

"*If* we do this, will he . . . be in any pain?"

Dr. Iverson shakes her head. "Quincy won't feel a thing."

Ms. B's fingers trace the elevator panel, like she's deciding if she should push the button, step back inside, walk into her empty house, alone. "He deserves more time," Ms. B says finally. "You're right. Everyone deserves one last word." Her hand drops to her side. "Doctor, you'll take good care of my son?"

"I'll personally oversee the entire reanimation."

Ms. B nods, and Dr. Iverson takes her hand. "You're making the right decision."

Dr. Iverson glances at her watch, smiles. "I apologize, but as I mentioned, we don't have a lot of time. I should've already left the hospital. If you'll follow me back to—"

I cut in. "Left for where?"

"The Center," she answers.

"What center?" Ms. Barrantes asks. "You aren't doing the . . . procedure here?"

"Reanimation is . . . very involved. There's a lot of equipment, a lot of people at work."

I clear my throat. "And all of this is legal, right?"

Dr. Iverson grins. "It's not *not* legal. But of course, discretion is important."

Dr. Iverson's pocket vibrates, and she holds up a finger to us as she accepts the call.

"Yes," she says into the receiver. "And the room's prepped? Good. I'm on my way."

I steal a look at Ms. B, but she's leaning against the hallway wall, her eyes closed, her lips pursed in a low hum.

The doctor rattles off a sequence of numbers, and before she ends the call, she's corralling us back down the hall. "I promise you. It won't be long now."

80

There's a door behind the grief specialist's desk.

I hadn't noticed it.

Seconds after Dr. Iverson's apology-filled exit, this other door opens; a lean, immaculately groomed man in pressed gray pants, a stark white dress shirt, and a gray wool bow tie enters.

My first thought is *he must be hella hot*; Elytown is unseasonably blistering.

My next thought: everything about him feels designed, staged, like a house you were trying to sell.

His smile.

His perfectly square silver-frame glasses matching his gray eyes.

This kind of guy, anything he offers, you read the fine print twice.

He extends his hand to Ms. Barrantes, then to me: a cold, tight grip.

"I am Mr. Oklahoma."

"Nice to meet you, Mr. Oklahoma," she says, glancing at me like she wants me to exchange pleasantries.

But that's not happening. This dude, one of those *I can't quite put my finger on what's wrong with you* people. "Why do I get the feeling that's not your real name?" I ask.

His customer-service smile doesn't wilt the slightest. "I will be your personal reanimation liaison, Ms. Barrantes. Your case is my only assignment. As such, day or night, I am at your call. Should you require anything, I will do my level best to bring it to fruition. Should you have questions or concerns, I will work to address your inquiries. It is our expectation that this experience be the very best for Quincy. For you. And for your family. We demand of ourselves your full satisfaction."

"It sounds . . . too good," Ms. Barrantes says.

Mr. Oklahoma hands her a paper-thin, transparent tablet.

"This is a transfer of care authorization," she says.

"It will allow us to move Quincy to our facility."

She looks up. "But how do I know any of this is legit?" And for a second, I expect her to tell me to stand, say we're leaving. But instead, her finger glides across the signature line.

"You will not regret this," he says, in a voice that makes me wonder how long it is until we do.

79

Two years ago, my freshman biology teacher burst into the lab with too much excitement for nine a.m. and asked his students if we'd watched the hearings.

We hadn't.

"They're saying they can bring someone back from the dead," he'd said.

What? How? Had they already done it? we all wanted to know.

"Not yet," he admitted. "But they're close, and . . ."

But he'd already lost us.

Except now, here I am.

On the verge of seeing the amazing.

But this is night and day compared to what my teacher explained that morning.

He'd said researchers were working to extend human life for a few minutes, maybe several hours. That this technology would also restore them to their prior level of health, pre-illness, pre-accident. The hope was, with more time, family and friends could make it to the bedside of their dying loved one, exchange a few lucid words before they passed.

The time could be used to sort one's estate, to finalize last wishes.

To share passwords. To reveal secrets.

Not every case would qualify, but still—even reanimating the healthiest person seemed implausible.

But this—what the Center's offered—is so far beyond.

And I can't help but wonder what Ms. B and I aren't seeing.

What are we missing?

Why did the Center choose Quincy?

What do they stand to gain?

78

Two black men in black polos and slacks slide the black bag into the black van in the black night.

The setup for an awful joke that no one should finish.

One secures the rear door, the other slides into the driver's seat. They pull away, carrying my friend—can I call him that again?—to the Center.

"The Center for what?" I ask Mr. Oklahoma.

He frowns as if the answer's obvious. "It's just the Center."

"You guys wanted to give your marketing team a lot to work with, I see."

But no one laughs. A thing I don't like about myself—when I'm uncomfortable I make crappy jokes.

"Our car arrives in four minutes," he says, tapping his phone screen. "We have a bit of a journey ahead. I suggest taking advantage of the hospital facilities prior to departure. I will wait here."

Ms. B steers me down a corridor. "Closest bathroom's a one-seater. I'll go after you."

"You first," I insist, and just before she slips inside, I call her name.

My throat tightens. "I think . . . I feel like maybe it's best if I . . . if I leave you to this . . . uh . . . it feels rather . . . personal. Like a family-only thing. And I just think that maybe you'd like some privacy to . . . uh . . . reanimate your son?" I intended a statement but presented a question.

She blinks, her hazel eyes watering again. "As you know, it's just the two of us, Quincy and me, here in Elytown. It's just us . . . anywhere, really. I'd like you to come with me, Jamal. Unless you, or Whit, object. Have you called her?"

I shake my head, and she looks as if she might scold me, but she manages a half smile. "We should call her from the car. That is, if you're coming. If it's not too much." She rubs the back of her head. "What am I saying? Of course it's too much. You should go home. Right? You should go home to your sister. To the baby. But I'd appreciate it if . . . tell you what, I'll use the restroom. If you're not here when I come back out, no hard feelings?"

I nod.

"Okay," she says, holding my eyes a second past comfortable. The piston exhales as the door closes behind her.

"Okay," I say to no one.

Except it's not okay. I can't do this.

I should go.

I have to go.

But which way? Why does every hospital hallway look the same? I walk ten yards south (I think south), but that doesn't feel familiar. I head back, but . . .

Someone's coming, the clap of their shoes louder and louder, closer and closer. I duck inside a door marked Maintenance just as the walking stops.

The sliver of hallway light coming from under the door goes dark.

They're here. Right outside.

I hold my breath. She's looking for me. A couple of steps, then they stop again. It feels like forever before they leave. I wait for the loud click of the heavy exit doors, then slip back into the hallway, walking briskly in the opposite direction.

I barge into the main lobby—the purple-haired receptionist stares but says nothing.

I exit everything.

The cold night air grabs me by the throat.

I shouldn't be there.

Q wouldn't want me there.

A few hours ago, we were ready to end each other.

And even if by some miracle, Q wanted me there, I'm not sure I want to be.

I tap Whit's number and bring the phone to my ear.

But it doesn't ring.

No service.

"Hey," a voice calls out. "Told you he was a fighter." Q's paramedics back-and-forthing an e-cigarette in the ambulance bay, next to a No Smoking sign. "Not gonna lie, it looked bad. But sometimes the world breaks good."

"Thank you," I say.

She tips her head, a reel of smoke rolling from her lips.

And then I'm dead-sprinting down the entrance ramp, hopping the median. I cut the corner too sharply, and a horn blares, tires squeal, as I nearly kiss the hood of a minivan. If it hadn't jumped the red-painted curb, they'd be rushing me back inside the building.

"Are you freaking insane?" the driver screams, flipping me off.

I raise my hand in apology, but there's no time. At the south exit, I spot a black car methodically negotiating the narrow lane.

I barely get my fist on its bumper as the car glides into the street.

It jerks to a stop and I walk around.

The tint on the front passenger window dissolves, Mr. Oklahoma's silver eyes glaring through the perfectly clear glass. "There can be no more indecision, Mr. Anderson," he says through the window. "Do you understand?"

"Yes."

Mr. Oklahoma turns back, his window redarkening. The locks click and I slide into the back seat next to Ms. Barrantes. She's crying, and I'm embarrassed, and I don't know what to say.

She squeezes my hand.

"Thank you," she says so quietly it's as if I merely imagined it.

77

I ask again. "Are we still in Elytown?"

Our headlights impale the darkness ahead.

This far out—with no white noise to swallow it—you hear yourself think, your smallest thought booms like a shotgun.

The world so still you wanna shake it.

When things were especially quiet, Mom held a finger to her lips, as if she'd just rocked the world to sleep. *Listen*, she'd say, *even the bad guys nap*.

Mr. Oklahoma doesn't turn around. "We are, Jamal."

He'd make an excellent play-by-play announcer for the end of humanity.

I bet his *I love you*s sound like a eulogy.

I stick my head into the front seat, but before I can *are we there yet*, we pull sharply off the road, and I fall back, my face smacking the door.

"You wanna use that brake next time," I say, gravel popcorning beneath the car.

The driver taps a sequence onto the car's center console touch screen.

Mr. Oklahoma speaks quietly into his phone.

And Ms. B, her eyes wild, scoots to the middle, leans forward to stare out the front windshield, as if she doesn't believe what her own window's showing her.

"Is this some sick joke?" Ms. B asks.

76

What had I expected?

A building of iridescent glass. A gleaming steel fortress.

A feat of engineering and design that auto-slackened your jaw, made you wish you'd sprung for the phone with the better camera.

An architectural beanstalk shooting from the earth.

But this?

"The GPS working out here? We miss our turn?" I ask, glancing out the rear window.

"We are where we are supposed to be," Mr. Oklahoma says.

"Which is where?"

"The old milk factory," Ms. B answers. "Why are we at the old milk factory?" She reaches for her door handle. Looks at me. And for the first time, she looks terrified. Maybe she's realizing what I'm realizing. That we're in a strange car, in the middle of night and nowhere, at some defunct dairy plant, and no one knows we're here, or who we're with. *We* don't know where we are, who we're with.

Maybe we're coming out of the *bring Q back at all costs* spell.

Maybe it's finally dawning on us that this promise isn't real.

People don't wake up from death.

And even if they could, it wouldn't be in a room filled with milk crates.

I pull out my phone, but Mr. Oklahoma shakes his head. "There is no service here. My apologies."

"I need to call my sister. She's probably freaking out."

He nods. "You can call her when we're inside, Jamal. But we have already notified her. She is aware of the situation."

"You call my son dying a situation?"

Mr. Oklahoma frowns. "Please forgive my poor choice of words, Ms. Barrantes. I assure you I do not take your son's untimely death lightly. As for Whitney, Jamal, she has been fully apprised. Both her and the baby are fine."

What the—did he just—

"How do you know my sister's name? That she's pregnant?"

"When on the cusp of the incredible, Jamal, we must take every precaution. We must leave nothing to chance."

I'm not satisfied, but I know he won't say more.

But if he spoke to Whit, then he has her number. And somehow he knows about the baby. He probably knows where we live. Was he watching our house right now?

The gravel gives way to asphalt and we pull into a clearing invisible from the road.

And that's when we see it.

The first trace of modern technology.

Running north and south, a series of bright-orange light beams spaced evenly as far as I can see in either direction, like fence posts.

Mr. Oklahoma opens the glove box, removes two lanyards, a plain white badge dangling from each. "Put these on. It is vitally important you not remove them while in the lab."

I want to ask *what happens if we do*, except I'm too busy staring at what's ahead. I wait for us to brake, to slow down as we get closer, except we actually gain speed. Ms. B and I exchange looks.

We zip through, all of us illuminated in orange, and it's as if somehow we've stopped *inside* the lights. Like there's an entire room inside the beams. And I swear, on either side of us, I feel like there are eyes on us.

But in the end, we pass through without so much as a chime.

"This is where thousands of cows once crossed," Mr. Oklahoma says, randomly, I think, until I spot a rusted SLOW DOWN, COW X-ING sign.

"What happened? Why'd it shut down?" I ask.

"Weird things were happening with the cows," Ms. B says, and we persist down the dark road in silence.

75

You know that saying, don't judge the Center by its cover?

The inside is everything you'd expect from a facility claiming to resurrect the dead. An expansive lobby filled with soft blue light that caroms off the concrete floor. You can see clear to the top, five levels, stacks of square glass rooms.

The black woman at the front desk, her head shaved, lips lavender, greets us. "Welcome to the Center."

Mr. Oklahoma nods. "Cassandra will escort you to our chief scientists. You already met Dr. Iverson."

"Where are you going?" I ask.

"A few matters require my attention. I will find you after."

"This way," Cassandra says, stepping toward a glass panel. "Please, Ms. Barrantes, Jamal, follow me."

She leads us across a glass bridge, and there's Dr. Iverson. She introduces her colleague as Dr. Langdon.

Dr. Langdon clears his throat. "Before we proceed, you should know that neither Dr. Iverson or myself, nor the Center, are in any way affiliated with the Elytown hospital, or with any hospital system. We are entirely separate entities. The Center is a privately funded medical research facility. You understand?"

"I do, yes." Ms. B clasps her hands. "Rich people own this technology and control how it's used."

Dr. Iverson cuts in. "Luckily, the people who make this place go aren't only generous but also operate with the best intentions." Dr. Iverson smiles. "But that's not why you're here. As we confirmed prior to Quincy's transfer here, he does indeed meet all of our major reanimation criteria."

I meet the doctor's eyes. "Those being?"

"He is healthy, his body is largely unscathed, and he had a good amount of brain and heart activity postexpiration."

"Postexpiration? You mean, his organs were still working after he died?" I ask.

Dr. Langdon grins. "Did you know that right before you take your last breath, there is a large chemical surge within your brain? In fact, it's more activity than your brain ever experienced during all your life. That was the start of all this," he says, holding his arms out like he's selling us a house. "That surge is the key."

Ms. B presses for more. "But how does it work? What if something goes wrong?"

"While I cannot go into the specifics of the reanimation

process, I can tell you that each phase is closely monitored," Dr. Langdon says.

Dr. Iverson adds, "The technology is new, yes, but we employ many of the world's most advanced scientific minds. Quincy will be our tenth reanimation. Each time, as with any procedure, we've improved the quality of the experience."

Dr. Langdon frowns, takes a small step forward. "There is . . . a psychological component to reanimation that you should be keenly aware of."

Ms. B shifts. "Which is?"

"For the reanimation to hold, we need to rewind Quincy's memory to several moments prior to the moment he jumped into the water."

"Why?" I ask.

"Because the trauma of that incident, its severity, could untether Quincy's mental health."

"You said there'd be no pain, but now you're saying my son could go crazy," Ms. B says, her voice rising.

"No, no," Dr. Langdon says, holding his hands up. "The rewind prevents that. It lessens the shock to the system. As such, our team is also determining the ideal window in which to restart your son's memory of last night."

Ms. B nods slowly. "There's a *but* coming."

Dr. Iverson tilts her head. "Quincy will not recall any aspect surrounding his death."

"I don't understand."

"We're saying . . ." Dr. Iverson clasps her hands together in that doctorly way. "Quincy will not know he's dead, but in a few weeks' time, he will die again, Ms. Barrantes. Physiologically and psychologically, memory rewinding is the safest way for us to reanimate. But once Quincy's fully regrounded into his old world, it may be beneficial to . . . alert him to the nature of his situation."

"You mean, you want me to tell my son that he's dead, that he was temporarily *reanimated* in a milk factory, and that in however many days, he'll die again?"

Dr. Langdon's face tightens. "It's very much a question of ethics. The moral thing to do."

"So, you're suggesting withholding this from my son makes me immoral?"

Dr. Iverson cuts in. "We understand why you might opt not to tell Quincy. You want him to be happy. To enjoy his last days without being consumed by some countdown."

"I want my son to live in peace. Without worry. Free to be his normal self."

"And that is your legal right." Dr. Iverson nods. "We'll need you to sign a document acknowledging this conversation."

And clearly, this is not my decision, no one's asked for my opinion, but. "Wouldn't you want to know the truth?" I blurt.

Ms. B glares. "This isn't about me. This is what's best for Quincy."

"You agreed he deserves more time. Doesn't he also deserve to know what's happened to him? I think he'd want . . ."

"You know Quincy better than me, Jamal?"

I take a step back. "No, I'm just saying maybe we should consider . . ."

"We? *We* should consider," Ms. B repeats, her rage flaring. "When's the last time you had an actual conversation with my son?"

Technically speaking, it was on the beach, but that's not what she means. "Longer than it should've been."

She nods. "I appreciate you being here, but I know my son, and I've made my decision. No one is to tell him a single word. Not one. Is that clear?"

Finally, I nod.

Do I agree? Absolutely not. But I'm going to support Ms. B's decision.

Until I can't.

74

When Mr. Oklahoma returns, Ms. B rubs her hands together.

"What's next? You mentioned tests?"

He nods. "There will be a formal analysis. But first, we need to collect blood samples from each of you."

And I know I said I was gonna back-seat this thing, but—

"Blood samples for what?" I ask.

"It is essential we maintain a clean facility. As such, we need to ensure you are healthy, lest we expose Quincy to unnecessary risks."

I'm about to follow up when Ms. B touches my arm. "We'll do whatever's required," she says.

"That is the spirit." Mr. Oklahoma removes his glasses, rubs each lens with a cloth from his pocket. "But first, showers. You will find fresh linen and clothing in the dressing rooms."

"How soon until you bring my son back?"

"Very."

Ms. B holds her head. "I still don't understand how this is possible. We can't eliminate cancer, or solve world hunger, but you can resurrect the dead?"

"It is challenging to grasp. I admit there are times I too wonder if this is real. If this work is . . ." He pauses. "World hunger is a by-product of greed and could easily be resolved. As for solving cancer? We are close. The work we are doing, Ms. Barrantes, we are reverse engineering death itself. Conquer death and every domino falls swiftly—pestilence, every senseless killing, every affliction. Gone forever."

I jump in. "No one's mentioned a price. How much is this gonna cost?"

Mr. Oklahoma shakes his head. "This reanimation has been gifted."

"*What?*" Ms. B shakes her head. "By whom?"

He adjusts his glasses. "An anonymous donor." Mr. Oklahoma holds up two fingers at a camera mounted in the corner. "Apparently, someone believes your son to be a hero."

"A hero?"

"There was a report he saved someone from drowning."

Ms. B's voice is tinged with confusion. "Wait, what do you mean? What are you saying?"

And I remember Q's question: *Is she okay?* Had this been what he'd meant? Had there been someone else out there in that water? And if so, how had Q managed to save her?

"All will be explained in due time," Mr. Oklahoma says.

"No, *now*," Ms. B says firmly. "How about you tell me right now?"

But then a woman in gray scrubs materializes, waits at Mr. Oklahoma's side. "I understand your desire to know what happened tonight, and we will make time for it. But right now, the most important matter is that we restore your son safely. Now, if you will excuse me, I will gather you shortly."

Ms. B starts to object, but the woman in gray scrubs motions for us to follow. And I decide to keep Q's words to myself. At least for now.

"This way, please," our new guide says.

She leads us down a long white corridor, stopping at two doors. "Return here when you're finished, please."

And then she's gone.

Ms. B and I exchange a look.

"Am I crazy, Jamal? Am I crazy to do this?"

"What do you have to lose?"

She squeezes my shoulder. "My son again," she says, then disappears inside her dressing room.

The shower? More like a car wash.

Large enough to bathe a whole herd of cows.

Which, gross.

Anyway, the shower is fully automated.

117

There are no visible controls. No knobs, handles, buttons. No touchscreen. I step through the glass door and it closes silently behind me.

Three transparent arms slide up the three surrounding walls, shooting a warm, massage-like jet stream on all sides of my body.

And then a purple mist.

A rinse.

A yellow mist.

Another rinse.

The water snaps off.

I half expect an arm to pop out of the wall and dress me, but instead I slip on the new clothes, a powder-blue jumpsuit and house shoes.

Ms. B already back in the hallway.

The woman in gray scrubs leads us to another area of the Center.

A room with a wide window overlooking an enormous all-white lab, women and men wearing hospital masks and jumpsuits like the one I have on, except white, seated at work-stations with rows and rows of interconnected monitors. Jumbled letters and numbers fly across the screens at a rate I can't process. Even if I could slow it down, I wouldn't know what any of it meant.

Mr. Oklahoma, standing with a man and woman dressed in lab coats, smiles, waves us over. "Ms. Barrantes, Jamal, these are our clinical modelers, Marcus and Kiana."

"Modelers?"

"They will conduct your interviews. The information they gather will assist in Quincy's personality recovery."

"Wait, why . . . are you saying Quincy might not have the same personality?"

"He will be the same Quincy, but the imaging smooths any potential wrinkles we might discover during the last phase of reanimation. Likely it will not be needed, but we prefer to be proactive rather than reactive."

Kiana pushes the door, holds it open. "Ms. Barrantes, if you'll please follow me to analysis room one, we'll get started."

"So that means it's you and me," I say to Marcus.

He doesn't smile. "Come," he says. "It's important we don't fall behind the reanimators."

73

Marcus is not a small-talk person.

"And Quincy's mental state at the party?"

"I'd say, uh, fairly normal, initially."

"Numerical value only, please."

I refer to the tablet he gave me. Columns of emotions, each with a half dozen subemotions, all assigned a number range. Get it?

Yeah, me either.

I tap the screen. "Right. Sorry. Eight. No, seven, I guess."

Marcus glances up from the terminal. "*All* of your responses are guesses, Mr. Anderson. As I explained, the majority of Quincy's recall will be directly downloaded. This work, it's simply a facade. Window dressing. All you need to do is answer to the best of your ability, yes?"

"Honestly, I don't understand how any of this helps."

He sighs. "The better we understand the way Q was perceived by those closest to him, the better the imaging. Make sense?"

No. Not really. "Yeah. Sure. I'm just . . . I haven't slept and I'm just . . . any idea how much longer this is gonna take?"

"You have better things to do?"

"Definitely not, but . . ."

"You want the best outcome for your friend?"

"Of course."

"The best outcome takes as long as it takes. Now, can we continue, or do you require a brief intermission?"

"No, no, you're right. Let's . . . let's keep going."

"Our next session is long-form questions. Use as many words as you need to answer. Clear?"

Not especially. I nod.

"So, it is our understanding, you and Quincy are no longer friends? Why was this relationship terminated?"

I wring my hands in my lap. My lips, throat, dry up. "What do you mean?"

Marcus shakes his head, sighs for the hundredth time since we sat down. "Jamal, tell me why your friendship ended."

72

two months after the funeral

QUINCY: Hey, just thought you'd want to know it's not looking good. Doctors said he probably only has a few weeks left so I thought you might wanna come and see him, you know.

And then a week later.

QUINCY: he's gone

QUINCY: not that you care

My finger brushed the doorbell, but I didn't push it.

I'm not sure how long I stood out there, on the Barrantes porch, before the door swung open.

Before I got what was coming to me.

"You're too late, Jamal," Q spat. "Why'd you even bother?"

And I couldn't even look at him.

"Q," I said. "Q," I said again, the words not coming.

For two months, I'd been so angry. All I could think was if Q hadn't called, my parents would be here, in our kitchen, in their bed, on our porch. And the more Q tried to be there for me, the angrier I became.

I was so stupid.

But as usual, I made matters worse, ignoring his texts.

And of course, he thought it was because I didn't care.

But the truth is, I couldn't stand to look at him. I couldn't separate Q's face from theirs.

"I'm . . . I'm so—"

But Q waved me off. "Don't you dare," he said. "Don't fucking dare."

And I couldn't even roll another word to the tip of my tongue before the door slammed, rocked so hard the hand-painted sign fell of its hook.

Bless This House, it said.

But I was too late.

Even before I stepped off that porch, the lesson was clear: There comes a point when, no matter what they'd done to you, you couldn't justify continuing to treat someone terribly.

There comes a point when it's no longer their problem, only yours.

And you could forgive and heal, or you could keep clutching that hurt, like a hot coal against your chest.

71

Quincy: Hey guys, so this is more of an announcement than anything. I know you all have been asking, What's going on with you and J? Well, I'm not gonna get into all the details, because honestly, I'm kinda wondering the same thing. But I'll say this, as of now, we won't be making any more videos together. Because, as it turns out, it's kinda hard to make videos with someone when you're not even talking, so, haaaaaaa.

But, never fear, I'm still gonna be here.

Yep, the UNCY in Jauncy ain't going nowhere . . .

So, I hope you guys stay put too.

Keep checking back every Saturday for new content, okay!

Quincy out!

Peaaaaacceeeee!

70

I can't tell you how many questions I answer.

How many numerical values I assign.

We take intermittent breaks, and at some point, they lead us to a room filled with enough food to feed all of Elytown. *Hopefully you'll find something you like*, they said before leaving me and Ms. B alone, a white table with two place settings in the center of the room. The room is made of glass, same as all the others, except on their way out, our guides made it a point to press a panel beside the door, the clear glass darkening to a translucent frost. *We'll collect you in thirty.*

And when they return, we're taken to more tests.

Except for our meal, Ms. B and I are separated the entire process, but then, at the very end, I'm led to a large room the shape of a half circle. It's like a college lecture hall, but grander, plush seats, synthetic wood detailing, and a massive screen in the center of the front wall.

"Any clue why we're here?" I ask her.

But then the lights dim and the screen glows.

A woman in a tailored suit smiles at us from the screen. She's standing in the Center's main lobby.

"On behalf of everyone here at the Center, we'd like to thank you for your hard work today. Your willingness to participate in the reanimation of your loved one does not go unrecognized," she says as she walks the lobby floor.

She goes on like this for a while, highlighting each phase of the reanimation process, except her version is even more watered down, and I struggle to understand the point until finally she looks into the camera and says:

"And to ensure your loved one the optimal reanimation experience, we must ask that you follow three basic rules."

She holds up a finger. "One. Immediate family and close friends aside, you must not communicate what you've seen or heard during your visit here. For Q's safety, it's important that we limit knowledge of his procedure and this facility only to those who need to know. And this should be obvious, but please, no social media posts."

She smiles. Holds up two fingers. "You have been assigned a personal reanimation adviser. In the unlikely event something unusual should occur with your loved one, under no circumstances are you to contact your local authorities. Your loved one is under twenty-four-hour monitoring, and as such, it is likely a team of trained professionals is already on their way. But, for your peace of mind, please feel free to relay any concerns directly to your adviser."

Three fingers. "This is perhaps the most important rule. Enjoy these precious moments with your loved one. This is the second chance you didn't know you could have. Have fun with it!"

If this is what's required of Ms. B and me, I can't even imagine what they're putting Q through: rifling through his DNA, analyzing this, diagnosing that.

When the lights come back on, we're no longer alone.

"One for you, and one for you," Mr. Oklahoma says, handing us vacuum-sealed bags, our personal clothes compressed inside.

"Thank you for your help and your patience. Quincy's reanimation will be all the better for it," Dr. Iverson says.

"So, that's it? We're done?" Ms. B asks.

Mr. Oklahoma nods. "Now you go home and do your best to sleep. We will notify you an hour prior to our arrival."

"And you just, what, drop him in his bed and he wakes up?" I ask.

"In simplest terms, yes," Mr. Oklahoma answers.

Dr. Iverson clears her throat. "There is one more thing to discuss. The death window. You understand it, as it was explained?"

Ms. B nods. "Quincy will . . . there's a four-hour window, during which he will again . . . expire. And just . . . for emphasis . . . Quincy will not experience any pain?"

Dr. Iverson nods. "Except maybe the pain of being a teen-ager."

Mr. Oklahoma cuts in. "There is good news to share. Quincy's projected length of stay."

Ms. B holds her hands together, like prayer. "How long does he have?"

"Quincy's projected LOS is twenty-four to twenty-eight days."

Ms. B cuffs her face with her hands, and I even hear myself gasp.

Q has nearly a full month to live.

Dr. Iverson smiles. "Quincy will obliterate our previous record."

Ms. B can't stop crying. "Thank you, thank you," she says over and over.

"Of course," Dr. Iverson says. "We're honored you've accepted our services. You will not be disappointed."

"Now, please, go home and rest," Mr. Oklahoma says. "Time is our most precious commodity. You want to be at your very best when *your* son, and *your* friend, reopens his eyes."

69

When we exit the Center, three things carousel in my brain:

1) I have to make things right with Q. There's zero time to waste.

2) Quincy should know the truth.

3) I wish my parents were also coming home.

68

We're not halfway to the main road when the Center disappears.

And when we pull out, I'm dizzied with the feeling we've left something behind.

Something we'll never get back.

The drive home's even quieter.

Ms. B's face presses against her door; I can't tell if she's sleeping or submerged in thought.

Given the pendulum of the last twelve hours, I'd guess the latter.

Twenty minutes into the ride, I feel funny.

And then I realize where we are.

On the back road to my house.

The road I've avoided for two years.

Then I see the flashing lights.

And it's like my body's hijacked.

Like the knob that controls my senses is suddenly cranked to the extreme right, and then the entire panel smashed to pieces.

And now I can hear the driver's hands tightening around the wheel as we approach the bend. And I smell burning pine. And then we're right on top of those lights, they're in our car, and we're turning the corner, and every photon is leaping into my eyes.

And I can't see.

But also, I see them.

I see us, smiling, laughing, our family car filled with blinding light.

Our love is at an al-pine high! Our love is at an al-pine high!

"I'm gonna be sick," I say.

I barely make it two feet out the car before I torpedo vomit onto the side of the road.

Ms. B glides her hand up and down my back. "Feel better?"

"Yeah, I think so. Maybe," I say. "Just woozy."

She frowns. "Takes slow, deep breaths."

And so I do.

I play a game with myself where I concentrate on each breath and pretend as if my stomach and throat aren't inside-jobbing me.

"We should get you checked out, Jamal." She grips my wrist. "Your pulse's out of control. You're clearly dehydrated. And . . ."

I raise my hand. "No. I just need rest," I assure her. "Like the doctors said. It's been a long night for all of us."

Which, true. Behind us, the sun is escalating, the sky brightening.

I have to promise that I feel better, that I'll tell her the second that changes, that once home I'll tell Whit if that changes, and then I'm slipping back on my seat belt, my phone buzzing in the door pocket.

I unlock the screen as we angle back onto the road.

Autumn: Hey, what's going on??

Autumn: You there?

Autumn: Will you please update me when you get a chance?

Autumn: I'd rather know, even if it's bad. Don't decide anything for me

Autumn: OMG, JAMAL CALL ME

Autumn: JAMALLLLLL, SRSLY?! 😠😠😠😠

I tap a quick response back, hating that I can't tell her the truth.

Me: Hey, I'm so sorry!!!! But everything's okay.

She responds almost immediately.

Autumn: OMG, were you trying to kill me??? You can't leave me hanging like that, Jamal. Not when the last time I see you, you and Q are in the back of an ambulance!!

Her next text, a half-dozen rows of alternating angry emojis and crying emojis.

Me: You're right. There was just so much going on and we weren't allowed to use our phones back there with all the equipment and I just wasn't thinking straight.

Me: I'm really really really sorry.

Autumn: Are you still at the hospital? Where's Q?

Me: Yeah, they're keeping him another few hours for observation

And I feel massively crappy lying to her. But that's the only way this whole operation works, right? Funny, grown-ups always preaching honesty.

Autumn: You think it's okay if I go up there?

Me: tbh I'd wait. He was mostly sleeping.

Me: the only reason they let me see him was because I lied and said he was my brother.

Autumn: Okay. Think it's cool if you gave me his number? I wanna text him later. Maybe call.

Me: Yeah, I'll send it now

Me: Hey what about you?? You ok??

Autumn: other than the fact that I didn't sleep at all because I was worried sick? Yeah, I'm okay.

Me: And . . . what about us.

Me: Are we ok?

Autumn: No.

Autumn: We shouldn't be.

Autumn: You hurt me and that doesn't just go away.

Me: Yeah I know ☹ ☹ ☹

Autumn: But.

Autumn: And this is gonna sound real morbid and prolly selfish but whatever cuz it's real.

Me: I've been warned.

A few minutes pass and I wonder what she's doing.

The wait agonizing.

Was she trying to decide how to say it, if to say it?

Was she distracted by another text from someone else?

Had she fallen asleep?

Decided I wasn't even worth a morbid, selfish thought?

My phone vibrates, but it's just a text from the library, my books overdue.

Me: Hey you still there?

But my phone buzzes the same time I tap Send.

Autumn: I can't stop thinking what if the worst happened today . . . like . . .

Autumn: what if you'd died in that water? On that dumb-ass beach?

Autumn: Like, that fight would've been our last moment together.

Autumn: How horrible would that've been???

And I want to say, I know *exactly* how horrible because that's how I feel right now. About Q. That fight on that dumb-ass beach was our last moment together.

I tap the crying emoji but delete it.

Me: I don't want to think about that.

Autumn: me either but it's basically ALL I've thought about so thanks for that dude.

Autumn: story moral: don't lie to me!!!! LIKE EVERRRR.

Me: I won't.

Me: EVERRRRRRRR.

Aside from the earth-shattering lie I just told you about Q.

But really, what choice do I have?

Me: do you wanna come over later?

Autumn: I'm glad you and q are okay but . . .

Autumn: honestly I don't really wanna see you rn.

Which, fair.

Me: I'm so sorry, Autumn

And I wait for her reply, but it never comes.

There are dozens of texts from Whit.

A few from kids who'd been on the beach too, asking if Q's okay.

As far as anyone's concerned, Q is alive and well; just waiting to be cleared by the doctors, after which he will return home, Mr. Oklahoma had explained.

I scroll Whit's thread.

Her first texts are frantic, worried.

But then her tone completely one-eighties.

True to Mr. O's word, she knows what's happened, she can't imagine, can't believe any of it. Says how bad she feels because she was relieved that I was okay when Q wasn't.

Whit: I'm waiting up.

Whit: You don't have to talk. Not tonight. But I'll be here, waiting for you.

67

six weeks after the funeral

For six weeks there were flowers.

A mound of daisies and tiger lilies, a heap of sunflowers and dandelions, a bouquet of roses with thorns intact, in assorted states of decay.

Decay, a slow march to oblivion.

A month after we buried Mom and Dad, the city added rows of bright flashing lights at the bend, affixed a large sign: HIGH ACCIDENT AREA.

Which seems odd, right?

Shouldn't they add USE CAUTION?

Or SLOW DOWN?

At least a generic DRIVE SAFE?

Instead, they're politely tapping your shoulder, hey, so um, I see you're busy driving recklessly and endangering the lives of others, but listen, just so you know, and please do with this what you will, but uh, there are *whispers* a decent amount of accidents right here, so.

DRIVER: Oh. Wow. Thanks for letting me know. Should I slow down? Use caution?

That's entirely up to you. We're empowering you to use your own sound judgment.

The city also made a plaque, a vertical oak rectangle with a high-gloss bronze plate, like the ones in our school display case that read: Charles County Division II Softball Champs. Except this one was stop-sign-sized and drilled into the tree closest to the road.

In fancy lettering:

JADA & ANDRE ANDERSON. NEVER FORGET.

Never forget what? I asked Whit. That they're gone? That Dad's body was flung somewhere in those bushes? Not to mention, it's ridiculously weird. Like, who immortalizes a tragedy with a tree plaque?

You're overthinking it. It's a nice thing, Whit said.

Which is what people resort to when there's nothing real to be done, nothing useful—something nice.

Two nights after the city workers put it up, I snuck over and crowbarred it off.

It left gashes in the tree. Plus holes where they'd sunk the screws. I was still working on the fourth screw when the plaque splintered. I tossed the screws into the woods and nearly sent the plaque in after them.

I'm not sure what stopped me.

But there was no way I was keeping it.

At home, I tossed it in our trash bin.

And later, when someone from the city stopped by to apologize for the vandalism and to assure us a replacement plaque would be mounted, I told them *thanks, but no thanks.*

You sure, he'd said, his eyes looking behind me, waiting for confirmation from a grown-up. But Whit wasn't home.

We're sure, I told him.

Because Mom and Dad died there.

In the bend beside that thicket.

They didn't win a tournament.

66

Approx. 24–27 Q Days Left

"Hey, welcome back to the land of the living." Whit winces. "Jeez, terrible choice of words."

I uncrust my eyes. "How long was I out?"

But I never hear her answer.

My bedroom spins like a runaway carousel. The ache in my head crescendoing.

Shutting my eyes doesn't take away the pain, but it slows the whirling.

My exhaustion so heavy, yawning feels like work.

"Whit, I'm sorry . . . I'm so groggy . . . I . . ."

And then, silence.

Sleep caving in on m—

65

"This is Earth to Jamal. Earth to Jamal, do you read me?"

My cereal's officially cream-of-flakes soup.

I barely remember entering the kitchen.

Clearly, I opened the fridge. Unstacked a bowl and spoon.

Except how I got here, when I got here—I can't tell you.

Like when you're suddenly at your destination only you don't remember driving.

It's that wake-up-in-the-middle-of-a-dream feeling.

Where you have to touch your nose because it was just being eaten by zombies.

You look out your window because a meteor just leveled your garage.

"Jamal, hey." Whit shakes my arm. "Hey, man, you still with me?"

Whit tries disguising her worry with a smile, but keeping feelings wrapped isn't her specialty. I like to tease her she's the fashionista of feelings, always wearing them on her sleeves *and* leggings.

I shake my head. "Huh? Sure. What?"

"I didn't know you took your cereal well-done. How is it?"

I spoon up the brown gruel, gulp it, lick my lips. "Actually, it's under-soggy." I eat another scoop. "Yep, definitely needs more sog."

We laugh, which immediately reminds me that my skull still hates me. I massage my temples.

"Why are you looking at me like that?"

Whit frowns. "You mean like a person who watched his best friend die last night? Is that the look I'm giving you?"

"Nailed it," I reply. And before I can reel off more groggy retorts, she's third-trimester walking around the table to me, unable to wrap her arms around me because she's growing a baby. But she tries anyway. Settles for a tight side hug.

"Look, J, I'm so sorry for Q, for everything that's happened. I don't know where to start, but . . ."

I squeeze her shoulder. "Don't be mad, but can we put a pin in this?"

"Umm, Dad much?"

I shrug. "Dad was the king of postponed conversations."

"Yeah, and we both loved it. Dad, can I go to the movies with Carla?"

I fall into Dad voice. "I'll let you know, Whitney."

"Deeper. Dad's voice was, like, *way* deeper. Almost guttural."

"How's this?"

"Better, but deeper."

"This is all I got, Whit."

"Fine." She sighs. "Okay, but the movie starts in two hours."

"Two hours? Well, you shoulda let me know four hours ago. You know I hate to be rushed."

"If Dad was here, we couldn't talk about last night because we'd still be catching up on stuff from two years ago," Whit says.

And she's right. And we do this sometimes, riff on our parents. Make fun of them the way the four of us always teased each other. Except right now it feels off.

Our normal broken, again.

"Whit, I know there's a lot to talk about, that last night is a thing I'll be talking about for the rest of my life, but right now I just wanna sit here and not eat my cereal and hang out with my sister like a regular morning. Can we please do that?"

"Okay, I hear you, but I just think we should probably . . ."

"Whit, *please*."

"We can't keep sweeping things under rugs, Jamal. We can't let the bad things fester inside. Remember what Dr. Ocean said, 'If we're gonna heal, then we've . . .'"

"I know. I'm not asking for forever. Just not now."

She sighs, and I feel it coming. "You know, it's one thing to skip school. But it's another thing entirely to lie to me about it."

"Really? You wanna throw that on me *now*?"

"Jamal, *you've* been throwing that on *me* for *two years*."

"Don't you get it? I could die on my way up those stairs. In the shower. You could . . . What if you . . ." But I can't say it.

And honestly, I couldn't survive that.

"What's the point of school, Whit? Of calculus or biology or any of it?"

"Jamal, as lonely and as personal as losing Mom and Dad feels to you, to me, we aren't the first to ever be dealt a crappy hand. And we aren't the last. And you're right. You probably don't need calculus. But life isn't only doing the things *you* want. And you definitely don't get to use our parents' deaths as an excuse to detonate your life. If *you* wanna fail high school, own that. If *you* wanna make poor choices, do it in your own name. Not theirs. Don't dishonor them."

And I want to run out of this kitchen. Climb the tallest mountain. Scream every curse word I can think of, and when those run out make up my own, until my voice gives. Except life isn't only doing the things *I* want, so I'm told.

Whit takes my hand, lowers herself onto the chair beside me.

I can't tell you how many minutes go by before either of us speaks again. I take out my phone, cycle through a few apps, try to pretend I'm unfazed, but.

"Angeles hopped in his car, soon as I told him what happened."

My brow arches. "Wait, word? But it's finals week, he can't

just . . . he doesn't even know Q."

"No," Whit says. "But he knows you."

It's easy to picture Angeles running to his old sedan, driving down whatever road it was that took him from Chicago to Ohio.

"I mean, I get it. And it's, like, really cool of him, but also not something he should do."

"Oh, you're worried about someone missing school, huh?"

And I try not to laugh, but Whit's got that look on her face, like Mom when she called us out.

And we both laugh.

"Don't think because I'm laughing, we're done with all that. We're meeting with your counselor tomorrow."

"Damn, *tomorrow*? Can't it wait until next week?"

But Whit shoots me a different look, this one entirely her own, and I let it go.

"So, Angeles is gonna pull in our driveway any minute now?"

"Nope, I made him turn around. He was upset, but he knows I'm right."

"Good," I say. "I mean, I love the guy, but him skipping his finals after everything you two have sacrificed so he could finish school, like, nah."

Whit nods. "I told him, 'Angeles, I love you and I appreciate how supportive you are of me and Jamal, but I need you to keep your narrow behind at Northwestern for one more week and then you can come make my brother laugh and smother me, okay?'"

That word *smother* teleporting me to the beach. Autumn's voice a razor. The pain in Q's face at once vivid and fleeting—like the pinch from a needle.

"He's a good dude."

"He is. He's the best. And he probably could've gotten his absence excused, and maybe I should've let him come, but . . . he already does a lot, you know?"

"I've hated all your boyfriends except for him. Like, seriously, he's so cool I have to stop myself from asking him what he sees in you." I laugh.

Whit punches my arm. "Oh, trust me, I've actually asked Autumn the same thing."

Hearing Autumn's name, it's like another blow, except this one I feel inside. I nearly lost her on that beach.

"Whatever," I say. I sit straight up, smooth the front of my shirt, pose like I'm in the middle of a cover shoot. "I think it's pretty clear what she sees in me."

"An abnormally large head? A penchant for jacking up punch lines? A person who refuses to use plates but goes through seventy-four glasses every day?"

"Okay, okay, I get it." I shrug. "I guess we're both hella lucky," I say.

"And also, hella not," Whit adds.

And no truer words.

"I swear the way this kid kicks, they'll be a star on the pitch."

"God, I hope so. I need someone to explain soccer to me."

Whit scrunches her face. "Umm, I played all four years in high school. You came to my games, but you still don't get it?"

"Correct."

Whit shakes her head. "You're like the dumbest smart kid alive sometimes."

We both crack up. And it feels good. And no, not feel-better-about-Q good, obviously. But a tiny reprieve.

A temporary stay.

"Also, I'd like to reenter into the record that I strongly disagree with you and Angeles's decision to not know the sex. Like, it's wrecking me, for real. Plus, there are clear advantages to knowing. For instance, I could be painting the nursery."

She punches me again. "What's the sex got to do with the paint color?"

I tilt my head. "Fair. My bad."

She rubs her belly. I swear sometimes I see the baby's face peering out at me, their tiny hands poking out. It's so weird that humans, women, can grow life. Weirdly beautiful. And I get that at the end there's unspeakable pain—a pain men will never understand—but women keep doing it, you know. Because, wow.

And now Whit's due date is only two weeks away.

She'd already scheduled a C-section for the following week, *in case the natural thing doesn't happen naturally*, she'd said.

Which means the baby could potentially be born the same day Q re-dies?

What would it mean—that forever my niece or nephew's birthday would roll in tandem with the anniversary of my former friend's second death?

Whit stretches her arms. "I admit in the beginning I was curious, but now . . . I already love her or him more than I can explain, you know?"

"I didn't know it was real, but you have it. That pregnancy glow."

"You hang around a lot of pregnant people?"

"I swear your silhouette's shimmering."

"Stop it."

"You're going to be the best mom ever."

She lowers her eyes. Ping-pongs her coffee mug the two inches between her palms. "Not the best. There was only one of those."

"You stop it," I say.

We sit there, silent, letting our parents wash over us. We used to resist it, ward them off. We took turns being overcome; we'd rifle through cabinets, suddenly gripped by a desire for fruit snacks, cashews, anything so long as it distracted us. And when we ran out of things to open, when only our tear ducts were left, we'd scurry away, a sobbing mess. But now, we mostly let the ghosts do their thing.

This entire house a blurry time-lapse of their lives, a continuous loop of their hazy outlines walking the floor, marching upstairs, opening doors, flopping onto the couch, brushing their teeth—Mom and Dad, burned in, like negatives.

How can I shave without Dad appearing beside me, showing me how to glide the razor and not bleed out? How can I sit at this table and not see Mom swiping through the news on her tablet, more lipstick on her grapefruit juice glass than her lips? Why did she do that? Put her makeup on first? Why didn't she wait?

Why didn't Dad wait? Hold the brake five more seconds and everything's okay. I used to wonder if there'd come a day that memory no longer haunted me. But now I know, there are things that never leave you. Things that become you.

Height's the only thing I have on my sister, so I stoop down, burrow my face into her cottoned shoulder. And her hands insta-grip the back of my head. We cling to each other like this kitchen's a mountain face and we are dangling on its precipice.

And if we let go . . .

We can't let go.

"I'm so tired of everyone leaving," Whit says softly into my ear.

"I know," I say. "Me too."

"I wanna be a good parent, you know? But no matter how hard I try, no matter how hard I wish otherwise, I'm not Dad. I'm not Mom."

"No," I say. "You're here."

64

My phone skitters atop the kitchen island.

"Jamal? Are you awake?"

If I wasn't, I am now—why do people ask that?

"Yeah, Mr. O. Just enjoying a bowl of flavored milk. What's wrong?"

"Relax. All will be fine." Except the long pause that follows seems to contradict his reassurance. Also, am I the only one who hates being told to *relax*? In the history of Homo sapiens, no one's ever been told to relax and then actually relaxed. *Plus,* it's hella condescending, no?

"We do have a new development." I can feel Mr. O weighing his words. Cycling through what to say, how to say it, and in what combination—like a slot machine called How to Not

Freak People Out in Otherwise Extremely Freak-Out Situations.

"What is it?"

"As I explained during your visit, we needed to rewind Q's memory." He waits for me to acknowledge this factoid.

"Okay. Sure. I remember."

"Our initial reset target is no longer viable. We need to rewind Q a bit more."

"I don't understand. How much more?"

"He'll remember the house party, but not the beach," Mr. O says.

"Wait, does this change—"

"It means . . ." Mr. O cuts me off. "Quincy's reanimation could be more . . . eventful than anticipated."

"What does that mean? More eventful?"

"It means we would like you to be there when he awakes."

"Me? What about Ms. Barrantes?"

"Ms. Barrantes is having a hard time this morning. We need you there, Jamal. Can you do this?"

Why is it Mr. O strikes me as the kind of person who calls in sick to a doctor's appointment?

"I'm heading over now."

"Whitney is there with you now, no?"

What does that have to do with anything? "Umm, yeah, why?"

"Perhaps I should speak with her. Confirm that she is okay with—"

My turn to interrupt. "It's fine. There's no need for that. But I'm a little lost about what you want me to do here?"

"Nothing, Jamal. Your presence will merely help stabilize the reawakening. All of our data points indicate you as an important figure in Quincy's life. When he sees you, sees his mother, he will be more firmly cemented into our reality. You *were* his best friend, after all."

Were. Damn, how does *he* know to use the past tense?

But then I recall the twelve thousand personal questions I was asked, the majority centered on my relationship with Q, and yeah, of course he knows.

"I'm on my way."

"You're on your way where?" Whit asks, as I drop my phone into my pocket. She follows me into the hallway, watches me zip my jacket.

"Q's reawakening."

"Wait, I'm confused. I thought . . ."

"Yeah, I thought so too, but I guess after all that's happened, nothing should surprise us."

"So, what are you supposed to do? Just sit there until . . ."

"He opens his eyes, yep." I open the front door. "I'll call you in a bit."

"What do you say to someone when they're headed to a reanimation?" Whit asks. "Good luck?"

I nod. "I'll take that."

I'm nearly to Dad's car—when my chest starts to burn. Just the idea of driving this car makes me want to vomit again, twists a million daggers into my heart. Maybe it won't even start up.

Except I know it will.

Whit drives it from time to time for this very reason. She even took it for a tune-up the other day. *Whenever you're ready, it's there,* she's said more times than I can count. Not even blinking when I've turned down the keys, when I bummed ride after ride from her, as if she didn't have a thousand other commitments.

The front door swings open. Whit teeters down the walk. "Are you okay?"

I turn around, walking backward down the driveway. "Yeah. No. I'm not sure. Am I?"

"You're driving Da . . ." She catches herself, probably afraid to jinx it.

I shrug. "Miracles just happening all over the place." I slip into the seat and nostalgia floods me. It smells like Dad. How many times had he sat where I'm sitting now?

I don't even want to adjust the rearview mirror; which is silly, because Whit's driven it, has probably adjusted it, but still. I don't want to disturb a single thing. I just want to sit here a moment. But a moment, the one thing I don't have. I press the Start button, the engine growls to life. Whit's still walking toward me, nearly at my window, but far enough away that I throw the car in reverse without fear of hurting her.

I just need to take my foot off the brake.

I just need to—

Suddenly, I'm in the passenger seat and I look over to my left and there is Mom, and she's reaching across to pinch my cheek in that way that I absolutely hate, except she's smiling her *I love you no matter what even if you killed someone which I naturally wouldn't condone but I'd certainly give you the benefit of the doubt I'd definitely hear you before rushing to judgment* smile and who can resist *that* smile?

"Jamal, my love," Mom says. "I'm proud of you. For doing this. For making it right."

"Mama, I don't know if . . . what if I can't . . ."

She nods slightly, in that way she does when she's assessing the situation, when she's giving you all of her attention, funneling her energy into this singular moment in time with you.

"Baby, you are made for moments like this. Don't you see?"

"Mama," I say, softly. And then my hand is moving up to her still-cheek-pinching hand, except then my hand goes through hers and like the snake-shaped smoke that curls away when you blow out a candle, she disintegrates into a wisp.

"Mama," I call out.

But she's gone and I'm back in the driver's seat.

And my hands are shaking on the steering wheel, and c'mon, J, get it together, Q needs you, just release the brake, man. Just lift your heel, your toes. Just—

"You got this, Jamal," Dad says from the passenger seat.

And now I can't stop the tears.

I can't bring myself to look at him. Not straight on.

Not just to watch him dissolve, disappear into nothing.

"Jamal," he says. And now his hand is on the radio. "Listen, I know Mom says you shouldn't listen to music while you learn to drive. But it's relaxing sometimes. Like, you want your mind on the road, but also you don't want to overthink, overcompensate, okay? It's important not to overreact, okay, son?"

I'm not going to look.

I can't.

His heavy hand covers mine. "Son, you're gonna be fine. Just lift your foot, okay?" A commercial ends, and a song slides into the car. "Jamal, why won't you look at me, son?"

"Dad, you're not there. It's not really you."

"What are you talking about? Of course it's me. Jamal, who else would I be?"

"Dad, I'm going to stop talking to you. Please, stop talking to me. I can't . . . I can't do this . . . please. Not now."

"Just look at me, son. Just look. One look . . ."

And I give in and he grins wide enough I can see his gold molar, bottom row, right side. "See," he says. "Not so hard, right? Not so—"

He starts to fade, flicker.

"Not so. N-n-n. Not s-s-s-so."

He smiles harder, and then he's fainter, a dissipating cloud. Until only his outline is left. Like if he'd lie down on paper and you traced him, and then you cut out the outside of the shape and then you cut out the inside, too, and all that was left was your thin line. This Dad shape.

And then that's gone too.

My head falls against steering wheel, and there's a sharp horn blare.

But it doesn't matter.

Because I can't do this.

Why did I think I could do this?

Any of this?

And then a chime is repeating itself. My driver's side door is open, because Whit is standing there, looking in at me.

"It's okay," she says.

And I can't stop my body from quivering.

From shaking.

"J," she says, taking a step toward me. "I'll take you."

I try to say *okay. Thank you.* But my brain is still loading its language programming apparently, because it translates into a low grunt.

I slide over to the passenger seat.

Actually, I contort my body over.

And the car leaps backward, and I lower all four windows, the wind slapping everything as the neighborhood slips by faster, faster.

Because I don't want to talk about it.

Because I know Whit will feel obligated.

Because I'm tired of talking to ghosts.

Because that's what we're on our way to do.

63

Ms. B fumbles with the latch, her hands trembling.

"I told them not to call you," she says. Her voice is thin, eyes pink. "I'm sorry, Jamal. You should be at home with Whit." She looks past me. "Is that her in the car? She knows she can come in."

I shake my head. "She's nauseated. And she said she didn't want to have her head in the toilet when Q comes back to life."

We force a laugh and I follow her into the kitchen.

"I know this sounds crazy but . . . I'm not sure I can watch." She shivers. "I mean, I'm a nurse. I've seen a lot of wild stuff, but this is my son . . . what if it *does* hurt? What if he doesn't . . . what if it doesn't work? Maybe this was a mistake. I should call it off. Is it too late to . . ."

"Ms. B, do you have any tea?"

She looks at me wide-eyed.

I smile. "Mom always made me tea when I was nervous or afraid. She said it wasn't only for soothing throats, it soothes your spirit too."

And okay, it's possible Mom didn't actually say that.

But I think she'd approve.

62

Nothing prepares you for the moment your dead friend opens his eyes.

I must've missed that day in health class.

And while my parents fumbled admirably through the birds-and-the-bees talk, they totally bombed the *what to do when your friend comes back to life* chat.

So, yeah. Color me ill-prepared.

And yet here I am.

Sitting in a desk chair, staring at my dead friend lying still in his headboard-less bed, his thick arms casket-folded atop his chest.

There is a wake, after someone dies.

And this is a wait, before Q un-dies.

I hear Ms. B downstairs, moving around the kitchen. I

exhausted every argument I had to convince her to come in the room with me, but in the end I promised her I'd be okay alone. That Q was gonna be okay. That when Q woke, I'd find her.

"I can't ask you to do this," she said, lips quivering like a divining rod.

"You didn't have to."

I was halfway up the stairs when she called my name. "What happened between you and Quincy?"

"What do you mean?" I asked. But I know what she means.

"Why did you suddenly stop being friends? He wouldn't talk about it."

I swallowed hard. "Respectfully, Ms. B, if Q didn't tell you, I feel like I shouldn't either. I'm sorry."

She stared a beat, then tipped her head, like a guard waving me through a checkpoint.

I remember what the lady said in the Center's video: "Rest assured, we'll monitor the entire reawakening from a safe distance."

What if I'm being watched right now?

The video hadn't explained *how* they monitored.

I assume they have some kind of chip embedded into Q's brain or something, but . . .

What if they meant *literal* monitoring? Like cameras, mics?

I glance around, looking for spyware, or anything I don't recognize.

I used to know Q's room like my own. I could pictograph it from memory, every detail, from the Mighty Moat: Live in

Concert posters on the wall to what he keeps in all five dresser drawers. And even after all this time, not much has changed. Nothing obviously out of place. Or weirdly in place. Or monitor-y.

But also, if the Center could resurrect the dead, I don't think they'd have a hard time bugging Q's room undetectably.

My eyes fall onto Q's laptop.

What if they were watching me, listening to me, through the laptop camera?

Q's left eye twitches, or maybe I imagine it. Maybe it's my eyes flickering. It's hard to know what's real anymore.

Q's eyes flutter but don't open, like flicking a lighter that won't stay lit.

He sits up, turns his head toward me, eyes still closed, his mouth opening and shutting, but soundless.

Like watching Frankenstein wake with the volume muted.

And then Q suddenly falls backward, head thudding against his pillow, arms falling to either side, all ten fingers twitching.

He does this several times.

Rising, falling.

Like he's installing a new update, rebooting after each cycle.

I remember another video line: "Likely, there will be false starts. Several," she'd said. "Don't be alarmed."

Don't be alarmed when your dead best friend tries to come back to life, sputtering like an old mower.

The third time it happens, Q doesn't stay upright, just snaps up and back like a tripped mousetrap, and, startled, I fall out of the chair, bump into his desk, his laptop waking.

Which is symbolic, right?

Or at least kinda ironic.

I pull myself up, ready to resume my focus on Q's bed routine, except the cursor's blinking at me from the password screen. Almost like it's talking to me. Like it's saying, *trymetrymetryme.*

And I wonder if he changed it.

Not that I'm gonna know, because I'm not even gonna try it.

Breaking into my ex–best friend's laptop, even for a semi-good reason, is still an invasion of his privacy. Another betrayal to add to the list.

I look back at Q, waiting for him to spring to life any minute.

If he woke up and saw me . . .

But I have to know. Because if it's still JAUNCY19, that means something, yeah?

I slide the laptop closer, my hands hovering over the keys.

I have to know.

I type.

Press Enter.

The screen flashes.

The browser comes into view, and there are a hundred open tabs, because Q can't let anything go. But the current tab is what gets me.

Q's vlog. I read the description beneath the video, and I can't resist.

I click.

61

Quincy: Hey guys! We're back with your new favorite segment here at Jauncy.

Jamal: That's right! It's time for . . .

Q and J: Jauncy innnn the STREEEEEETSSSS!

J: The segment where we take Jauncy to the streets . . .

Q: Uh, J, that's kinda why it's called Jauncy in the Streets. Kinda feels . . . self-explanatory.

J: Umm, maybe if you'd let me finish, friend. The segment where we take to the streets AND ask people questions about things they apparently know nothing about.

CUT TO: a skateboard park

Q: Hey, man, mind if we ask you a question?

Sixteen-Year-Old Skater: Sure. You're not gonna make me look stupid on camera, though, are you?

Q looks straight into camera and grins

Q: I promise you, man, we're not gonna make you *look* stupid on camera.

Skater: Good.

Q: Okay, these questions are all about how well you know the Constitution, okay?

Skater: This is like that Kendrick show.

Q: You got it. You ready?

Skater: Let's do it, bro.

Q: Okay, name any one article of the Constitution.

Skater looks seriously perplexed

Skater: Article? Bro, the Constitution, I'm pretty sure, isn't like a newspaper. There aren't any articles. It's just laws.

A buzzer sounds and WRONG flashes on the screen

Q looks back into the camera, camera zooms in on his face

CUT TO: an ice cream stand

J: Hi, ma'am, is it okay if we ask you a question about the Constitution?

Forty-Something-Year-Old Woman Eating Fro-Yo: Okay?

J: Name one of the individuals responsible for penning the Constitution.

Fro-Yo Woman: Well, I know they're all white dudes.

J glances over his shoulder and gets an off-screen confirmation from Q, then turns back to the woman

J: We'll take it!

A chime plays and CORRECT flashes on the screen

Jamal holds up Fro-Yo Woman's arm in triumph and Fro-Yo Woman blesses them with a victory dance

Fro-Yo Woman: C'mon, now, dance. You can't let me dance by myself.

Jamal looks into the camera, shrugs, then joins the woman, the two of them doing the running man side by side

60

I don't have time to cycle through the questions now orbiting my brain—e.g., *why had Q been watching this old video of us*—because there's movement on the bed.

And when I turn around, Q's eyes are still flickering, except ten times faster, and then boom—his eyes pop open.

I wait for them to close again.

But they don't.

Q stares up at the ceiling.

Oh my God, Q's head . . . he's turning . . .

He's turning his open-eyed face toward me.

What should I do?

His body jerks back, his eyes pop, and his mouth plunges into a frown before snapping off into startled confusion. "Yo, what the hell are you doing here?"

And I don't know how to answer—not because I'm incapable, but because nothing prepares you for seeing your friend come back to life.

It will be a surge of emotions. It is completely natural to feel overwhelmed.

But this isn't a surge.

This isn't overwhelming.

This is a goddamn tsunami and hurricane falling in love and having quintuplets.

This is everything that ever was, anything that ever will be, swallowed by torrential downpour and knock-you-off-your-feet wind, and monstrous claim-everything waves, everything rushing, rushing.

"For real, why are you in my room, man? And staring at me like while I sleep? Are you drooling, bro? What time is it? Yo, did you spike my ginger ale at the party? And why won't you freaking answer me?"

And I don't know what to do.

With my hands.

With my face.

With my voice.

And I'm glad it's dark because my eyes start doing that thing that eyes are sometimes prone to do . . . you know, that go-blurry-because-whatever thing.

But honestly I don't even care, because, Q—

Q.

You're . . . alive, man.

YOU'RE ALIVE.

"Are you okay?" I ask him. "You're feeling, like, not weird, or whatever?"

"Other than the fact that you're staring at me like you're deciding whether to have my babies or to stab me in my throat, yeah, I feel great."

And this normally would've been funny.

But it's too much.

Everything is too much.

All of this, especially this, is a mistake.

And so I do what I do best.

The thing I'm arguably most proficient at.

I stand up.

I smile.

And then I run as fast as I can.

I nearly crash into Ms. B as I fling open Q's bedroom door, and she calls after me as I race down the stairs and out the glass front door and down the block, down, down, down. And I may never slow because I'm not only a proficient sprinter, I have stamina for days. I run fast and I run hard and I never stop.

I can't stop.

59

I'm sitting in an empty parking lot when she rolls to a stop, lowers the window.

"I didn't think you'd come."

She shrugs. "I wasn't going to. Still not sure I should've."

After we hung up, I wondered how it would be to see her. This would be the first time since the beach.

Normally, she would've bounded from the car when she saw me, and we'd race to meet in the middle of this street like it was some grassy knoll.

Normally, her sandpaper eyes would tractor-beam me into her body and her wide-open arms would finish me off.

But nothing's normal anymore. Only an hour ago, I fled Q's reanimation.

"So, you getting in, or you wanna walk beside the car?"

I fasten my seat belt. "Autumn, I'm . . ."

But she shakes her head and it's a silent twenty-minute drive to the lake.

She gets out first, and I watch her walk toward the water so resolutely I half expect her to walk right in. But she stops at the edge.

Stands there like she's waiting for me to join her.

Or waiting for me to disappear.

And then she's stooping low, gathering stones from the grass-pocked sand, using the bottom of her shirt like a basket. I climb out, dig until I find a cat's-eye. I hold it out to her, but she walks past me back toward her car, her collection of stones like rain on tin as they tumble onto the car hood. I watch her scoot herself up; she loses one of her sandals to the ground.

When I bend down to pick it up, she kicks off the other.

It's not funny but I nearly laugh.

I can't help but appreciate her dedication to reminding me how little she needs me.

I slide onto the car, the rocks dividing us.

This part of the beach is nearly always deserted, save an occasional flurry of kids searching for sea glass or chasing their runaway dog.

Autumn reaches into the pile, flings a stone into the water. I track it, watch it plop and disappear below.

And it occurs to me just how much time we've spent here.

On the water.

In the sand.

Listening to the waves like a favorite song.

She makes a face when I steal one of her rocks. I hurl it as hard as I can, but I lose it in the sun.

"Autumn, I'm sorry," I say finally.

Because it's true.

Because the only thing worse than her being angry with me is her being angry with me *while with me*.

A few more rocks sail from her hand.

"What are you sorry for?"

And I nearly say *everything*. But this is a moment for specificity.

"For how I behaved on the beach. For being an idiot. For making you feel like I'm taking you for granted." I scoot closer. "Because the thing is, I *don't* take you for granted. Every day, I wonder how long before you realize how far out of your league I am."

"You know I hate when you say stuff like that." She shakes her head. "There are no leagues. There's you and there's me and we're both here. And either we're here together or we're not, Jamal. That's it."

I nod. "No, you're right," I say. "But can I ask you something?"

She shrugs.

"Have you ever felt like I didn't love you?"

She turns toward me. Looks me right in my face. "Have you ever felt like telling me?"

"What? Yes. Of course, but . . ."

"But what, Jamal? There should be no buts."

She turns away, back to lake-gazing.

"It's not that I don't feel that way about you. Because I do. I do hard. You're . . ." I reach for her arm, expecting her to jerk away, and she does move, but slowly, like she's deciding how it feels, considering it. "Autumn, you're my person. And I hate that I made you feel anything less than amazing, because that's how I feel when I'm with you. Because that's how I feel about you. Honestly, I'm not even sure I knew what love was until you came along."

"Don't be stupid. What about your parents? Whit?"

"I mean, yeah, but . . ."

"And you loved Q, right?"

"I guess. Maybe."

"Why's it so hard for you to admit what's in your heart?"

"Truthfully? Because . . . because it's like if I put it out into the atmosphere, I can never reel it back in."

She makes a face. "Why would you wanna reel it in?"

"Because . . . I'm dumb?"

"Jamal."

"Because then . . ." My throat clenches. "Because then maybe it won't hurt as bad when it's over."

She frowns. "Why does it have to be over?"

I shrug. "Because everything ends."

"It doesn't have to."

I shake my head. "Yeah, well, it's the only version I know."

"Yeah, well, maybe it's time you take responsibility for that."

"What's that mean?"

She turns to face me. "It means maybe you'd still have a few good things if you weren't so determined to be an asshole to everyone."

I nod. "I'm sorry I lied. I guess I wanted to erase Q from my brain. I didn't want to acknowledge he'd ever meant anything to me."

"You can't change that. And even if you could, what good would it do? You're only hurting the people who've stuck by you. And you're only hurting yourself."

"You're right."

"Pain's never a reason to be shitty. And I'm telling you, right now, if you *ever* treat me like that again, it'll be the last time you see me."

"I know. It won't happen again."

"It better not."

"So, does this mean you forgive me?"

"It means you've got some work to do."

I scoot closer. "Autumn, I . . ."

But she puts her finger to my lips. "No," she says. "Don't say it. Not now."

"But I . . ."

She slips my arm over her shoulders. "Wait until it's right. When *you* want to say it."

Her cheek falls into mine.

"Okay," I say, even though right now feels right.

"But don't wait another two years, or honestly another two

weeks, because you will be saying it to yourself at that point." She pulls her head away to see my eyes. "You got me?"

I stare right back. "I got you. Always."

I slide over a bit more, and this time she does too. Meets me in the middle, which is all anyone can ask for.

She slowly lowers her head to rest against mine, like she's not certain it belongs there anymore.

"You scared me, Jamal. When they pulled you from that water, I . . . I . . ."

"I know," I say, squeezing her tighter.

"You can't scare me like that again, okay? Like ever."

And of course, we both know there are things beyond our control. Things we can't truly promise away.

But also, sometimes, that's not the point. "I won't."

With her free arm, she flings another rock—but attached to me, she can't get the same velocity, the same arc, and it just barely finds the water.

Which, sorry, but uh, can you say metaphor?

Sure, you might sail faster, farther, alone.

But what was the point of accomplishing anything if you had no one to share it with?

Whether you plunked into the middle of the lake or you barely cleared the edge, you were in the water.

"Tell me about Whittier again," I ask her.

She makes a face. "For someone who claims he prefers spontaneity, you love talking about the future."

And she's smiling, of course, she's teasing me, but she's also right. I do love talking about the future, but more so, I love hearing other people talk about it.

As if somehow the fact that other people see me, see us, together, in their imaginations meant it was more likely to happen.

She finds my hand, interlaces our fingers. "Well, we'll both be at Whittier or maybe U of Chicago, and naturally, you'll be undeclared for three years, while I double major in business and urban planning, so that, you know, I can . . ."

"Save the world," I interject.

She punches me, laughing. "No, so I can do my part to preserve the planet. You do realize, at our current rate, even if we focus only on the ozone, this place will be radically different in less than a decade?"

"So I've heard," I say, because she's forever reminding me—the earth's dying a slow, painful death, Jamal, and all of us are guilty.

But aren't we all dying slowly, painfully? Why should the earth be exempt?

But I don't say these things. Ask these questions. Because they're not real.

They're just by-products of heartache and regret, anger and disappointment.

Because I believe in Autumn and her dreams, maybe, probably, even more than my own. Because at least she dares to dream. And who was I to punch holes in them?

"Okay, so while I try to help save the planet, you'll be finding yourself, and we'll get an apartment together off campus, and we'll cook together, and have movie marathons, and take long walks along the shore."

I grin. "So, basically, we'll keep doing the things we already do."

"Except we don't live together, silly." She sticks out her tongue. "But, if you want any of that to actually happen, you're gonna have to pick your grades up, and you know, maybe fill out some college applications."

I barely resist rolling my eyes. Jamal's Lack of Academic Ambition, another favorite Autumn topic. Although, to be fair, she's not alone.

Between her, Whit, and seemingly anyone even remotely affiliated with Elytown High, the Get Yourself Together, Jamal chorus was singing louder and louder.

"College isn't the only way you can be successful," I argue.

She nods. "No, that's true. So, you have a noncollegiate plan mapped out for your success?"

"Yep."

Her forehead creases, eyes squint, as she taps her chin. "And remind me, babe, because you know how shaky my memory can be . . . umm, what exactly do you intend to be successful doing?"

She waits because this is normally where my defense falls apart.

Except, I don't know, it's like spending that time in Q's room woke up something in me, too. I shrug. "I was thinking

I wanna start writing again. Maybe, and don't laugh . . . but maybe I take some improv classes."

She stares at me so long I ask her what's wrong.

"Nothing," she says. "I've just never really heard you talk about a thing you wanna do. And it's making me happy, but I'm trying not to overreact because then you'll get all weird and not wanna share more with me."

"It's not a big deal. I mean, it's hardly a plan. It's barely anything."

"It's a start, babe. A start is something." She brushes my cheek. "Hey, stand up, I wanna show you something."

"What? But then I'll have to stop touching you and that sounds terrible."

She shakes her head. "C'mon, silly."

I grumble, but I slide off the car, stand beside her. I hunch my shoulders. "So, what are you supposed to be showing—"

But I don't get to finish.

Autumn wraps her arms around my waist, squeezes me like I'm toothpaste.

Autumn's hug is a kind of irresistible extraction that compels you to spill your whole guts. Makes you release everything about anything.

Because you know she is refuge and a half.

Because she knows the hurt you've inflicted.

Because she also knows how hard you love.

She's seen you so happy, you were vibrating.

Because she is wholly convinced you are redeemable.

177

Because she knows the secret to being forgiven is first forgiving yourself.

This is a single, midmorning, standing on a random patch of beach hug from Autumn.

Everyone needs this hug.

And even when we finally pull apart, her right hand slides up, then down my arm, until her hand finds mine, until her fingers every-other my fingers.

We stand there, hands held, waves coming at us like they mean to wash us away.

And then she asks: "What are you gonna do about Q?"

"What do you mean?"

"You know what I mean."

"I dived into the water for him, isn't that enough?"

"J."

"I don't know yet. I'm still working it out."

She brings our hands up, kisses my knuckles. "As long as you're actually working on it."

"I am. I will."

And I want to tell her the whole truth.

She more than deserves it.

Because every makeup deserves a peace offering.

But for now, instead, this: "So, you wanna know why they named you Autumn?" I ask her.

And she shakes her head, begs me not to say it. "Babe, we've exceeded our dad joke quota for the night."

I nod my agreement. "Okay, okay. You right." I kiss the top of her head.

She grins. "Thank you for the self-control. Look at you out here showing personal growth and . . ."

"Because how could I not *fall* for you?"

And then she's pretending to push me, and I'm pretending to stumble backward, flailing my arms like a baby bird attempting to fly for the first time.

And we're laughing, laughing.

Driving home, the sky applies its dusk filter, everything a moody gray.

And the highway lampposts hum to life, their light gliding and swirling along both sides of us, like electric-orange butterflies.

In my driveway, Autumn leans across the seat and we kiss.

We do that awkward car-divider-between-us hug. "Thanks for the ride."

"Everything's gonna be okay," she says.

I shrug. "How come the more people say that the less true it feels?"

58
the funeral

I was hiding behind the funeral parlor when we met.

I slipped through the sea of nose-blowing and eye-dabbing and stepped out a door marked Do Not Open.

I needed air and I needed a wall, because it had only just hit me:

How many things I wanted to tell them that I couldn't.

And there were only gonna be more things, all the time.

I took a breath, cracked my neck.

"The first undertakers were actually furniture makers," a voice said.

And I nearly jumped clear of my skin.

I turned to see a girl sitting on a wide sill, the window behind her boarded with plywood.

She laughed. "Sorry. Thought you saw me up here."

I shook my head. "I definitely did not. Why are you up there?"

She shrugged. "Why are you down there, man? Why are we anywhere? It's a tad early for existentialism."

And I didn't know what that was—if the universe thought it was doing me a solid, mashing this girl's world with mine, I was not into it. Especially that day. I pivoted toward the door, but she hopped down from the window.

"It makes sense, though, right?" she continued.

"Huh?" I asked. "What does?"

She sucked her teeth. "That the first undertakers were furniture makers. The casket game was a logical move. You already had the materials and the skill. You just needed the bodies, and God knows, there's no shortage of those."

"Umm, you do realize a funeral home is a sad place, right? Like, I enjoy trivia as much as the next guy, but . . ."

"You come from the party?" She motioned toward the door I'd just disobeyed. "You know the people that died?"

"Yeah," I said. "You?"

She wagged her head. "No, I just work here on Saturdays."

"Oh. Cool?"

She laughed. "Is that a statement or a question?"

"Definitely more question."

She laughed. "Well, today's my first day. Somehow, my grandma knows the funeral director, so here. I. Am." She pulled a granola bar from her pocket. "Halfsies?"

I hadn't eaten all day. Hadn't really eaten much since. But I found myself nodding anyway, watching her as she unwrapped it and broke it in two.

"I'm gonna be nice and give you the bigger piece, but don't think this is how it's gonna always be."

And even though she was only joking like we're gonna hang out again, it was not an idea I entirely hated, which, odd, because I'd been in full-on *hate everything* mode for days.

I said, "Cool." And then added: "Statement."

And I didn't know how but her laugh made me wanna laugh.

"It really sucks," she said. "I heard they were young."

"Who?" I asked but then I got it. And then my lip was trembling, tears threatening rain.

"Heard they have three kids."

"Two," I say quietly.

"What was that?"

"Just two kids."

"Hmm," she said. "Well, it still blows. Can you imagine? What on earth do you say to a kid who's just lost the two most important people in their life?"

"I don't know." I turned to her, wiped my eyes. "But here's your chance."

She made an *Ooooh* sound, blanketed her mouth with both hands. "Ohmi—"

But she didn't get a chance to finish this awkward moment because the Do Not Open door opened once more.

"Hey, man," Q said, stepping out onto the cracked pavement. "Everyone's looking for you, so I, uh, I figured you'd be wherever they weren't. And . . ." He spied the girl and stopped. "Oh, my bad, am I interrupting . . . ?"

I didn't meet his eyes. The energy had been off between us. But if he'd noticed it, he did not let on.

The girl stuck out her hand. "Hi, I'm Autumn. And no, you aren't interrupting anything except me making a fool of myself, so perfect timing."

Q smiled. "Nice to meet you, Autumn. I'm Quincy." He glanced at me. "Uh, Q, actually. Jamal's friend." And he paused like he was waiting for Autumn to explain how she knew me, or for me to interject, but honestly the only thing I wanted was for this dude to vacate the premises. Not just my presence. Not just this grimy alleyway. The whole funeral home. The block. The damn world.

Of course, he could have just let it go. Be content with not knowing this one thing about me and my life. But he couldn't help himself.

He shook his forefinger at her. "You look familiar. Wait, are you from Indiana? Are you the daughter of . . ."

He looked to me for help, but I shrugged. I knew who he meant, but I didn't understand why he didn't feel it: the fact that I didn't want him there.

Autumn laughed. "No, I'm an Ohio kid through and through. Actually, we only just met." She touched my shoulder and I flinched—not because it hurt, or because I didn't like it, but for the exact opposite of those things. I made a subtle move back toward her hand, but she pulled away, an apology on her face. "I don't mean . . . I have this bad habit of touching people. All my friends are used to it, or don't mind telling me to screw off. I'm sorry."

"No," I said too quickly. "Don't be. It's . . . okay."

And there was a long pause there.

A beat where it was just her and me in this dark alley and it was a world where my parents were still at the forefront of my brain, where their death was at once tender and searing, but it was like her eyes were time travelers.

And she'd been sent here to give me a glimpse of future Jamal.

A Jamal who was still hurting but who'd found a way to not be so broken.

"Damn, man, I haven't seen you smile since . . ." Q's words split. His voice softer. "I'm just saying it's good to see you smile."

"That's weird because I was actually just shoving both of my feet into my mouth before you came out." Autumn turned to me. "You don't know me and this means shit even if you did, but I'm so incredibly sorry for your loss. And I'm sorry for being here when you were trying to find a place to be alone."

I shook my head.

"He's been alone a lot lately. I imagine he's happy to have some company," Q says before I can get any words out. "I was actually gonna ask J if he wanted to, later tonight after the dinner thing, just hang out and just, I don't know, reminisce or . . . anyway, you're welcome to join us, right, J? She should join us?"

Autumn was smiling, which was a good thing. A great

184

thing. But I didn't want to hang out or talk or reminisce about how awesome my parents *were*. Especially not with him.

"Actually, if you don't mind, man, could you go find Whit, let her know I'm out here if she needs me."

"Huh. Oh. Yeah, man. Uh . . ." He nodded—and it was there, the perfect friendship cocktail, a finely shaken blend of reluctance, jealousy, and earnestness. "It was nice meeting you, Autumn. Hope to see you later."

A reluctance to leave me in my time of need.

A jealousy for the fact that I wasn't actually alone, for the fact that I was actually with a girl he did not know.

An earnest desire to do whatever would make me less shitiful.

Even if the only way to do that meant he couldn't be there.

So, why wouldn't I want my best friend around? Why would I want distance? What's changed, you ask?

The answer was everything.

Nothing the same.

And a sliver of happiness.

"We just moved here," Autumn said.

"You and your parents?"

She shook her head. "Nope. Me and my grandma."

"Oh," I say, wanting to ask more but also knowing it was none of my business. "That's cool. Well, uh, welcome. You two could've chosen to live anywhere in the world. Chicago, NYC, Paris, but yet here you are in . . . Ely . . . town."

She laughed. "That's what I thought too. But then . . ."

"But then . . . what?"

"Nothing," she said, shaking her head, breaking our eye contact, but not breaking this trance she'd magicked me into.

"Say what you wanted to say."

And she turned back to me, and her smile was gone, but the light in her eyes was not, it was somehow more, and she finished her sentence. Punctuated the hell out of it.

"But then, you," she said. "But then, you."

POSTREANIMATION
DAY 1

Approx. 23–27 Q Days Left

57

Two things get me through the seven-hour daily void that is high school.

1) Autumn Gregory.

2) Fixating on whatever school break's next on our academic horizon.

So today, I feel doubly fortunate—Autumn's leaning against my locker *and* spring break's two days away.

She wraps me in a hug. "You look like regurgitated shit."

I rub my chin atop her head. "Awww, babe, you always know just what to say."

"What're we doing after school?"

I sigh. Pop open my locker. "Can't."

She flashes mock horror. "Who's the side chick?"

"Mrs. Sweat."

"Ugh, gross."

The bell rings and Autumn stands on her tiptoes, my arms returning to her waist. "Baby, say that thing you know I like."

She grins. "You're gonna be a father."

And we both laugh. "Your grandma would whup your ass with her cane."

"And yours too."

"Yeah, she would." I pull her closer, but this time she stiffens.

"What's going on in that head of yours?" she asks.

"Guess I'm wondering if Q's gonna be at school today."

The one-minute bell rings.

Autumn studies my face. "The important thing is he's okay, yeah?"

"No, yeah. You're right."

She reaches around, smacks my ass. "Okay, well, leave already so I can watch you walk away."

We kiss and part ways. And I can't help but stare at her, too. Because, sweet baby Jesus, she's poetry.

My pocket buzzes.

Whit: Don't forget mtg w/Sweat.

Me: sorry I already have plans not to be there, so.

Whit: ✊ 💥

56

Usually I'm the last person to trickle into seventh period English.

But today I'm nearly the first.

And even though I try to play it cool, I can't help it. My eyes are fixed to the fourth chair in the third row.

Feeling—I guess, eager, maybe—for Q to show up, even though, to date, we've rarely even made eye contact in this class.

So I'm all kinds of disappointed when Ms. Taylor closes the door, Q apparently absent.

Which, I know is not my business, or my problem, or whatever—

But I wonder if he's okay.

If I'm honest, a part of me half expected him to text me after I fled our little bedroom showdown. Figured at the very least

I'd get a *don't ever come here again.*

But instead, nothing.

And nothing, in a way, is worse than anger.

When someone yelled at you, or sent you an all-caps text, at least you knew how they felt. And yeah, the last time I saw Q—okay, really the last two times I've seen Q—he was angry, so maybe that's where things still stood.

But what if, like, the reanimation gave him a change of heart that, like, wasn't immediately evident? What if, after I'd run out his front door and across the lawn like a track-and-field champ, he'd had an intense moment of self-reflection, had suddenly realized *why* things had gone south between us?

Felt beyond terrible? Wanted to sincerely apologize, except he was afraid of how I'd react? Intense moments of self-reflection didn't mean you lost all your pride.

Maybe he was waiting for me to make the first move?

Waiting for an opening?

And I'm feeling slightly better until the classroom door swings open.

I stare in a way that suggests I'm willing to have the conversation, but either Q's possibly embarrassed by his previous behavior or he's content to keep things status quo, because he avoids eye contact.

I maintain my *it's cool man* stare, but Q's eyes look everywhere but at me.

I study him from afar. He seems normal. Same posture. The

go-with-the-flow look on his face, just as before.

And it's strange, knowing that someone I knew, someone I was once so close to, was, in the most literal sense, living on borrowed time.

And I'm struck once more with guilt.

Because this sucks.

Because if Q knew, there's no way he's hanging out in seventh period English right now.

Because how were you to grieve a loss that wasn't currently a loss?

As sad as I feel, it's nowhere near the way you feel when someone actually dies. Because I'm also happy he's alive again.

So, maybe when Q . . . you know . . . I'd grieve retroactively, twice as hard?

Maybe I—

Wait, why is everyone staring at me?

Oh, probably because our teacher's staring at me and calling my name over and over. Damn. How long had I spaced?

"Jamal, what do you think? Was Beowulf's life a tragedy?"

Okay, apparently long enough to not know we'd already started discussing our reading assignment.

I shrug. "I don't know."

She motions for me to sit up straight, which I reluctantly do. Ugh, is there anything more annoying than a Try-Hard Teacher?

"There's no wrong or right. I just want your opinion."

"Honestly?" I shake my head. "I feel like the whole thing's a tragedy."

Her face lights up. "How so?"

I laugh. "Tell me you weren't disappointed when you found out dude's not an actual wolf."

The class cracks up. The kid in front of me swivels for a fist bump.

Ms. Taylor nods, smiling. "Okay, okay. But do you think Beowulf would've been more or less heroic had he been an actual wolf?"

"I mean, he's fighting all these monsters but he's just a regular dude. How's that fair?"

"True. Except he's successful, right? In the end? He slays the dragon."

"But he dies doing it."

"So, what's one message you take from his life?"

And I know what she's doing. She's *engaging* me. Proving to me that I can do this if I want. If I try. But I lob her question back. "What do *you* see?"

She studies my face. "Okay, I'll play. What do I see? Hmm. How about there's no greater honor than fighting for others, even at great personal sacrifice?"

I shake my head. "No offense, but that sounds stupid."

A few kids *oooooooooh.*

"Nah, for real. He was a hero, right, but when he needed his people the most, everyone except Wiglaf abandoned him. All that time he was loyal, kept his word. So, where were they

194

when he needed them, huh? They were back at the crib watching some bullshit on Netflix."

More laughs.

"So, you shouldn't do anything for anyone, Jamal?" Ms. Taylor challenges me with a smile. "You should just keep to yourself? You'd rather live longer and die alone than die sooner alongside your friend, for what you believe in?"

"This ain't about me." I slide down in my chair.

She folds her arms. "No, you're right, Jamal. It's not. But I'm interested in what you think. In what we all think."

I don't say a word. She stands there, in my aisle, our eyes locked.

And okay, if this is what she wants, fine. "I'm saying Beowulf played himself. Those dudes didn't leave him when he fought the dragon. They were *never* with him. He was *always* alone. And in the end, he got the dragon, and the dragon got him."

I glance over at Q, to see if he's following, but nah.

He's smiling at his phone.

And okay, maybe I feel the smallest tinge of jealousy for whatever's making him grin so hard. And okay, maybe I tell myself it's an old Jauncy video.

And maybe that conjures up memories of a different time.

A better time.

Because what if Beowulf and the dragon had put aside their differences and become a renowned comedy duo?

55

two years before the funeral

I clicked an inactive tab on Q's laptop.

We were supposed to be researching sea lions for science class, but of course we were watching highlights from last night's NBA games.

"Yo, what's this?" I asked, as I took a bite into some leftover tostadas Mr. Barrantes had made the night before. "Q's Comedy Hour?"

And Q's face had erupted in panic. "Don't click that . . ."

But it was too late.

It was a TuberOne video he'd posted.

And it was just Q in front of the camera, sitting at his desk, telling jokes. And listen, I always knew Q was funny, but this . . . this was different.

He was beyond funny.

He was freaking hilarious.

"You kinda remind me of Donald Glover," I told him. "Like his old stand-up stuff."

And his face lit up. "Yeah? You don't think it's corny?"

I shook my head. "Nope."

"Donald's funny, but I was kinda going for someone else."

"Well, I was gonna say Kendrick Fallon, but I d—"

Q grinned extra wide. "You got it."

"You wanna host a TV show?"

Q shrugged. "Maybe. Or, I don't know, maybe write jokes for Kendrick. I heard an interview where he said that's how he got started in comedy. Writing jokes for other people."

I smiled. "I could totally see you doing this."

"Yeah? You just saying that?"

"Bro, I don't just say stuff. You know me."

And then Q had gotten this weird look in his eyes. "Well, I'm glad you feel that way because I was thinking you'd want to team up together. Be a comedy duo."

"I'm not nearly as funny as you."

Q laughed. "We're just different funny. You're like observational humor. But that's still funny."

I still wasn't sure. I wasn't seeing it. "I don't know, Q. What if kids at school find our videos and think we're stupid?"

"No one will ever find them. I've made thirty already and you had no idea."

He had a point. It was almost like this secret life Q'd been leading without me. Alter-ego Quincy.

"Okay, but if we're gonna do this, we've gotta make it good. I mean, what if it went viral? Q, this could be your ticket. You could be Kendrick one day."

"Let's not get carried away, but . . . thanks, man."

I took a giant bite of tostada, guac juice running down my chin. "So, what should we call ourselves?"

"Jauncy," Q said with zero hesitation.

"Jauncy?"

"Yeah, Jamal plus Quincy. Jauncy."

"I guess I don't hate it. I mean, that first part, Ja, sounds great, so."

Q pretended to pinch my cheek. "Awww, look at you! Already got jokes!"

I always imagined that one day, when Q was famous and, like, hosting the Academy Awards, he'd tell that story in an interview. The interviewer would say, *hey, so look what we have here, we've gotten our hands on THE original Q comedy shows Jauncy.*

And then they'd play a couple of our most famous skits.

A few seconds of our funniest moments.

And I'm not a toot-your-own-horn-often kinda guy, but we made a great team.

We had a great run.

The same way I was the basketball expert, helping us perfect our pick and rolls and our pick and pops, Q was our comedy guru.

I'd assumed we'd just film ourselves being crazy, but nope, Q took it all seriously.

"There are no rules in comedy," he said. "But rule number one is this, everything's always funnier when it's true. Even stuff that might not be *funny* funny is still funny when it's something people relate to. Yeah?"

It made sense.

"Rule number two, just go with it. Commit to the joke, especially when you're in a group situation, like improv, or in our case, a comedy duo."

"A dynamic duo," I sang, pointing upward, as if to suggest we could fly. "So, how many rules are there?"

Q smiled. "Only one more. Rule number three, have fun."

54

Mrs. Sweat tents her hands. "Whitney, Jamal's truancy is not our only concern. We're equally . . ." She stops, slides a manila folder across her desk. "Here. See for yourself."

Whit flips it open.

"Those are Jamal's grades for the quarter. He's failing or nearly failing four of his six courses."

"Jamal," Whit says, her voice like a gasp. A sound that says *how could you not tell me? How could I not know?* She tries to meet my eyes, but I look away. She turns back to Mrs. Sweat. "Isn't your job to . . . aren't *you* also failing *him*? Last semester, we got him tutoring and an individualized learning plan and . . ."

Mrs. Sweat motions to the papers in Whit's hand. "On

average, he's missing a day every week. And that's not counting the classes he's skipping."

"I've been sick," I say. "I have doctor's notes."

Whit rubs her nose with her sleeve. A few tears drop onto her jeans. Whit says my name again, softer, quieter. "He's had a hard time. We've had a . . ."

Mrs. Sweat frowns. "Look, we all know Jamal's . . . not had an easy go of it. But I'm afraid that despite our best intentions, this school's been complicit in Jamal's failure. We've let him slip for two years. But now, it's clear to us that if we let him slip anymore, it'll be through our fingers. Through the cracks." She pauses, her voice the right percentage of firm. "We're of the mind that Jamal needs more help than what's available at our institution."

"Wait, you're kicking him out?" Whit asks.

I sit up in my chair. "Wait, what? You can't kick me out." I look from Mrs. Sweat to Whit back to Mrs. Sweat. "Can you?"

She opens her drawer, pulling out a glossy trifold pamphlet and handing it to Whit. "It's my strong recommendation that Jamal transfer to Elytown Prep."

"What? The school for problem kids? That's not me!"

And I won't lie, Mrs. Sweat seems genuinely sad. The face she's giving me right now—I've seen that from a lot of adults these last couple of years.

I've seen it from Whit. From Autumn.

"So, he has a choice, though?" Whit asks. "He doesn't

201

have to leave Elytown High?"

Mrs. Sweat shakes her head. "Honestly, I don't want to see Jamal go. I want Jamal to stay here and succeed the way we all know he's capable of. But I don't want to lose you entirely, Jamal."

"Lose me? I'm skipping school, I'm not participating in organized crime."

"No, Jamal. I don't want to lose you to grief." She frowns. "I can't watch you get eaten whole. Not anymore. I have to do something. *We* have to do something."

I sit back in my chair.

I'd never thought of it that way.

That I'm being swallowed by grief.

But maybe it's true.

Except it's not exactly like Mrs. Sweat thinks.

I wish I'd been swallowed whole. That would've been a mercy.

Because the way I feel? It's like being eaten slowly. Like I'm being gnawed.

We spend another twenty minutes dialoguing about my academic future.

In short: I can stay at EHS. But I'm on probation. No more skipping school, or even a class. And my grades have to show improvement.

Which, ugh.

But fair.

And then we're out of Mrs. Sweat's office.

Out of the main office.

Out the school foyer.

Out onto the front lawn.

Nearly out into the visitor lot.

But then I'm running back toward the north end, Whit calling after me.

And was this the best post-probationary-meeting choice I could make?

From the outside, not even close. But it was something Mrs. Sweat had said—*despite our best intentions*. In the end, it doesn't matter what you were *trying* to do.

Only what you did.

And now I'm jogging down the side of the humanities building, running my fingers along the brick facade, glaring into each of the open rectangular windows.

And then I see my calculus teacher seated at her desk, and she meets my eyes, but I'm looking past her, I'm looking at the kid who, when I sprained my ankle playing neighborhood football, carried me off the grassy knoll and the entire quarter mile home.

The kid who'd seen me at my worst but had still wanted to stay.

The teacher walks over to the window. "Jamal, you can't disrupt our club meeting. In fact, why aren't you headed home already?"

"Excellent question, Ms. Haddish," I say. "One that deserves a considerate answer." I poke my head inside the window frame so she can't close it.

"Jamal, please move along. You can't cause a disturbance. Now if you don't wanna be here, fine, we can't force you to stay, but . . ."

I shake my head. Because why did everyone think *that*?

That I didn't want to be in the places I was at?

Why had no one ever asked me *why* I didn't want to be here? Instead of just deciding *oh well, it's your loss.*

Maybe Mrs. Sweat was righter than she knew.

Maybe I was being swallowed up.

Maybe I'd forgotten how to be me. The old carefree Jamal. Silly, fun-loving Jamal.

"You're right, Ms. Haddish. And I'm really, truly sorry for interrupting your club, and I promise I'm gonna leave in like fifteen seconds, but please, please let me just say one thing first."

She crosses her arms. "Jamal."

"Please," I beg, tenting my hands together in prayer. "Fifteen seconds. That's it. I just need to tell my old pal Q something."

"Jamal, if this is some kind of vendetta or . . ."

"It's not that." I wave my arm in Q's direction. "Hey, man, are you . . . hey, c'mon, can you just look at me for a second?"

But Q keeps staring straight ahead, as if he can't hear or see the guy flagging him down in the window.

Ms. Haddish sighs. "Q, will you please just . . ."

Q turns my way.

"Q, I . . . I don't know how to start this, but I'm just gonna . . . I'm just gonna try . . . okay, it doesn't matter . . ."

Ms. Haddish taps her watch. "You have like five seconds left."

I shake my head. "Okay, look. I'm sorry, Q, for treating you like crap when . . . when my parents died. You didn't deserve that. I know that. And I'm sorry it's taken all this time for me to tell you as much. I'm sorry that you had to . . ."

Whoa, Jamal, easy, boy. You nearly spilled the reanimation beans.

"You see, the truth is . . . the truth is . . . I blamed you, Q. I blamed you for what happened."

Q's face twists in confusion, but he says nothing.

"Yeah, I did. You called that morning to tell my parents happy anniversary. I don't know if you remember."

And I can't be sure, but I think Q's head dips in the smallest nod.

"And maybe you don't remember, but I know you remember how terrible Dad was with technology," I say. And now I feel my eyes beginning to water. And I want to stop this whole thing in its tracks. Because I can't fall apart here, in front of a school that's wiping its hands of me, in front of kids who still whisper about why I'm so messed up. I should just leave. Do what I do best. Turn and sprint to safety, but—

I'm here.

And I want to be here.

I wipe my eyes. "Anyway, just as we . . . just as we pulled out . . . you called, and Dad's phone was connected to the Bluetooth and . . . and . . ."

I look down and away.

I take a deep breath and a step back, ducking out of the window.

Just say it, Jamal. Say the words and let them go.

I look back up and now Q's standing in front of the window.

And I force a smile, because I appreciate what he's doing.

That he gets it.

What I'm trying to do.

And he's meeting me halfway.

He's meeting me where I stand.

I nod. "Thank y—"

But I don't get the *you* out before Q sticks his arm out through the open window.

And this is unexpected—he wants to bump fists with me. Or possibly pull me into a bro-hug. Which is even better. Means even more.

I smile, and this time, it just happens.

"Hey, Q, I really am happy you—"

Except Q isn't reaching out for a hug.

Or to hear my apology more clearly.

Or to prepare to deliver his own apology in return.

No. I watch, Ms. Haddish watches, her entire after-school club watches, as Q's fingers wrap around the window handle and pull the window closed, all while maintaining perfect eye contact with me.

And for the briefest moment I think he's joking as he fumbles with the window, rattling the glass pane.

That it's stuck but he's about to push it back open.

That this is his way of sticking it to me a bit.

That he can't just let me off easy.

But I couldn't have been more wrong.

The latch was stuck, but he wasn't trying to reopen the window, Q's *locking* the window in place.

And when the lock finally clasps, he's still looking right at me.

The whole episode, he barely even blinks.

And well, reader, I wish I could tell you that's how things ended.

That I chose the emotional high ground.

But, uhhhh—

"What, you don't wanna hear me say how you killed my parents, Q? What's the matter? You still too much of a punk to admit what you did? You killed my parents, Q! You, man! You did that! Not the dude driving the other car! It was you and only you! And you wanna know what the stupidest thing is?" I pause to laugh and rub my belly the way you do when something's epically hilarious. "Like, this is the real zinger, bro. You're gonna love it. Haha. Listen. Ms. Haddish, you guys can hear me in there, right? Everyone, check this out. It wasn't even their anniversary. You get it? He called to wish my parents a happy anniversary, and not only was he wrong, he was soooo wrong. If his wrong was a grenade, it would still be so far from the truth, it would inflict zero damage. Because, get this. This kid, my former best friend, wait for it . . . he had the wrong fucking month! He called them on June seventh, but their anniversary was July seventh." I squeeze my face together, like I'm so mortally embarrassed for him. "So, wow, egg on his face, right? How freaking embarrassing for Q, huh, guys? He killed my parents for absolutely no reason. So, yeah, fun."

And then Whit's materializing at my side, and she's tugging my arm, and I'm resisting at first, not in an *I'm doubling down on my assholery* way, but because for a moment everything in the world has fallen away, like I'm the last living thing on earth, and it doesn't feel good, and it's terrifying, but she's saying over and over again *that's far enough, Jamal, Jamal, that's enough*, and she's right, she's so right, it *is* too much, I *am* too far gone, it's enough, it's enough.

All of it, everything, more than enough.

And then we're finishing what we started—we're out.

Out the school grass.

Out the parking lot.

Out the premises.

We're out.

All the way out.

53

Our drive home quieter than death.

52

I lock my door, fall onto my bed.

Wake my phone, tap Videos.

Scroll to the hidden folder.

I promised Whit I wouldn't watch it anymore.

Swore I'd deleted it.

Dr. Ocean warned me to be careful. Your obsession with this video isn't healthy, Jamal. There are better ways to address your feelings.

But I'm not looking for better.

I slip in my earbuds.

I tap Play.

51

I zoom in on Mom's face and she blocks her eyes with her hands. Behind her, about twenty yards from the road, the electronic Elytown Greenhouse Emporium sign spells out WELCOME in white pixelated animation.

"It won't kill you, Jamal." Mom says this matter-of-factly, like she just wormholed here from the future. Dad, wearing a flannel shirt for probably the first time ever, nods his agreement. The three of us made fun of him the entire ride here. *Wait, are we buying trees or chopping them down*, we joked. And we called him "Paul *Bunion*" until he blasted the radio to drown us out.

"I think only *I* get to say what's gonna kill me or not," I reply. "We need a bigger car. Or maybe we can plant five trees instead of, you know, *twenty*-five."

"We'll be fine. It's a short drive to the preserve," Dad says. He loads the last sapling into the back seat, its thin branches poking my forearm. "Besides, this is *your* Carpet Denim, Jamal. And now you have to *leaf* with the consequences."

Mom and Dad exchange way-too-enthusiastic high fives, which quickly accelerates into a super involved and probably overly complicated routine complete with 360-degree spinning and shoe-tapping, culminating in a leaping, grunting chest bump—they'd been working on this for weeks in our living room, ever since they saw NBA players flash their own signature handshake exchanges during a game.

Yes, these are my parents. No, I don't know why they're like this.

"You're killing it today, babe," Mom says. "You're on *forest* fire."

Dad half frowns. "I don't know if I can laugh at that."

"Yeah," Mom says, nodding. "That was highly insensitive."

Dad rubs his chin. "Maybe if you'd said *controlled* forest fire."

"Yeah, I wanted to be clever, but I got *stumped.*"

"Ohmigod, nice freaking recovery, babe!" Dad exclaims.

High-five routine round two.

"Did you get that on tape?" Dad asks me. "You got that, right?"

"Unfortunately," I confirm.

A man parked next to us stops loading purple flowers into his red pickup truck, apparently so that he can laugh hysterically. He pumps his fist in a way I think is meant to encourage my parents to continue their semi-embarrassing-but-also-kinda-impressive routine; Dad calls these moments PDAs—public displays of awesome. Is that me groaning or you?

"Oh, man, you guys rock," the purple-flower man declares.

"They're for sale," I tell the man. "What's your best offer?"

Whit's face pops out at me from between two small dogwoods; her arms sweep their foliage in either direction. I'd nearly forgotten she was in the back seat. "Jamal, I can't believe you're not into this! You're one of the *sappiest* people I know!"

Mom's and Dad's faces light up like a holiday window display. "Oh *snap*," Dad says. "Welcome aboard the Awful Joke Train, favorite daughter!"

"Thanks for having me, Dad," Whit says. She lets the trees go and they smack her in the face. "Oww!"

And okay, I can't resist. "Guess a dogwood's bark *is* worse than its bite."

Mom, now in the front passenger seat, reaches through the foliage to high-five me. "There he is! There's my corny son! Welcome back, my friend."

I laugh. "Hey, I was just trying to *branch* out!"

"Now this is what I'm talking about! You feeling what I'm feeling, Andersons?" Dad says, starting the car. "Our love is at an *al-pine* high."

Dad's grinning. I know this because even with all these trees in the way, I can just barely see his eyes, his face, in the rearview mirror.

He sees me looking and he winks.

I wish I'd winked back.

Dad pulls the car onto the road. The car speakers ring, an incoming call. Dad fumbles with the phone controls, taps random buttons because he and tech, water and oil. And I see his head snap to his left, I see his eyes widen, the horror, his shoulders twitching as he reaches for the car horn, as his foot slams into the gas.

But both reactions are too late.

Whit screams. Four tires shrieking. Metal crumpling, folding, we fishtail across two lanes as our car origamis into something new.

But it's the second impact that does the damage.

I don't look out my window.

I don't leave Dad's eyes.

Their horror, abrupt and savage.

Like opening a door and finding fire.

We spin three and a half revolutions before the car finally stops.

Somewhere in the middle, I drop the camera.

But it keeps recording.

The impact jams the horn, and it's hard to hear anything else—*Jamal, are you okay? Jamal! Jamal!*—the horn just keeps blaring that one awful note, long and loud.

We're perpendicular to the road, our front end tipped into a drainage ditch.

Nine baby trees still fill our back seat.

Ten trees rocketed through the broken windshield, through the shattered driver's and front passenger windows; when the firefighters slowly pull us out, I see them, dogwoods scattered across the road. I don't know why I count them, but I do. It feels like it'll be important later. Like maybe knowing things like how many trees or that it was 11:34 a.m. or that it had come down to Saturday or Sunday and we'd voted 3–1 Saturday because the weather was supposed to be perfect.

Not surprisingly, Whit voted for Sunday. She always chose the furthest date for everything. *I like having something to look forward to for as long as possible*, she said.

But now, sitting in the back of a yellow ambulance as the paramedics examine us, the pungent smell of antiseptic stinging my eyes and nose, all I see is fear on Whit's face—her pain as bright as the red gash cut across her cheek.

They find five saplings seventy yards from the scene.

The last one?

It's the only thing left in our front seat.

"Hello," says a voice detached from the scene. "You there, Mr. Anderson? Mrs. Anderson?"

It's not until several hours later, in the middle of the night, that it occurs to me who'd called.

"Happy anniversary," the voice said. "I know it's technically not until tomorrow, but I just wanted to get a jump on—"

50

I drop my phone, then pick it back up.

To Autumn: Can we talk? Can I call you?

49

Autumn: I forgot these things even made calls, haha.

48

I nearly pee myself when Autumn taps on the window, and she laughs, smushes her lips against the glass like a Picasso smile.

I shimmy open the window, my heart thumping, banging against my ribs like an animal thrashing in its cage.

"Thanks for the heart attack," I say as she climbs into my bedroom. She brushes herself off and I laugh. "You're not a fan of the front door entrance anymore, or?"

She wags her head, grins. "I was being romantic. This was a shout-out to the old days."

"You mean all those times we snuck each other into our rooms and got caught?"

She shoots me with a finger gun, winks. "That's it."

I frown. "Yeah, well, I'm starting to think that's my whole problem. Clinging to the old days. That maybe the best thing you can do is leave the past behind."

"Assuming this has to do with your one-day-only perfor-mance outside the after-school film club window?"

"You know?"

She shrugs. "Pretty sure everyone knows. People keep text-ing me to see if you're okay."

I groan. "Seriously?"

"You have to make it right," she says softly.

"What if it's too late?"

"You feel like you made your very best attempt today?"

I shrug. "Probably not. I mean, it happened so fast. It was all on the fly and . . ."

She nods. "So then there's more work to do," she says. "Doing the right thing isn't only about Q forgiving you, J. You can't control that. But when you look back next week, in ten years, whenever, you wanna know you did all you could."

I know she's right.

She taps the center of my chest. "The letting go you keep talking about? It's not you letting go of your bad feelings about Q. It's about you no longer blaming everyone else for *your* choices, for *your* actions. It's about actually meaning all your *I'm sorry*s. Or better still, just stop hurting people, man. Stop running away. You deserve to be happy. We all do."

And tears fall free, hers and mine.

And when Autumn leaves, I take a deep breath and dial Q's number.

47

AUDIO MESSAGE to Q: I don't expect you to text me back. Maybe you'll never talk to me again. Maybe I'll never get the chance to really talk to you.

But the idea that what I said today could be the last words you ever hear me say. I can't let that be.

See, the thing is, there's this angry, ugly Jamal lurking inside me. And for the longest time I let him do whatever he pleased. He was so hurt. So broken. But then one day he wasn't just inside me. He was me.

I was him.

If I were you, I would've climbed out that window and kicked my ass across the country. I thought because I was finally forgiving you, that I was finally telling you *my* truth, that it meant you had to accept it. You had to understand.

I imagined us hugging it out.

Maybe even crying.

Okay, that would probably be me crying more than you, I admit it.

You know what else?

You're gonna laugh your ass off when you hear this.

I imagined we'd exchange *I love yous*, but like, totally nonironically.

Because that's the kind of friends we used to be.

Because once upon a time, that was the kind of friends I thought we'd always be.

But here's what I didn't understand.

When you leave someone, even if you see the error of your ways, even if you apologize profusely, it doesn't matter. They don't owe you forgiveness. They don't have to take you back.

To be honest, Q . . .

The way I treated you, you shouldn't take me back.

You shouldn't even take the time to listen to this long-ass audio message either. And maybe you won't. Maybe you stopped listening a long time ago. If so, bravo to you. I get it. And I hope you get all the happy you deserve. That your next best friend is the kind who'd never hurt you the way I did. But Q . . . on the off chance you are still listening, I'm sorry. And this time, there's no excuses, no explanations attached. I'm just incredibly, wholly sorry.

And there's more to say.

But I'm not gonna keep going because you never have

enough memory on your phone as it is, and so if I go too long maybe you won't even get this.

Okay, I'm acting like that's still something true about you, when in reality, that was only true two years ago. Maybe you've got lots of memory left. Maybe you're flush in gigabytes. I just said the stuff about not having enough because I was looking for a reason to end this message and ask you to meet me in person.

To maybe hear me out.

So.

That's it.

The whole enchilada. The whole kit and caboodle.

Did you know that it's not *kitten* caboodle, as in, baby cat?

I just found that out. All this time I thought it was kitten caboodle.

Like it was some super feline.

Which, come to think of it, I still like that better.

Bye, Q.

DAY 2

Approx. 22–26 Q Days Left

46

I don't get much sleep.

Because the prospect of burying our emotional hatchet? It's exciting.

Like, I feel genuinely enthused.

And I can't help but wish I'd only reached out sooner.

I slip my phone in and out of my pillowcase, checking my messages, even though tone *and* vibration are both on, so I'd hear *and* feel if he messaged back.

But I check anyway.

Maybe that's part of my penance too, you know?

Not knowing what's happening.

Which, full circle.

Because that's what I did to Q.

Left him without answers.

Without closure.

Never knowing why.

And then, ten minutes before my alarm sounds, a chime.

45

Q: Lose my number forever.

44

And okay, I won't lie to you. It stings more than a little.

43

And I consider skipping school altogether.

Because who needs it?

I don't even want to risk seeing that dude.

But Mrs. Sweat pops into my brain and she's all, *don't be swallowed up, Jamal.*

And Whit's like, *yeah, think about your future.*

And Autumn squeezes in, wearing a Whittier U sweatshirt, *OUR future, babe.*

And I've never won an argument against them individually; there's no way I can ward off a whole We Care about You trinity.

So I moan, I groan, then roll out of bed.

I'm not gonna pretend my insides aren't knotty as hell.

For most of the day, my stomach hangs out exclusively in my throat.

But after Autumn listens to my audio message, she tells me she's proud I finally did the right thing, reminds me that even still, Q doesn't owe me forgiveness.

And the entire day, even when her class is a million miles away, Autumn's popping up outa nowhere, like a ninja, but with hugs and kisses.

Even still, the closer seventh period creeps, the more nervous I feel.

But then I realize something cool.

The reason I wanna avoid Q isn't because I'm angry.

Because I'm nursing a grudge.

Yep, I've officially stopped grinding my two-year-old Q-sucks ax.

No, I don't want to see Q because I'm sad.

Because I wish our ending could've been happier.

Which, in a weird way, is progress.

"I think I'm getting sick," I announce, rubbing my stomach between fifth and sixth period. "Yeah, like maybe the flu. Or . . ."

"It's not flu season, Jamal."

"Yeah, okay, I didn't claim to be a doctor. I'm just saying I don't feel—"

"You're not skipping seventh. No more skipping, remember?"

I sigh. "Yeah, but I wish I didn't."

But of course, in the end, all that angst is for naught.

This time, for the entirety of seventh period English, Q's empty chair stays empty.

When the final bell rings, I toss my bike into the back of Autumn's car.

And she lets me play all my favorite songs.

And at least between the two of us, it's like old times.

But then. "Hey, you missed the turn," I say, glancing over.

"Oh, did I?" she asks, winking.

"Where are we going?"

She shrugs. "Guess you'll have to wait and see."

As soon as we hit the exit ramp, it's like my face has a mind of its own, I'm cheesing hard. "Waaaiittt. Are we going . . ."

Autumn raises her eyebrows twice. "Oh yeah, baby."

And then we're slapping uncoordinated fives across the seat, but who cares about our inslaptitude, because this place.

THIS PLACE.

A mile away, you whiff the excitement: a combo of extra-powdered-sugar funnel cake and metallic adrenaline. With every This Way sign you pass, your chest hums like you're a live wire, and your stomach's a sloshing whirlpool of *I'm so happy* and *I need to throw up*. It's the best.

We pull up to the parking attendant and we practically sing her a *good afternoon*.

"You two picked *the* perfect afternoon to come to THE BEST AMUSEMENT PARK ON THE PLANET," the attendant says, handing me my change. "Gonna be an awesome day!"

"We think so too," Autumn says.

"Every day is awesome with this lady," I say, grinning.

"Aww," the parking attendant says, clutching his heart. "You guys are totes adorbs."

"Map?" asks a blond kid wearing the park's uniform, red polo with blue sleeves, skinny-ass shorts.

"Map?" I wave him off, hit him with *pshhhh*. "We don't need no stinking map. This is our park. These coasters run through my veins."

"We've added three steel coasters, two wooden, and ten additional rides since last summer," the blond kid says, smirking.

I take the map, but I don't look at it right away 'cause principles.

We pause for a quick entrance pic with a park photographer; *on the count of three say 'rocking roller coast'!*

"*ROCKING ROLLER COAST,*" we scream, leaping into the air.

"So, what should we ride first?" Autumn asks.

"You already know," I say.

"Hold up," Autumn says. "You sure you wanna go right to *that*?"

I nod extra enthusiastically, rub my hands together like I'm starting a fire.

"You don't want a warm-up ride first?"

"What, you scared?"

Autumn scoffs. "Never scared. I'm just saying, far as I know you only brought one pair of undies, so."

I grin, palm her head. "We should probably make sure you're tall enough first, right?"

She jerks from my grip. Pushes my arm away. "For that, I'm making you ride up front."

I shrug. "How is that a punishment?"

We stand in line for the Atlas Destroyer nearly two hours, but finally we push through the turnstile. Our time's arrived and it feels seventy-nine levels of glorious.

I clutch Autumn's shoulder. "Still time to back out. I'll only tell a few people."

She laughs. "Giving yourself a pep talk, J?"

"How tall is this again?" I ask a roller-coaster attendant.

She chuckles. "Three hundred and fifty feet, with four loopty-loos, six hills, and five pitch-black tunnels."

"And no one's died?" I motion to Autumn. "Asking for a friend."

"Ohmigod, J! OH. MY. GOD. That was incredible! Best ninety-three seconds of my life!"

I wink at her. "Hmm, I feel like you've had better, you know what I'm saying," I say, gently elbowing her in her side.

"Noopppeeee, this was the best," she sings.

She runs down the ride exit ramp and I chase her.

Your favorite amusement park and your favorite person, what could be better?

And then we're in line for our favorite loaded fries, and I'm like, *okay, Universe, out here trying to make amends, I see you.*

But then a voice calls my name from behind and I wave my fists at the sky because, *nope, still up to your same tricks.*

42

I can't believe my eyes.

What were the odds?

"You're not here to physically delete your number from my phone, are you?"

And I try to smile, but it's hard when all you feel inside is terror.

What if he *is* here to delete his number?

Or to kick me to Jupiter?

Or...

Q closes the gap between us, slaps his meaty hand on my shoulder. "Bro, do you wanna talk or not?"

"Huh?" I say. "Wait, you *want* to talk?"

He shrugs. "What, you thought this was like the movies where two principal characters get into a seemingly impossible-to-resolve conflict, effectively severing their relationship not only emotionally but also physically, until lo and behold, they run smack-dab into each other in the least coincidental but ultimately super-conveniently super-cool setting, i.e., an amusement park?"

"That's exactly what I thought, yes." And then I finally get it. And I stare into Autumn's eyes, and then Q's eyes, and then back to Autumn's, then back to Q's.

"I smell a conspiracy. You two set this up, didn't you?"

And I barely pin the question mark on my sentence's end when the two of them, in unison, shout: "OH MY GOD! YES, JAMAL!"

41

Q isn't making a blink of eye contact.

His hands are on the back of his head, like he's chilling in a hammock as opposed to sitting outside the park's petting zoo with his former best friend.

And initially, I was fully prepared to begin this conversation.

But when I began, he waved me off.

So, here we sit. Silently not looking at each other.

And then finally: "I kept waiting for you to come. I knew you would. But my dad kept getting sicker and sicker and you were nowhere to be found."

"I know," I say, because it's true. Because the only thing to say is: "I'm so sorry."

"Why?"

"Because I was angry. Because I blamed you for . . ." I look away but force myself to turn back. I hear Autumn's voice. *Accept responsibility, Jamal.* "I blamed you for the accident. I convinced myself that if you hadn't called, they'd still be alive."

"I can't believe you'd . . . wow, that really hurts. I loved them like my own parents."

I nod. "I know. I was wrong."

"Yeah, you were."

"I blamed my dad too."

"Why?"

I shrug. "Because he was trying to answer your call, but he couldn't figure out how." My voice breaking. "But that's just as wrong. Those were lies I told myself because I was angry, and I was afraid."

"What were you afraid of?"

"A lot of things. Suddenly, I realized how little control I had over so many things. That the massive amounts of love you have for someone didn't protect them from being hurt. *I* was afraid to be hurt again. I decided . . . I decided that if I could stop feeling, then nothing could ever make me feel that bad again."

Q shakes his head. "And I get all that, but still, I wouldn't have done that to you. I *didn't* do that to you."

"Q . . . I . . ."

Q's finger jabbing into my chest. "You think you're the only one who's ever hurt, Jamal?"

"That's . . . that's . . . not . . ."

"No one knows pain like Jamal. No one hurts as deeply as Jamal hurts. Your parents, they were only *your* parents, not Whit's, too, right? Only you felt that loss? And you feel bad because your sister, what, wanted to be there for you? You think she took a goddamn deferment at her dream school so you could flush your life away? That's how you thank her? That's how you honor your parents' legacy?"

I try to slow this down, because it's going too far too fast, but Q's showing no signs of braking, of letup.

"Q, listen to me . . . you don't understand . . ."

His finger back into my chest. "You have no clue what I understand. Or Whit. Or my mom. Or anyone. And how could you, Jamal? For two years, you've only cared about you."

"Q . . ."

"Contrary to what you think, we aren't born to sit and wait for the bad stuff to happen. We aren't born to die. But . . . but it happens to all of us. And what that means is we're gonna lose people along the way, people that matter a whole lot, people we can't imagine living without. We die, Jamal. And it's okay. You can talk about it. We can talk about it. Otherwise, it's gonna eat you whole, man. Instead, we need to be living the best we can. Without fear, when we can help it. Without anxiety, when possible. And carrying as little grief as humanly possible, okay?" He grabs my shoulders. "But you gotta stop walking around like you're dead because *you are killing everyone*, man. Because all of us are tired of watching you self-sabotage and self-destruct. Because it's awful wondering when you're gonna finally succeed and blow up into a gazillion pieces. Because your pieces are great, J. Because when your pieces are clicking... when they're really humming... they're some fucking rad pieces, man. They are. You are alive. And it's okay. It's more than okay. It's great. Let it be great."

And I can't hear any more, but also I want to hear it all again.

And I grab Q and at first he's pushing me, pushing me, but for the first time I can remember in forever I don't just give up, I'm holding tight, tight, and he's way stronger than me, but I'm feisty, I'm resilient when I need to be, when I want to be, and I hold on, man. I hold on tight. And he could flick me away easily if he wanted, but he doesn't, and that's something.

And then, after dozens of people give us weird looks as they pass by, he finally hugs me back.

Okay, more like he kinda pats my back.

With like the very tips of his fingers.

And we stand there.

Eliciting an innumerable amount of weird stares.

My arms locked around him, and him kinda fingertip-patting my back.

And no, I can't tell you for how long.

Because duration—how long a good thing lasts—is never the point.

"Can I ask you one more thing before we end this therapy session?"

He gives me a look, like *shoot*.

"What made you change your mind? What made you come today?"

"Autumn told me that I wouldn't have real peace until I forgave you."

More confirmation I don't deserve her.

"But really, that was the icing. This morning, after I sent you that text, I went down for breakfast. And like, on the surface, there's nothing all that different than any other morning, right? Me and Mom a perfectly orchestrated routine. She's making huevos rancheros, I'm making the coffee. And I'm not sure if you remember, but she's not exactly a morning person."

I nod. "You kidding? That was one of the best parts of sleeping at your house. She never woke up before ten."

"True." Q laughs. "Except this morning, she's talking both my ears off. Says she was up all night, tossing and turning. Says she suddenly had this weird feeling she was supposed to find something."

"Like what?"

"She didn't know. Just had the feeling. So, she's walking all over the house, and she's standing in all the rooms, and she's just looking for . . ."

"A sign."

"I was gonna say message, but sign works. And then she's in Dad's old office, which she's been slowly cleaning out. I know you remember Dad's bulletin board?"

"Umm, I couldn't forget that if I tried. That's the most inspirational thing I've ever seen."

And it is. When Q's dad was first diagnosed, back when we were ten, he'd been feeling depressed, naturally. So he came up with the idea that he'd hang a bulletin board and he'd pin happy things up. The things he was thankful for. Things that made him smile. Or laugh. He pinned comic strips, poems, fortunes from fortune cookies, articles from magazines, and when he heard something he liked, he'd write it down and tack that up too. And then he asked Ms. B and Q to add whatever they wanted too. And then he moved it from his office to the living room, and anytime someone visited, a friend, a family member, coworker, even the delivery-truck guy, he'd show them the board and tell them the next time he saw them, he wanted them to add something to the board. And almost everyone did. There was even something from my parents on that board. The board was overflowing with slips of paper.

"Yeah, it's great. Well, after Dad passed, she moved it back to his office. Honestly, I assumed it made her more sad than happy. Because after his cancer went into remission, Dad used to tell everyone it was the board that had fought it off. But then, of course . . . it came back. Anyway, Mom is standing in his office and she glances at this board she's seen a million times and she's walking back out when one of the fortune cookie slips catches her eye."

"It was some thought-provoking phrase?"

"Nope, there was something written on the back."

"Wait, for real?"

"Yep. A web address. In Dad's handwriting. Mom had never noticed it before. So, she types it into her phone, and she says she's instantly mesmerized. And that feeling she'd had is like changing inside her, and she knows this is it."

"What was the website?"

"It was a TuberOne video. And I'm like, okay, I'll watch it after school, because the thing is twenty minutes long and I'm still groggy. But then she's plopping her laptop in front of me. And now I'm watching some video about living your life with no regrets. About generating good energy in life. About never taking time, or love, for granted."

And for a second, I wonder if this is going where I hope it is, that she's told him about the reanimation. But that's not possible, right? No way he's in such a generous mood, if he knew.

"And then the video ends, and I'm like, thanks, Mom, because I don't know what else she wants me to say. But then just as she's sliding two sunny-sides onto my plate, she puts her spatula hand on my shoulder and she says, 'Quincy Michael, I want you to promise me one thing.' And I say okay, what? And she says, 'That this month, you'll work doubly hard to live your life the way your father did. With grace and honor, love and mercy. That you will let go of any anger and hurt, and that every day you'll do one thing that makes you happy.'"

"Oh, wow. That's . . . that's deep."

Q nods. "Yeah. It just got me thinking, what would Dad do? What choices would he make? He used to invite strangers into our house because he believed there was something good in everyone. People loved him because dude abounded in positivity."

And that couldn't be any more accurate. Mr. B may have

been the most genuinely joyful person I've ever met.

"So, here I am."

"So, you're saying it wasn't really Autumn that made you come?"

"Dad loved everyone. But he really loved you. He wouldn't want me to carry anything bad for you in my heart. But Autumn's the one who kept blowing up my phone until I promised to come here. So she gets credit too."

"Well, you gotta send me the link to this video. I wanna check it out too."

Q nods. "It's probably easy to find. It was by the Center . . ."

And my eyes nearly fall out of my face. "Did you say the Center?"

"Yeah, the Center for Orthopedics. I guess a bunch of bone doctors in Canada made it a few years back and it went viral."

Okay, okay, so, maybe not *the Center*, but still, c'mon, that's pretty dang close, and if that's not at least a little meaningful, I don't know what is.

Q grins. "Also, Autumn is very persuasive. And charming. And smart. And utterly gorgeous," Q says. "Not sure what she sees in you."

I push his smirking-laughing ass away, but I agree. "Whatever it is, I hope it never goes away."

40

Autumn's waiting for us at the entrance to Cursed Canyon.

When we're close enough, I reach over and take Q's hand, and it takes him a second to realize, and then he's telling me he's glad to see I haven't wasted the last two years maturing. Autumn asks Q if he's a hugger and then the two of them are embracing and I make a joke that I'm lonely, that I like hugs too.

And what could be better than this? My current favorite person with my former favorite person on either side of me, the best Jamal sandwich ever constructed.

And how could I not be happy when they're both so happy?

We hit Battle Bayou, Annihilator II, Hedge's Revenge, and we've got so much more on our roller-coaster horizon, but for now we're waiting for fried cheese on a stick.

Q's still pumped from Revenge, throwing air punches like he's warding off the blue raiders. If he's stopped smiling since we got off that first ride, I haven't seen it.

Which is great.

But also, it makes me feel twenty-four types of crappy. Because I can't help but think all this fun is balanced on a lie. That Q should know the truth. That no one's ever owed anything more in the history of the world than me owing Q this.

I have to tell him.

Because friendship is someone willing to tell you the hard truth.

I throat-clear. "Hey, Q?"

"What up?" Apparently, the Hedge's raiders are quite the foe—he's ratcheted up his air-punching intensity several notches now.

"I was . . . uh . . . you . . . you'd want me to tell you if, uh, there was something kinda big and it was about . . ."

Q extracts his phone from his pocket, taps the screen, and slips out of line, holding his finger up at me like *hold on, be right back.*

"What are you thinking about telling him?" Autumn asks.

I shrug. "Nothing. Just being hypothetical."

Q returns a few moments later.

"My bad, J. That was Mom."

"Everything okay?"

"I guess. She didn't know I was coming here and she's acting all upset about me missing dinner." He drops his phone back into his pocket. "Anyway, you were saying something?"

I shake my head. "You know what? It's nothing that can't wait."

What? Give me a break, okay? Telling your friend he's dead is something you have to build up to.

Autumn laughs. "Smash these cheese sticks and then Steel Throne?"

I groan. "Again?"

Q clasps his humongous hands together in prayer. "It's my fave."

I pull up the ride in the park app. "Homie, that line's ninety-plus minutes right now."

Hands still clasped, he drops to his knees. Autumn drops to her knees beside him.

"Okay, guys, get up."

"You sure, because we're not above groveling," Autumn says.

"Actually, we kinda enjoy it," Q adds.

But I'm only pretending to protest, because truthfully, I probably would've waited twice that long, Steel Throne's that good.

I tell myself I'll tell him while we wait; an hour and a half is enough time to try to explain the last two and a half days, right? But I can't figure out how to start: *hey Q, so you know how you think you're alive right now, hahaha, funny thing, you're gonna love this.* But I don't even get to bomb because there's a DJ playing music for the crowd, and the girls in front of us start flirting with Q—*oh my God, you're so tall. How tall is your girlfriend*—prompting Q to start telling jokes.

Seriously, he's like doing this entire stand-up routine, and you'd think his dark skin was actual chocolate, the way they're eating him up.

Before I know it, we're buckling our seat belts and bumping fists.

"You ready to do this, boy?"

"Let's get iiiitttt," I say as the ride squeals to life.

And I can't help but wonder if it's all a sign: first, the phone call from his mom, and then insanely loud wait-in-line music combined with the *you're so funny, are you gonna be a comedian* girls. And then him and Autumn hitting it off so smashingly?

Was the Universe conspiring to tell me that this *is* the best thing for Q?

To let him enjoy his last days and not worry about what comes next?

And really, the main reason I'd tell him is because I want him to maximize his last days on the earth; to do everything he wants. To go on his own terms.

But can't I make sure he gets all of that *without* telling him he's on borrowed time? What if I could help manufacture the best days ever? Wouldn't that actually be *better*?

When Autumn leaves us for the world's longest bathroom line, I decide to prod Q a bit.

"Q, if you could do anything you wanted the next few weeks, what would you do?"

Q sucks the bits of cotton candy from his long fingers. "You already know this."

"Okay, hmmm," I say, but I'm drawing a blank. "Give me a hint."

He does a voice, an impersonation, and it's killer. Dead-on accurate, so I pretend to not know who he means until he's just frustrated enough.

"The Kendrick Fallon thing? You still wanna host a late-night talk show?"

He shakes his head. "Arsenio Hall." He pumps his fist.

"Who?"

Q gives me a look like I just asked him for a back rub. "*Arsenio. Hall,*" he says with emphasis.

"Ohhhhh, see, I didn't get it the first time, but then you said it louder, and it clicked. Thanks."

We crack up.

"The guy in the club scene of *Coming to America* who *wasn't* Eddie Murphy."

"Why didn't you just say *that*?"

"He used to host a late-night show. Every star came on his show. Everyone loved that dude. Look him up. He's like the perfect balance of humor and charm. Like, he's not only the guy who invited you over, but he's also the guy who makes you feel like he's been *waiting* for you. He's dope."

"I'll check him out."

"Yep. Respect your black history." He takes a sip of his drink. "How 'bout you? If you could do anything you wanted over the next few weeks, what would you do?"

I look away. "I'm already doing it."

"Booo. That's weak, man," he says, laughing. "What, is this the part where you tell me I only have weeks to live and I'm stuck spending them with you?"

"Would that be so bad?" I attempt to ask casually, except I must make a face because Q shakes his head.

"Wow, why do you look like I just stole your puppy? I'm only playing with you, man. Of course you'd want to spend your last days on the planet with me. Duh."

And for a moment I wonder if somehow Q knows everything. Like, the truth is locked away in his subconscious, except every now and then it manages to sneak a message out.

"Earth to Jamal." Q stares at me. "You okay, man?"

I shrug. "I'm not sure what I'd want to do, honestly. I'm not like you. I don't have it all figured out yet."

"I don't have it all figured out, either."

"You're way ahead of me. All I know is I don't want to end up living in my sister's basement."

Q laughs. "Well, you've got time to figure it out."

That four-letter word again: TIME.

"And don't worry," Q adds, winking. "Even *if* you are camping in Whit's basement, you're definitely gonna be a guest on the show."

"Cool, I'll come on and tell embarrassing stories about you."

We laugh, bump fists, but two quick taps this time, the way we always have.

And then Autumn's back from her restroom sabbatical, and then it's Mission Mayhem, Cobra Cobra, those teeny-tiny ice cream beads, and my aforementioned all-time fave park amusement, FUNNEL CAKE, powdered absolutely, but hard pass on all that fruit compote crap.

"You shoulda got it. I woulda ate it. I love strawberries."

"Nope. Not a chance."

Autumn also disagrees. "Not even on the side?"

I shake my head vehemently. "I'm a funnel cake purist, sorry, guys. Those artificial preserves can't even share a plate with my sugar waffle."

And then bumper cars (I can't be stopped! I give Q all kinds of collision-induced headaches), and antique cars (always a classic! Autumn leaves us in her antique dust!), and an old Anderson household tradition (even Dad used to play and he swears all the games are rigged): a three-point shooting competition, which (whatever) Q wins handily, a giant purple panda to show for it, which he presents to Autumn.

And I pretend to be jealous.

"Man, don't be giving my girl presents."

Autumn squeezes the bear and says, "Finally, a *real* man."

And then more rides, more rides, more rides. Like, in between rides, I still feel like we're riding.

I can't tell you how many rides we ride.

Only that as we step onto our final coaster for the day—a day that's now night—my head is super achy but my heart's needle gauge can't even measure how full it is. Okay, that was terrible. Did I mention my head's achy?

This time we're in my favorite riding spot. The very last car. This ride with three seats in each car, which, if that's not kismet.

And then we're climbing a few hundred feet, only to drop fast enough to leave our stomachs behind—which, life, right?— the high winds making cartoons of our faces, gnats spattering like bug grenades, diving for our eyes and mouths, but we keep both open anyway, because we have to scream and howl and make fun of each other—*are you over there closing your eyes?! Look at you scared!*—because we don't want to miss a thing.

We're at the top of the final hill when the fireworks start.

Splatters of purple and yellow and blue falling with us.

You couldn't script a better ending.

Before we make it to the exit, Q's phone buzzes and I know it's his mom, except his face lights up in a way I'm not sure I've seen; he tilts the screen toward Autumn, who squeals with delight. Starts singing, "Q's got a *girl*, Q's got a *girl*."

"Hey, what about me," I protest. "I wanna see!"

And then he flashes it to me too.

A text.

Brianna: hey you guys leave yet??

"Dayuuuum, bro," I say, pushing him playfully. "These the girls from line? You gave them your number?"

Q shrugs like even he's surprised, but he can't keep his face from smiling. "Okay, don't laugh, but I've been really working on this. Trying to put myself out there more, you know. But to

252

be real, I didn't expect it to work like this."

"Why would I laugh and why wouldn't it work?"

"Because for all these years I've been a bit of a loser."

"Q..."

He holds up his hands. "It's cool, man. I'm good with it. I know who I am. Who I was. And it's okay." He turns his head, his eyes aimed at the rapidly emptying parking lot.

Autumn nods. "Q, none of us know who we are. We're all works in progress."

He doesn't answer.

I jump back in. "So, man, are you gonna text her back or you playing hard to get?"

He meets my eyes. "What should I say?"

Autumn grins. "Maybe start by answering her question."

He wags his finger at her. "Oh, you're good, Autumn." He taps the screen for a bit.

And then a moment later, Brianna hits him back:

> let's hit up the beach!! but ciara's making me drop her home first.
>
> Oh, and she wants me to tell you if I don't check in with her every fifteen minutes she's gonna send her Navy Seal brother after you! Okay, bye! Cya soon!

"You guys down, right?" Q asks.

Except all I can think is: I'm kinda getting tired of the beach. And I especially don't wanna be anywhere near water. I want to say: Q, if you knew what happened the other night, you wouldn't want to, either.

But the look on Q's face.

How could I crush him—the guy who just confessed he's trying to put himself out there?

"You kidding me? I got you, bro," I say.

And then we're in the car, crawling down the shore road, our headlights illuminating the lake's edge. It's after dusk, so technically this part of the beach is closed, but Q's face is pure determination. Brianna waves at us, leaning against their car when we pull up.

"You sure you're feeling okay?"

Q turns the car off. Takes a deep breath. "Physically, I feel normal."

"That's what I like to hear. Listen, it's okay to be nervous, but you got this, man. Remember, she hit you up."

Q nods. "You right, you right." He pulls the mirror down, does a quick once-over, then a breath check. Satisfied, he daps me up and then we're walking toward them.

Brianna's all dimples by the time Q closes the distance, and then they're walking off toward the water, leaving me and Autumn alone.

Autumn motions toward the shore. "You wanna help me find some sea glass?"

"Ha. You're looking at the reigning sea-glass-collecting champ."

She rolls her eyes and starts across the sand.

After we've collected a small fortune in sea glass, and Q and Bri have returned, the four of us roll up our jeans, discard our socks and shoes, and race toward the water.

Our feet detonate the beach—sand exploding up our legs, excavating shells and sea glass. Sea glass, jade and vermillion and cobalt, shimmering like fallen stars.

Our bodies propelling forward, hurtling, we run faster, faster, and for a moment our saw-toothed four-person line barely touches ground. We blast through the night like one-person rockets; erupting, flying straight into space, where time can't hurt us.

Bri goes down first, crashing into Q's legs, the two of them collapsing in laughter.

Autumn tries to hip-check me, but I keep my balance, my toes sinking into more seaweed than sand. "Cheater!" I call after her. She slows enough to look back at me, her face catching moonlight, and she's cracking up so hard I don't know how she's still running. I pick up my pace and now she's barely ahead.

"How do you like your dust," she calls over. "Medium rare?" But before I can answer she starts to pull away, grinning, her legs and arms and heart finding another gear I can't compete with.

I try to ignore the shells biting the bottom of my feet.

My burning calves.

But I'm no match for her. Autumn slaps the water before I reach the shoal, her hands raised in victory.

"You're . . . fast," I say, huffing, my hands on my knees.

"Yeah. Plus, you're slow," she says, scooping water and flinging it at me.

Except the second the water hits my face, I'm right back there. Back to that night. What wouldn't I have given in exchange for the two of us walking out of those waves together? But instead, each small paddle a struggle, each thrust slipping Q's face below the surface, again and again.

And it hits me. No, this isn't the same spot. Or even the same beach. But this *is* the same water. These *are* the same waves that claimed Q's life, changed everything forever, and it's too much. It's all too much. *We've gotta go. We should go.*

Another mini wave hits my face, snapping me from my thoughts. "You suffer defeat awfully well," Autumn says, her hands already delivering another watery assault. But I don't make a move back. "Hey, you okay?"

I'm the exact opposite of okay.

But this isn't about you, Jamal. This is about what's best for Q. So what, you have to stomach a secret you'd rather not keep? That's nothing compared to what Q and Ms. B are going through. You can't tell him. You can't.

"You still here, J?"

"Yeah, no. I'm sorry. Just . . . something popped in my . . ."

"It's weird being in the water, huh," she says. "After what happened."

"Yeah, I think even more than I thought."

"Well, it's a nice thing you're doing. For your friend."

"I want to do more."

"So, do more," she says, just like that. And then she's water-blasting me right in my eyes.

"Oh, now it's on," I say, returning the favor.

Both of us are soaked in seconds.

But mid-water-fight, Autumn nudges me. I follow her gaze and my wingman heart soars. Bri and Q, who'd already been holding hands and walking along the beach, have now paused under the pale moonlight to eat each other's faces off.

I nearly shout, *go, Q!* But I summon willpower I didn't know I had.

"Aww, they're cute," Autumn says.

But it only makes me question the Universe's decision-making.

Because how can the beach be an end *and* a beginning?

We scavenge for branches and dry wood. Handfuls of the tall wild grass that grows alongside the embankment.

Drop our collection into a pile that somehow Bri turns into a fire.

"Girl Scout troop leader, what can I say," she says, winking.

We wheel a cooler from Bri's car, and a giant plastic bowl of cut-up fruit materializes, is passed around and scooped into paper cups. I toss a grape at Q, but he ducks and I hit Bri instead.

And then it's on.

Grapes of wrath.

Grapes of rafts!

Okay, okay, damn, forget I said it.

Bri holds up a bottle of wine, looks at Q and me as if to say *is it cool?*

Q nods his consent and then we're sip, sip, passing.

The wine warm in my belly.

Sea wind warming my cheeks.

The fire jabbing left and right, dancing, dancing.

Autumn's fingers interlaced in mine, moon on her shoulders, her neck, her lips.

And I can't imagine a better place than here, now.

Autumn decides to check on her grandma and then Bri steps away to answer a call from Ciara, and I shoot Q a look like *maybe we should go*. But he's not close to ready.

"How about we walk a bit," I suggest.

"I live for long, romantic walks on the beach," he says, hopping up and swatting sand from his pants.

We amble down the beach, toward the now-closed amusement park, its million colorful bulbs reduced to soft white and pasty orange, just bright enough to prevent planes or birds from crashing into the coasters.

"Q . . ."

"This the part where you tell me you're sorry again? That you're trying to make up for lost time?"

I shake my head. "This is the part where I tell you I love you, man," I say. Because that's what you say on a night like this. And okay, maybe I'm feeling the wine more than I realize.

"I love you, too, man," he says back without hesitation.

"No, but I really love you."

"Okay, bro," he laughs. "Same."

"I don't want to live in a world you aren't in," I hear myself say. Which, I think, *okay, easy, J. Easy. Be careful here.*

"Good thing I'm gonna live forever."

"No one lives forever, man. I mean, we could . . . we could . . . die like right now, and there's nothing that we could do about it."

Q stares at me. "Hey, are you okay?"

"Huh? Yeah. No. I mean . . ."

"Because it sorta feels like you wanna say something, and if you need to talk . . ."

I cut in. "*I'm* okay, Q. It's not—it's not me who . . ."

But a shadow blitzes us, leaps onto Q's back, and then he's twirling Bri around and around, and she's *wheeeeeeee*-ing and singing: "I don't ever wanna come down! I don't ever wanna come down!"

"Everything has to, at some point," I say softly.

"What was that?" Bri asks.

"I said . . . I said . . . we had a fun day at the park."

"Best day ever," Bri shouts.

"Best day ever," Q confirms, spinning her faster and faster, no signs of ever slowing.

39

By the time I pry Bri and Q apart, it's three in the morning.

"You sure you're okay to drive, Q?" Autumn asks.

Q glances at her in the rearview. "I feel great. Promise."

I stare at Q. "You look a little pale."

Q laughs. "Thanks. I guess I'm a bit queasy, but I'm fine, really."

And then we're at Autumn's car. She hops into the driver's seat, and I follow.

"Q's following us, right? Autumn confirms. "You gave him my address?"

"Yep, we're gonna escort you home, and then I'll ride with him the rest of the way."

Fifteen minutes later, Autumn and Q exchange good nights,

and then she and I kiss outside her door, and thirty seconds later she's waving at us through her front window, and then I'm in Q's car.

"Hey, you checked in with your mom, right?"

"Negatory, my friend. My phone died hours ago."

"Well, you should've borrowed mine."

"We were having a magical time. Didn't want to lose our groove, you know. And I did text her earlier."

"When exactly? And what did you say?"

"I don't know. Five-ish? Just to let her know I was going to the park after school."

"Q, maybe she wasn't expecting you at six or seven or even eight. But it's three fifteen in the morning!"

Q laughs. "You're really getting yourself worked up. Stop worrying. Mom will be okay. I mean, she'll be mad for a day or whatever, but she'll get over it."

"I have a feeling this'll go another way entirely."

Q laughs. "Oh, you know my mom better than me, huh? It's fine, man. The world is right."

I shake my head. "Listen, I know you're still on the *I just made out with an awesome girl* high, but you should call your mom. Like now."

But Q shrugs it off. "Jamal, I'm dropping you off at your house, anyway, so if you're worried she's gonna give you a hard time, you're in the clear, okay? I'll tell her it was all me. We'll be home in thirty. Just relax."

I don't even bother objecting over *relax*.

I just plug my phone into Q's car charger, and we drive a few miles in silence.

Q looks over at me. "J?"

"What?"

"Bri is pretty awesome, right? Like, you think so too?"

I glance over. "She is, but it doesn't matter what I think. As long as you think she is, and she thinks you are, that's all the validation you need."

Q nods. "I think she's very awesome."

Finally, enough juice to power on, my phone buzzes and lights up for like two minutes straight, a string of texts and voice mails popping up in my notifications.

"Damn, someone's really tryna get ahold of you."

I hold up the phone so he can see the screen, which basically alternates Whit and a 216 number I'm assuming is Ms. B.

"Yep, that's my mom. She leave a message?"

"Several." I press Play on one from the middle, hold it to my ear.

> Ms. B: Jamal, I'm trusting that you're gonna take care of my son. I didn't want him to go so far, but . . . just make sure he stays safe. And remember, it's our secret to keep.

"Put it on speakerphone. I wanna hear too."

"In a minute."

He reaches for my phone, but I move it away.

He winks. "What, you and my mom got something to hide?"

262

"Huh? Like what?"

"I didn't forget all the stuff you used to say about her."

"Q, I was ten."

"Real feelings don't die."

"Okay, you got me. Me and your mom are having an affair and in this voice mail she's just told me I may be your dad."

"I hate you."

"What a rude thing to say to your father, son. You were so much nicer when you were still inside me. You had *so* much potential."

"That's beyond disgusting."

Q throws on his hazard lights and jerks the car onto the shoulder.

"What are you doing? What's happening?"

The color drains from Q's face.

"You gonna be sick?"

He shakes his head. "No. I don't know. Maybe. Yes."

38

Q's barely put the car in park, when he leaps out. He runs ten yards, his sneakers crunching gravel, glass, who knows— toward the scraggly underbrush, the freshly cut highway grass, and he lets it all go:

The pepper jack fried cheese.

The bacon cheeseburger.

Ice cream dots.

Enough varieties of soda to start a fountain drink stand.

Chili cheese french fries.

Blue cotton candy.

And yes, even my beloved funnel cake.

And it's weird, how it sucks to throw up, but also there's that instant relief of emptying yourself from the inside out.

I wish I could expel this secret.

Deception, the heaviest thing you can carry.

"You okay?" I call out, as he wipes a pearly string of saliva hammocking from his lips. I hand him a stack of napkins and a small pack of wet wipes from the car.

"Not gonna lie, I feel better."

And he didn't mean it that way but *lie* echoes up and down the highway.

Lielielielielielie.

"Like, so much better."

And I nearly say, *hold that thought.*

"Q, we need to talk."

"Okay, can we do it in the car? These woods sorta give me the creeps."

"I just . . . I just need to say it now. While I have the nerve."

"If a highway forest killer comes out of those trees, you gotta take one for the team."

I nod weakly. "Q . . . I . . . if it had been up to me, I would've told you as soon as . . . how do you even say something like this?"

"You're freaking me out, man."

"Brace yourself for more freaking out."

"J, whatever it is, you can tell me. I won't . . . I would never judge you. Not anymore, at least. You could tell me that you're the highway forest killer and I'd be surprised for sure, but then I'd get you the help you need to stop killing in the highway forest. I promise you."

"Q, it's not funny, man."

Q's hands go up. "When things feel dark, I go for laughs, you know that."

"Yeah, well, there aren't enough jokes to lighten this."

Q holds up his hands. "Why so glum?"

"You should've stayed your ass on the beach. You're a terrible swimmer. Why would you even try?"

"I feel like I'm missing something important."

"Because you are, Q . . . you're missing something monument . . . monumentally . . . very important."

"Or maybe someone's had a little too much wine."

"Everyone's lying to you, Q!"

"What are you saying?"

"Everyone's lying. Including me."

"Lying about what?"

"Everything. Your whole life. You're not even you. I mean, you're you but you're not you."

"I'm sorry, J, but you're not making any sense."

"*This* doesn't make any sense."

"Listen. Let's just get back in the car, okay. Let's get home and we'll talk in the morning when we're both thinking more cl—"

He grabs my arm again and again I yank myself from his grip.

"There's something you need to know. And I have to tell you right now."

"Okay, man. I'm listening."

And *now* reverberates in my brain, ricochets and rips

through whatever gray matter I still have. *NOWNOWNOW NOWNOWNOW.*

I wag my finger. "Yo, I'm serious, man. You need to listen."

Q scratches his chin. "I said okay."

NOW, JAMAL. NOW.

But I force it back down.

I gulp hard.

I swallow.

"My arms are different sizes." I extend both. "See, look. Weird, right?"

Q studies me. "I don't know why I take you seriously."

Because maybe Ms. B's right.

Maybe I only want to tell Q the truth because I feel guilty for being so crappy.

I want to make up for lost time. For being a terrible human to my best friend.

Prove I'm a good person, a better person than I would appear to be, because look, here I am doing something brave, taking a chance, keeping it real, doing the thing.

But maybe I don't get to throw up on the side of this road and feel better, lighter.

Maybe keeping this trash inside is the price for my mistakes.

37

It's funny how much of ourselves we never see.

Our most honest mirror, a friend.

A sister.

Whit raps on my mostly open door, a long pillow under her arm, her favorite blanket—Mom's favorite—draped across her shoulders like a cape.

"Sleepover?"

I drag in the rocking chair we put together for the nursery.

She settles into it, rocking slightly.

"You okay?"

"I could use another pillow," she says.

She leans forward and I reposition the pillow until she's most comfortable.

And then I tell Whit about our surprise reconciliation.

How I want to be a better friend to Q than I was before.

"Except how can I be better if I'm keeping such a huge secret? He has a right to know the truth, right?"

Whit shrugs. "It's all in our motives, man. You gotta ask yourself, *why* do I want to tell him? Because you're anxious to show you're new and improved, or because it's truly the right thing?"

36

In the middle of the night, I say: "Would you want to know?"

And Whit says, "Would I want to know *what*?"

But she knows what I mean.

So I don't rephrase; I let the question hang.

Let it breathe.

"Would you?" she asks.

"Yes," I tell her without hesitation.

"No," she answers back. "But I think you're asking the wrong question."

"What's the right one?"

"Should you know?"

DAY 3

Approx. 21—25 Q Days Left

35

Whit throws on my lights and shout-sings at the top of her lungs: "Carpet Denim!"

And I have insta-feelings.

Had I heard her right?

I shake my head, trying to clear space for her words to land. "We haven't done one since . . . can we even . . ." I think of the thing she said last night. "Should we?"

"I think they'd want us to. Truthfully, I think they've been waiting for us to. Like, all this time, us purposely avoiding Carpet Denim, we've been disappointing them."

"So, just you and me?"

"Umm, ouch! You saying I'm not enough for you?"

"No, you're more than." I look away, my throat tightening,

burning like someone lit a marshmallow on fire and stuffed it down my windpipe. And I'm not going to cry; it's not that. But it's like tears are lining up just on the other side of my eyeballs, ready to dive down my face if necessary.

Because this is the time for lots of things—but tears don't make the cut. Not right now.

"Okay, so let's get this party started. We got a day to seize!"

I roll out of bed. "Let's get it!"

"I'm excited." Whit claps her hands together. "Why'd we wait so long to do this?"

"We weren't ready to do this."

"So what's changed?"

I shrug. "Us, I guess."

Whit nods, takes a few steps into the hallway. "Okay, well, we can discuss our evolution more in the car. Get in the shower, because you smell like you've been lost in the jungle for weeks, and I'll meet your ass in the kitchen."

I sniff myself. "Your assessment's definitely a tad harsh, I feel really attacked right now, but okay, give me five."

Whit sniffs the same air. "Make it ten."

"Hahaha, you're so funny," I say, already walking into the bathroom. I poke my head back out. "Umm, Whit?"

"Yeah?"

"Is there a reason you're wearing a workout headband right now?"

Whit grins. "I figure we're gonna be very active, so."

I roll my eyes. "What you mean is, you've been looking for

274

an excuse to rock that headband forever, and now you're using Carpet Denim to justify it."

Whit shrugs. "Whatever. I'm cute." Whit makes a face. "See, baby's kicking. Two kicks means yes. They agree with me."

"Surprise, surprise, the baby you're carrying, who is incapable of audible responses, agrees with their mother."

"Sorry, I don't make the rules, but I mean, it's two against one. Basic math."

I laugh. "So, this is what I have to look forward to? A lifetime of being outnumbered, outvoted, out-everything'd?"

"Wait a sec," Whit says, holding her hand up. "Yep, two kicks."

"*Ohmigod*," I say in my best valley voice. "This is gonna be so much fun."

"Should Uncle Jamal jump in the shower immediately?" She holds her hand up again. "Yikes! You're not gonna believe this. Two more kicks. Baby Anderson has spoken."

"Fine. You win," I say, raising my hands in surrender. "But Baby Anderson, if you're gonna live here, in this house, a word to the wise. If you have any measure of pride, please, please, don't ever let your mom leave the house wearing a headband!"

I snatch the headband off her head and bound into the bathroom. I can barely lock the door, I'm cracking up so hard.

"Really? You just gon' victimize a pregnant woman? I know where you live, Jamal!" she shouts from the hallway. "Sleep with one eye open, buddy."

I turn on the shower. "I'm sorry, Whit. I'm having a hard

time hearing you right now because I'm really engrossed in my personal hygiene!"

"I hate you so much! Seriously, you're the worst!"

"You said you want me to flush your headband down the toilet? Wow, that's a really strange request but, and please don't take this the wrong way, I've heard hormones get all weird while you're pregnant, so, hey, if you really wanna flush your headband, who am I to stand in the way, you know?"

"Jamal Anderson!"

"I'm sorry, Whit, but I still can't hear you. Tell you what, give us two kicks for yes, one for no, okay?"

I pause.

"Jamal, I'm not playing with you!"

I hide the headband underneath the sink cabinet.

Then I flush the toilet, because siblings, amirite?

34

You're probably wondering *wtf is Carpet Denim?*

You're saying to yourself *shit sounds made up.*

And you'd not be wrong.

See, Carpet Denim's a by-product of four-year-old Jamal's inability to pronounce *carpe diem*. Although I'd still argue that—when said quickly—it sounds more like *carpet denim* anyway, fight me.

Showered, changed, and feeling extra clean, I track Whit in the kitchen.

"So, you ready to do this?" I open my fist, hold out my palm. "And look what I've got."

"The dice!" Whit exclaims.

And okay, I appreciate we're this late in the game and you're totally seeing another side of us. A Whit and Jamal duo prone to excessive exclamationing and insufferable amounts of shrieking. But it's Carpet Denim day, and if that doesn't get your blood racing, you're not human.

I slap her two dice. "You roll first?"

But she shakes her head. "We don't need the dice."

I scowl. "Uh, tradition? Whoever rolls the higher number chooses our activity. Then we alternate."

"Thanks for the rules recap, but we already did all that."

"Not following."

So, naturally, she speaks slowly. Like she's handcrafting each word with the finest materials. "Our last Carpet Denim. We never finished. Which makes it still your day, Jamal."

I wag my head. "No, no. That doesn't . . . that's different. We should roll."

I reach for the dice, but she slips them into her pocket. "Sorry, no dice," she says, laughing at her own joke and patting her pocket closed. "Rules are rules, man. And I don't make them."

"Umm, except that's literally what you just did. You just made this thing up."

"Nope. It's in the book. Look it up."

"There is no book."

"You're right. So that means it's gonna take you a while to find the rule, huh. Well, I guess in the meantime, we should get this Carpet Denim on the road!" She waves her car keys, slips out the front door. "You coming? I'm excited. Are you excited? Are we doing this? God, we're doing this. Mom and Dad, they would be so . . . wait. Wait. Ohmigod. Oh. My. God."

I rush over to her, stricken with panic. "What? What's happening? Is it the baby? Did your water, uh . . . I'll get the overnight bag and, damn, are you okay? Do you need me to carry you to the car? But also, no offense, but I'm not sure I want any of that fluid on me, so maybe we can . . ."

"Whoa. Whoa. Easy, cowboy. Let's take a deep breath, okay? Because you're about to need it." She grins, digs into her purse. Produces a circular piece of spectacularly ugly, bright-ass neon cotton. "Wait a minute, what do we have here? Is this . . . is this what I think it is?" She slips it snugly over her head and throws the biggest smile since the founding of our siblinghood. "Another incredibly awesome headband."

"Wow, Whit. Wow. Please tell me you don't have a whole package of those cheesy things?"

"So, I can't tell you that, but I can do this . . ." She drops her hand back into her purse and pulls out another terrible headband. "Uh-oh, *whaaaat*, this one has your name all over it? How did *that* happen, hmmm."

She flings the headband to me.

And sweet baby Jesus, she's not lying.

This lime-green bordered, pink-polka-dotted, orange-hatched fashion atrocity literally has my name on it. *Jamal*, in gaudy gold thread, right in the center.

"What the actual hell, Whit? There's no way you found a headband with *Jamal* on it at the store." The lack of already-made personalized merchandise is an ongoing saga in my life.

You could get Jack, Jordan, James. I'd even seen Trey dangling on a key chain at a rest stop. But never, ever Jamal. "You had these made, didn't you? You are officially out of control."

She laughs. "C'mon, J. We gotta be twins for the day."

I sigh. Fit the headband around my forehead. "Happy?"

She claps excitedly. "Super happy."

The doorbell rings.

I look at her. "You expecting someone?"

She pregnant-skips to our front door, swings it open with gusto.

And there stand Q and Autumn, back-to-back, their arms folded, posing like they're shooting a nineties hip-hop album cover.

"Hiiiii," they say in inspired unison.

"Somebody order a music video?" Autumn says.

"I'm starting to think the best thing about being friends again is this gal," Q says, nodding to Autumn.

"Funny, I was just thinking that was the best thing about being Jamal's girlfriend."

"Gee, thanks, guys."

Autumn's breaking into the running man, Q joining her.

And then Autumn's rapping over Q's beatboxing, and it's a whole-ass thing.

My name is Autumn, and this is Q.
Carpet Denim is what we 'bout to do.
We rock every party.

We get played hardly.
If ya step to him, or me, or you, or she,
Prepare to be sorry.
Buuh-huuh-huhhh-huuuuuh

"Wow," I say. "I don't even want to ask how long you two practiced that, or even whose idea it was, because wow. I can't unsee or unhear any of that."

"Let's hear you spit," Q challenges me.

But I wave them off. "Y'all ain't ready."

Autumn scoffs. "I told you he'd be scared, Q."

"Oh, never that. NEVER. THAT." I look over at Whit. "Yo, Whit you ready?"

Whit slants her headband, semicrosses her arms. "Yo, J, I stay ready."

"Okay, then drop that beat."

And then Whit proceeds to deliver *the* worst beatboxing performance in musical history. The only thing crappier is my rhyme skills.

"Yo, yo, yo, uh, uh, uh," I groan, the way rappers do when they're preparing to jump on some bars and spit a verse. But I basically keep doing that until Autumn and Q are laughing their asses off, and then I figure I might as well keep it going, considering Whit and I have already lost this battle.

"So, here we go, Whitney and Jamal. We back to give you that hot heat, to make you applaud."

"Boooooo," Autumn interjects.

"*Hot* heat," Q says, shaking his head. "As opposed to the well-documented cold heat. Got it."

Whit stops her highly irregular beat, and I pause my rhyming. "Yo, who invited these fools anyway, Whit? I thought you said it was just you and me."

"No, *you* said that. I asked if that wasn't good enough for you." Whit winks. "But c'mon, Carpet Denim is, and will always be, about family. And family isn't only what you're born into. Some family you're given, and some family you choose."

And we all nod our heads in agreement, because *church*.

And then Whit's tossing a headband to Q, one to Autumn, and yeah, okay, maybe we look like the last four kids to get picked for dodgeball, but so what?

I stick my hand out in the middle of us, and everyone piles their hand on top. "Seize the day on me, seize the day on three," I say. "One, two, three!"

"Seize the day," we all shout.

"That's what the hell I'm talking about," Whit says. "Now let's do this!"

So, yeah, I'm still kinda mixed-feelinged about this made-up Carpet Denim continuation thing. But one thing I'm not confused about: how much I love these three people. I can't imagine a better foursome.

33

And of course, we all see what Whit's doing.

That she's pushing us to heal.

But that doesn't mean I gotta like the salve.

Soon as I realized where we were headed, I started shaking my head. "Whit, I don't know about this." I said this over and over, until I lost count.

At one point she reached across the seat and squeezed my hand. "It's time," she said. "It's been time."

Autumn leans forward in the back seat, palms my shoulders in a show of support.

I spot the sign first. Elytown Greenhouse Emporium. We pull into the drive and I can't look.

I squeeze my eyes tight, like a belt that's skipped a notch.

"Jamal," she says softly.

But nope. Can't do it. I'm sorry. I can't.

"I come back here . . . a lot actually," she says. "I sit in that parking lot across the street and wait until they close, wait for the last car to pull out. And then I walk right over. Must've come here half a dozen times before I realized there's a small gate in the back that's always unlocked. Takes you right to the trees. I walk through them, around. All types of trees. Every type. And I remember the four of us moving up and down these aisles. You leading the way, because it was your day. Mom and Dad, they were extra corny that day. Dad kept nuzzling Mom with his new beard."

I laugh, but I don't open my eyes. "Mom hated that beard."

"It was pretty terrible. But like in this gloriously awesome way."

"Yeah. It's hard to tell, looking at us, but our parents were kinda cool."

She shushes me. "You can't say that out loud. They'll arrest you for that."

I smile. "God, can you imagine how big their heads would've gotten had we actually told them that? That we thought they were cool?"

"I don't know that I thought so back then. I mean, I loved them, but they had their things too. They're only perfect in our heads."

I nod. "True." I open my eyes. And my head is buzzy

and for a few seconds everything is a blurry technicolor. It's strange, how every time I remember that day, when I see this greenhouse vividly in my head, it seems so huge. Looming. But in reality, the lot's maybe large enough for ten vehicles, and the greenhouse is the size of a three-car garage. "You still come here?"

Whit bites her lip, maybe to stop it from trembling. "I do."

"Often?"

She nods.

"Makes you feel closer to them? In your own way? Makes them feel alive?"

She nods again.

"A fortress for your heart."

The greenhouse only has seven saplings.

"We could go to other nurseries," Autumn suggests.

Whit agrees. "Combined I bet you we get to twenty-five."

But I shake my head. "For this, I think it's less important how many trees and more important that all the trees only come from here."

"Fair," Whit says.

And we load the seven into the car, a perfect fit.

As the car rolls to the edge of the driveway, Q and Autumn busy watching clips on her phone, I'm increasingly desperate for any distraction.

Whit studiously glances left, then right, waiting for traffic to clear, the street seemingly infinite in either direction.

"So," I clear my throat. "How's Angeles's finals going? Any news yet?"

And yes, I do care about his tests, but mostly I conjure Angeles to redirect my brain, to wash away Dad's voice: *Our love is at an al-pine high! Our love is at an al-pine high!*

"He says everything's a lot harder than he thought it'd be, that he's probably gonna fail the quarter and get a job selling used cars, asks me if I'll still love him. Which, in Angeles talk means finals are going great," she says, grinning.

But then it clicks for Whit, and she quickly turns us around, cuts the car across the lot. And despite it leading us onto another street, essentially forcing us to drive in a circle and easily adding ten minutes to our trip, we use another exit.

We can't use that exit.

Because not everything should be as it was.

Because every trip should build in time for detours.

We swing by Q's to pick up his mom, and to grab shovels and rakes and other gardening equipment.

And then the five of us make the drive my family never got to finish.

It's odd.

How a road you've never traveled feels cursed?

How sometimes it's the things that don't happen that haunt us hardest.

286

We scour the preserve for the perfect spot.

Settle on a clearing encircled by spruce and evergreen.

Everyone sort of stands back while Whit and I argue over who should break ground first. But in the end, Whit wins, and after I double-glance her way to make sure it's really okay, I stab the shovel into the grassy soil.

And I hold it there a minute, half the shovel face beneath ground.

I wait for a sign, any indication that this is wrong, wait for Mom and Dad to materialize and voice their displeasure. But that doesn't happen, and all I feel is a happy-sadness.

Two years ago, I couldn't wait to be here. We'd had a program at school about protecting the environment, and every student was given a sapling to take home.

That same evening, I sunk my shovel at the back of our lawn, Dad looking on.

"Hole needs to be bigger," he'd said.

And I'd made it bigger.

"Still not big enough," he'd said. I kept digging.

We went on that way another few rounds until Dad bust out laughing. "I better stop you before you get to China."

Mom coming out to see what was taking so long and then telling Dad he was wrong for that. "Boy's too gullible," Dad said.

"He gets it from you," Mom said.

"Please, that's from your family."

Mom pointed near Dad's shoes. "Dre, you dropped your pocket."

Dad glancing down, Mom and I cracking up.

He'd spent the rest of that day trying to trick us. Happy when he'd finally fooled an unsuspecting Whit.

That night, at dinner, I announced my Carpet Denim.

"Did you know every day nearly two hundred thousand acres of forest are cut down? Well, I want to put a few trees back into the ground."

If that stupid assembly had never happened, if I'd never brought home that tree, if . . .

If.

If.

A game that never ends.

Whit digs the next hole and her tears drop into the hole ahead of the sapling.

We sculpt and pat the earth around each small tree.

And there's an eagle gliding back and forth across the horizon and Ms. B says it means this work will be blessed. I don't push her for what blessed means, because it's not what matters. Two years later, there is finally dirt beneath my fingernails, there are new trees in the ground.

Whit and I each plant two, and Q, Autumn, and Ms. B each plant one too.

When the final tree's earthed, Whit walks back to the car, returns with two metallic vases filled with our parents' ashes. I nod my approval.

"Yeah?" she verifies. "You sure?"

"I'm sure."

We stand there in silence, until Whit reaches for my hand. Squeezes my fingers, just as a plane buzzes overhead. I reach for the tree closest to me. Rub one of its waxy leaves between my fingers.

And I say, "Mom, Dad, our love for you is at an al-pine high."

And then everyone's hugging and crying and generally all in our feelings until suddenly Whit's all *hold up hold up hold up.*

And we stop in our tracks and wait for her to say whatever she needs to say.

Except it turns out she doesn't want to *say* anything.

Well, not exactly.

"There is one more thing our trees need to be complete," she says, reaching into a large garbage bag, which I'd wondered why it was there, but then naturally assumed it was for . . . garbage.

But what Whit pulls out of that trash bag is garbage.

And also it's gold.

And I know my face is all kinds of bewildered. Astounded. "How in the world did you get that?"

Whit shrugs, smiles. "When I saw it had been ripped down from the tree, it didn't take me long to piece together the *who.*"

"You found it in the trash bin."

"After searching around the woods for an hour and thinking it was lost forever, yeah. But then a couple of days later I'm walking out the cans to the street for trash day—your job, by the way—when *surprise, surprise,* guess what's sitting inside, upside down?"

Whit holds the plaque out to me and I feel more tears.

Whit points to the shovel at my feet. "I'm thinking we just kind of prop it up and slightly bury the bottom of it rather than screw it into the poor trees, whaddya think?"

And the tears just keep coming, they just keep rolling, as we dig a small trench, wedge the plaque inside.

And I don't know, whereas it was the dumbest idea before, it makes sense now.

It makes sense here.

JADA & ANDRE ANDERSON.
NEVER FORGET.

And that's how we came to finish my nearly two-year-old Carpet Denim.

With five people who in the last four days have had enough arguments to fuel a small war. And yet, here we are, somehow finding a way to band together. To put the past behind us.

Because sometimes the best family are the people you choose in spite of the bad stuff.

Five people who didn't always see eye to eye but loved each other regardless, scattering our two beloved parents among seven new trees in one lucky-to-have-them nature preserve.

32

"We should get an early dinner," Whit says before we're even out of the nature preserve.

Q votes Chinese food, but Ms. B overrules him, says nobody wants to be around him post–Chinese food, which, *truth*.

I toss out Italian and everyone agrees, pasta's it.

"But homemade noodles," Ms. B insists.

So we hit up the grocery store, then lug our haul into our house, Ms. B immediately asking Whit where we keep our pots and pans.

"Go deep," I say, and Q pretends to run a go route into the living room and I deliver the bag of garlic right on time, hitting his hands in perfect stride.

"Okay," Ms. B says. "If you two drop any food, or break anything, you'll be handwashing every pot and pan after dinner."

"Welp. So much for that," Q says.

"Fun while it lasted," I chime.

Ms. B rolls up her sleeves and puts in serious *work*, whips together a batch of her killer spaghetti, homemade sauce with ingredients she won't let us see her add, the four of us taking turns trying to ambush her, or distract her, but all our efforts are for naught and Ms. B's recipe stays secret.

She doesn't even crack when Q, Autumn, and I offer up our garlic-bread-seasoning recipe in exchange for her sauce recipe—she actually kind of offends us, the way she turns her nose up, as if we somehow aren't offering items of equal value, but whatever, her loss.

Our recipe's basically an entire loaf of sliced Italian white bread that we olive-oil-drizzle and then embellish with a carefully curated seasoning blend, sprinkled liberally.

And by curated, I mean, we take turns shaking shit on we think looks cool or adds a unique flourish of color.

Except Q's last addition has even me perplexed—me, the person who adorned a few pieces with a dash of cinnamon, you know, for an unexpected *boom*, before the other slices were expeditiously removed from my reach.

"Bro, star anise? What the heck is anise?"

"Opposite of a nephew," Q replies.

"Duh," Autumn adds.

And yeah, it's officially a thing now: double-team Jamal when possible.

31

We're asking Whit and Ms. B for their bread-seasoning preferences when the color drains from Q's face and his eyes go droopy and he complains of dizziness.

Autumn doesn't fully grasp the situation, because she has no idea Q's dead, but she does appreciate that something's really wrong.

"Sip your water slowly," Ms. B tells him, and I remember she's a nurse, but then I also remember the kind of nurse she is, and I wonder if all nursing translates the same.

I suppose, at the very least, assessing someone, checking their vitals, their level of consciousness, would.

Ms. B stands up from the table just as Q draws the water to his lips—his hand trembling.

"Q, what's happening?" I hear myself say. "Q, are you okay?"

But now Q's entire body's convulsing and before Ms. B or I can make it to him, the glass drops from his grasp, a mosaic of clear-blue glass scattering beneath the table.

"Noooo," Ms. B calls out.

But it's too late.

I'm too late.

She's too late.

Q's pupils shrink to nearly a pinpoint, drool rappelling from both corners of his mouth, until his neck snaps forward and his entire face crashes into his plate, noodles leaping, sauce squirting like blood capsules.

We stop Autumn from calling 911 even though I think all of us wonder if that's the right move, if that's actually in Q's best interests.

Instead, Ms. B frantically dials Mr. Oklahoma, immediately launching into Q's pertinent health info as soon as he answers.

I can just faintly hear Mr. O's reply: *we're already en route*.

But I can't even concentrate on what else he says, what else Ms. B relays, my eyes glued on my friend, my hand resting on his back. Autumn picking noodles from his hair, his face, because I think we just want to be useful and how do you do that when you don't have anything of real value to add, other than concern, other than hopes and hastily heaven-sent prayers, even though you seem to only pray when shit sucks, when you're all out of options.

I don't even know how much time passes before the men

in black come streaming through our front door, this time adorned in stethoscopes and other, more-complicated-appearing medical instruments.

Autumn whispers in my ear. "Who are these people? They're not paramedics."

"No," I say. "I don't think they are."

They remove Q's shirt, attaching a series of circular sticky pieces to his chest and stomach—*leads*, Ms. B calls them. These leads are connected to a battery-pack-looking thing, and that's plugged into a large tablet, operated by one of the non-paramedic women, who taps feverishly on the display screen, shakes her head, and then taps more.

Meanwhile, the others administer oxygen, check Q's blood sugar, heart rate, blood pressure, respirations per minute. They check his blood gases, whatever those are. And a bunch of other labs, whose results instantly feed back to the large tablet.

"He's stabilizing," the woman says matter-of-factly to her coworkers. And they continue their work until finally she announces *stabilization achieved*, and they quickly detach and remove their equipment, reshirt Q, then slide-board him onto a gurney.

"Excuse me," Ms. B says. "Where are you taking my son?"

The nonparamedics cast each other looks like who's talking to this upset lady, one-two-three not it.

The woman asks Ms. B to follow her into the hall, and I hear their voices but not words. A few minutes later, Dr. Iverson shows up with Mr. Oklahoma, joining Ms. B and the woman in the hall.

That's when voices spike.

Especially Ms. B's.

But then, after a while, she returns to the kitchen, stoops over her son, kisses his forehead. Strokes his temples, his wrist and fingers.

Then it's *one-two-three-lift* and we watch as they carry Q out and down our front walk. We follow them, watch Q slide into the back of a black van. The van plain and new.

"Where are they taking him?" I ask Ms. B.

But Dr. Iverson says, "We need to run a few tests we're unable to perform here in the field. Don't worry. Q's fine."

Mr. Oklahoma nods his agreement. "Nothing to be concerned over. Quincy is a fighter." The second person this week to say that.

And then as swiftly as they came, the three men and one women re-van and pull away. Meanwhile, Mr. Oklahoma opens Dr. Iverson's car door, then walks to the driver's side, looks back at the four of us over the top of the car.

He waves like he's not sure he should.

Then they're gone too.

We stand there, silent, unsure what to do.

And then Autumn turns to us. "So, what the hell's going on?"

We take turns lying to her.

It looked worse than it was, our company line, which is only slightly better than hahaha, that was a joke! They're gonna bring him back any minute now, hahaha.

But Autumn knows me. My lying face, my half-truth face, my squeaky lying voice.

"Something just happened, and I seem to be the only one who doesn't know what," she says, her eyes sweeping across our faces for a crack in our unified front.

But we don't cave.

And then Ms. B's climbing into her car, ignoring the stop sign, skidding around the corner.

"You gonna tell me the truth?" Autumn asks.

And I know this is it.

A make-or-break moment.

We both feel it.

But I can't. It's not my truth to tell. And I tell her that.

And Whit tries to convince her to stay, but she can't peel out of our driveway fast enough. I wave my arms for her attention, yell through the driver's side glass that I'll call her later, but she rolls down her window, so I can see her face when she says it, so I can see she really means it.

"Don't bother," she shouts, her eyes welling up. "Save your breath and lie to someone else."

And then, she, like everyone before her, is gone.

Because, sooner than later, everyone leaves this house.

30

Later that night Whit's phone rings and she sets it on the couch between us, Ms. B's voice kindling-crackly, and I can't tell if it's the speakerphone or that she's been crying.

"They're bringing Quincy back home, but they tell me there's a new development to discuss."

Fifteen minutes later, Ms. B's pacing her living room.

Whit's in the bathroom.

I'm sitting on the couch, trying to not overanalyze what *new development* means.

A loud knocking evaporates our haze.

And I suppose I was expecting Q to come gliding in, ducking to avoid bumping his head the way he always did even when he could clear the threshold, a habit cultivated from years of knots and bruises on his face.

But there's no danger of that now, as they deliver Q in a gurney identical to the one they took him away on. Q in some sort of deep sleep.

Eyes and lips clenched. Hands folded flat against his chest.

Ms. B doesn't look surprised by Q's state, and she leads them up to Q's room.

As the men return, I hear Ms. B close the door, her body revealed from the feet up as she descends the stairs, like watching a picture leave a printer, a couple of lines visible at a time.

I don't hear Mr. Oklahoma enter the house.

I don't see him standing in the threshold.

But here he is, his demeanor all business.

"This will be hard to hear," he says. "The good news is we were able to reset Q back an hour prior to his collapse. He will wake in a few hours and he will have no recollection of what happened." He frowns. "However, Q did suffer a significant setback. There was an inexplicable surge in Q's brain that induced, in simplest terms, a coma. During this comatose state, Q's brain activity, along with the rest of his vital organs, began behaving as if Q were, in fact, dead."

"What are you saying? Just say what this means already," Ms. B demands. Her face a diagram of impatience: eyes narrowed, lips curled, forehead flexed.

"My apologies." Mr. O nods, throat-clears. "It means Q's length of stay was seriously impacted."

"Wait, you're saying he won't get four weeks?" I interject.

"Regretfully, no," Mr. O replies.

Ms. B's voice jumps like someone startled her from behind. "So, how much time are we talking? How much does he have left?"

"Three weeks?" Whit asks. "Less?"

Mr. O shakes his head. "It truly pains me to say, but it would be a miracle if Q lasted another forty-eight hours." He removes his glasses, gives them a quick buff with his handkerchief.

"No! No! You promised me . . . you said there was nothing to worry about!" Ms. B yells, and I have to step in front of her to keep her from crossing the room in a fury.

Mr. O, however, doesn't seem to notice his life's in jeopardy. "But we do have another option. We could put a hard cap on Q's reanimation."

"What does that mean?" I ask.

"We'd set the exact time Q would re-die. That way there are no surprises. That way everyone can prepare."

Ms. B wags her head in disbelief. "But you just said you don't know how much time he has. That it could be a day, two days."

"We would have to schedule him to re-die tonight. We could give you a couple of hours to say your goodbyes."

And I've never seen Ms. B move so quickly—even when we were racing to the conference room at the hospital. And then she's barreling into Mr. O, shoving him back onto the sofa, Mr. O's eyes like the first letter of his last name, wind knocked from him, he struggles to talk, to explain.

But Ms. B appears beyond all that.

"You lied to me," she says over and over. "I never would've done this! I shouldn't have done this! What was the point? Two days? Two days!"

I do my best to pull her away, the Center's team of transporters don't touch her, but they gradually slide between her and Mr. O, forming a human wall between them.

Mr. O stumbles to his feet, stoops to catch his breath, hands on his knees.

"You're a liar! I'm gonna report this! Don't you ever touch my son again! This is done! This is over!"

Mr. O holds a hand up, his face turned down. This, the first time he's appeared uncollected, noncomposed. "I am so very sorry," he's saying. "But at least you had more time, you still have more time, please, understand that we—"

"Get the hell outa my house! Take your machines and your people and I don't want to see you anywhere near my son! You hear me? If you come within a hundred yards of here, I'll shoot you. I'm not playing! I'll . . . I'll . . . f-f . . ."

Her words falling.

Breaking.

Into bits, into letters, into wet sounds.

Her knees buckle and I push myself under her body, do my best to lower her to the floor.

Mr. O nods at his men, and they exit the house, quickly, quietly.

Then he gathers his glasses from the sofa, finds one of the arms badly bent, the frames skewed. He slips them into his

301

shirt pocket. Runs his hand around his waist, retightening his tucked shirt. He moves slowly across the living room, the way you do when you're not sure you want to leave.

When you know you're leaving things undone, and worse than before you arrived. He stands with his back to us, the front door opened, framing his slender body, dusk dropping into the horizon like flour into a bowl.

The lamppost light in the yard spasms to life.

A dog barks a few doors down.

Ms. B sobs into my shirt.

Mr. O turns around, tilts his head at Whit, at me, at Ms. B.

"What happened?" I ask. "Please. What went wrong? Was it something we did?"

"Dr. Iverson told you Q was our first spontaneous reanimation?"

"So, you're saying this is all because you didn't have enough time to prepare?" Ms. Barrantes says, her voice broken. "You told me he'd be okay. You gave me your word."

"I am sorry that we did not fulfill the entirety of our promise to you, Ms. Barrantes. Truly sorry," he says. "But the work we are doing at the Center is good work. Important work. And it will go on." His words a promise and a threat.

"You should leave," Whit says. "Now."

His right hand plays piano on the door, and he nods again. Holds up the peace sign. "I do wish we could've given you more, but I know you will use the time that remains wisely."

302

DAY 4

<48 Q Hours Left

29

This time we don't know when Q will wake.

And although none of us say it, given the Center's unreliability, we can't even be certain that he will.

Twenty-four to twenty-eight days reduced to forty-eight hours tops?

Just like that.

Had this always been a possibility?

Was it a coin flip, or even a likelihood that they'd opted not to mention?

At one point, Ms. B suggests that maybe they've gotten it all wrong—that maybe Q *will* go on living for weeks. Maybe months, she says.

Whit and I exchange looks, but we don't challenge her. We

know this is grief talking. We, too, have tried to speak impossibilities into existence.

We, too, have rattled off miracles, as if they were as easy as asking.

Truth is, we'll probably never have answers.

Not that we'd believe them if they tried to explain what had gone wrong.

All I know is this:

Q likely has less than forty-eight hours left on this planet.

And as much as I despise Mr. O right now, he was right about this one thing:

Every minute was invaluable.

Every moment needed to be maxed.

We say *spending time* because time costs.

No moment's free.

Every second, a price.

> **To Autumn:** Hey, I'm so so so sorry!!! Please text me back.
>
> **To Autumn:** Or call me. Whatever you want.

And then, later.

> **To Autumn:** You're right. I did lie to you.
>
> **To Autumn:** But I didn't want to.
>
> **To Autumn:** I was trying to do the right thing.
>
> **To Autumn:** But the right thing wasn't completely right.
>
> **To Autumn:** Q's back.

And then later, still.

To Autumn: Q's awake.

His eyes flutter, he coughs, licks his lips, stretches, then leaps into the corner of his bed. "Why the hell are you guys staring at me while I sleep? Did you join a cult while I was out? Am I being sacrificed? Because you don't want me, I'm all bones. But J, on the other hand, he's a little meatier. Look."

Ms. B falls onto Q and he's clearly confused, concerned. But he pats her on the back. "What's happening?" he asks. "Am I okay?"

"Yes," she tells him, swiping her eyes, only for more tears to take their place. "You're fine, baby. Everything's fine."

And then my phone buzzes.

Autumn: I'm glad Q's okay.

Autumn: But until you tell me the whole truth, we still aren't.

But how am I supposed to tell Autumn the truth when Ms. B, even with Q down to his final two days, still won't budge on telling him?

"He deserves the truth," I tell her, following Ms. B to the kitchen.

But she's all no no no no no no no.

She's all, you might as well pour concrete around my feet, because I'm not moving off this decision. I appreciate the situation's gravity, the heaviness—how hard it would be for Q to

307

wrestle with *hey, man, guess what, you're dead* without adding the whole *oh yeah and then you were temporarily resurrected* thing.

The chances of *that* conversation going well?

That it *wouldn't* result in a trifecta of wailing, obscenities, and grave depression? Go ahead and write ZERO in every language here.

But even a difficulty rating of FREAKING IMPOSSIBLE is not an excuse.

The right thing's the right thing.

I finally want to do the right thing, no matter what.

And okay, I'm not saying there isn't an argument to be made for *not* telling him.

When Ms. B says, "I want him to enjoy his last days on this earth, not grapple with his mortality," I totally get it.

It makes a lot of sense. Deserves consideration.

But in the end, to me, it's not good enough.

When you're talking about someone's life, I don't think you should hang your hat on what *you want*.

On how you feel.

And yeah, sure, I get that it's easy for me to say.

I'm not his bereaved mom. Or his grieving family.

I'm a once-upon-a-time best friend, now wafting within the margins of Q's sadly all-too-shortened life.

But still.

Still.

Think how *you'd* live if you *knew* you had only days left.

Now think how you live most days.

Okay, so you tell me: would you rather have the time of your life doing the things you've always wanted, or would you rather spend twenty minutes staring into your sister's magnification mirror while you pluck curly nose hairs so long they resemble a pig's tail?

Guys, this is not a trick question.

And so I just say it:

"You deciding *not* to tell Q is wrong," I say louder than I intended. Both of us louder with every sentence.

Maybe that's why we never hear him come into the kitchen.

"Tell me what?" Q asks.

Ms. B and I both whirl around, stunned, jaws dropped, our eyes saucers, all of it.

"Nothing, baby," Ms. B says, shooting me a look that could've easily wiped out the dinosaurs. "Jamal was planning a surprise party and . . ."

"A surprise party," Q repeats. "For what?"

"Oh, uh, for, uh . . ."

And while Ms. B searches for the next lie to tell, internally I can feel it happening. The words. The truth. Swirling in my gut. Full of the worst shit and rising higher and higher with nowhere to go, like a clogged toilet, it's gonna spill over. It has to.

"Q, there's . . . there's something I need to tell you . . ."

But Ms. B's waving me off. Her death gaze on bajillion. "Jamal, shut up. That doesn't belong to you."

"I'm sorry, Ms. Barrantes. I love you. But this doesn't belong to you either."

"Jamal, if you say . . . if you do this, you will never . . ."

I shake my head. "Never what? Set foot in this house again? See my friend Q again? All of those things are likely no matter what."

"What the fuck's happening? Why won't you see me again?"

Her face changes from anger to fear. "I'm begging you. Please don't do this."

"What's wrong with you, J?" Q continues. "Are you sick?" And now he's palming his forehead. "Fuck, you're sick, aren't you? When are you gonna catch a break, damn . . . listen, it doesn't . . . you're strong, man . . . and I promise you I won't leave your side no matter what ha—"

"Q," I say. I repeat his name over and over until he finally stops, Ms. B slumped in the kitchen corner. "I'm not sick, man. Please, please, just listen to me . . ."

Whit appears in the doorway beside Q. Her face perplexed. "What . . . what's going on?"

"Your brother is about to ruin my son's life. That's what's going on."

Whit turns to me. "What are you doing, J?"

"The thing I should've done already."

"I won't let it happen," Ms. B says, holding up her phone. "I'll call the police."

But Q walks over to his mom, takes the phone from her hands. "Mom, I love you. But whatever this is, you can't protect me from everything. I don't need you to. I love you, but you've gotta let me be my own person."

"You don't think I know that? You don't think I want you to be? That I'm not already proud of the human you are?"

Q nods. "If you really believe that, then you'll let whatever this is, happen."

And she doesn't say a word.

"Whit, will you stay with my mom for a bit?"

Whit nods.

And Q turns to me, motions for the door. "Let's go for a walk."

We don't ask *which way?*

We just fall into stride.

Fall into our route.

How many times had we run down this sidewalk?

Hopped off and pushed our bikes past this house because the owner used to yell *sidewalks are for walking, not riding.* Hopped back on soon as we turned this corner.

"Q, I . . ."

Q holds up a finger. "We got time, right?"

I nod. "Yeah, man. Sure." Even though that's what all this boils down to. Time.

We walk past a pink house and Q nudges me. "Yo, your spot, bro."

"Dude, really?" I laugh.

"Caught you slobbing and dobbing Brenda Longfellow. It

was like you were eating each other's faces."

"Okay. Whatever."

"The same Brenda Longfellow who spent that entire summer calling you Janky Jamal and harassing you every time you walked past her house."

"Then the last day of the summer, magical." I sigh dreamily. "Ah, the mysteries of the heart."

And it's wild, how places keep our memories whole; a building, or a park, or a patch of grass between two houses, each like a preserves jar.

We pass an auto parts shop where all the employees knew my dad by name. And then the convenience store where Q and I spent all our lawn-cutting money buying fruit snacks, chips, *SLAM* magazine. Then we're in front of Dollar-A-Slice Pizza.

CUT TO: outside DOLLAR-A-SLICE PIZZA

Q: So, we're outside DOLLAR-A-SLICE PIZZA, where every slice of pizza costs just . . .

PAN TO: a fourteen-year-old kid wearing a personalized Lakers jersey and holding a paper plate with a slice of cheese pizza on it

Lakers Jersey: Like five dollars?

Q: No.

Lakers Jersey: Three dollars.

Q: No.

Lakers Jersey: Man, I hate math.

Q: You just bought a slice of pizza.

Lakers Jersey: And?

Q: How much did that slice cost?

Lakers Jersey: I don't know. I just handed him a twenty, bro.

Q: How much did he give you back?

Lakers Jersey: What, you want me to count it?

Kid fishes a wad of bills from his pocket, zoom in on Q's face

Q: We haven't even gotten to the actual question yet, but honestly, I'm . . . riveted.

Lakers Jersey: Wait, are you guys even famous enough for me to do your video?

PAN TO: Q's face like, whaaaat did he just say?

Q: We just hit twenty thousand subscribers, so.

Lakers Jersey: Aw, well, don't feel bad. You guys seem cool. You'll get there.

Q trying to hold it together, before busting out laughing

Q: Wait, so you a big Lakers fan?

Lakers Jersey (points to the front of his jersey with pride): Ride or die.

Q: So, help me out. I'm not familiar with any Laker named C. D'Brickashaw.

Lakers Jersey (laughing): Man, it's personalized. That's *my* name. Coyote D'Brickashaw.

Q (head tilted in contemplation): Wait. So. Hmm. Your legal name, what's printed on your actual certificate of birth, is Coyote D'Brickashaw?

Lakers Jersey: Yep. Why? Am I the first Coyote you know?

Zoom in on Q's face, nodding slowly

A chime plays and CORRECT flashes on the screen

Q: I never say anything with a hundred percent certainty, Coyote, but I am one hundred and eighty-nine million percent confident you are the first Coyote this entire planet knows.

A chime plays and CONFIRMED flashes on the screen

Q: You got any siblings, Coyote?

Lakers Jersey (smiling): A sister. Her name's Turtle.

Q passes out on the sidewalk, unconscious

CUT TO: Q, back upright

Q: I know you don't like math, Coyote, but this is gonna be a simple equation, okay? I'm gonna throw you an easy lob for you to slam home. You ready?

Lakers Jersey: Sure, man.

Q: On average there are thirty days in a month . . . if you take those thirty days . . . and add your two parents . . . of those thirty days . . . how many of them . . . would you say . . . your two parents . . . smoke weed?

Lakers Jersey (laughing): All of 'em.

A chime plays and CORRECT flashes on the screen

Q: You're awesome, man. Guys, this is Coyote D'Brickashaw, friend of the show for life!

Q and Lakers Jersey exchange high fives

27

We walk another block before I try again.

Cut through a playground kid Q and kid Jamal used to chase each other around.

And I want to say the words in the best way, the right way. But there is no best, no right. There is only:

"Q, what's the last thing you remember about the Hills party the other night?"

Q smirks. "You mean other than us yelling at each other in front of the entire school?"

"You remember what happened after that?"

"Honestly, it's kind of fuzzy."

"C'mon, Q. Think."

He rubs his head in that way people do when they're trying to recall something. "I'm sorry, man, but I've got nothing." But then he snaps his fingers. "Wait, wait, I do remember something else. I remember I was sitting on the edge of the dock."

"You don't remember seeing anyone else out there?"

He shrugs. "Umm, no, it was just me, I think. I feel like . . . wait, wait, there was someone. I remember there was a flash of red. And I thought it was some junk floating. But it wasn't . . . junk . . . it was . . ."

And I feel bad, helping him remember a night we all want to forget, but I don't know another way.

"Wait, wait," Q says, holding up his hands, his face twisted in horror. "I think I—I remember someone swimming . . . she was there. A flash of red. But she made it out. You told me she made it out."

I shake my head. "I never saw the girl. None of us there at the party saw anyone out in the water but you . . . and then me."

"We dived in after her?"

"No. You dived in after her. And then I jumped in after you."

"Why?"

"Because you were . . . you were screaming, Q. You were sinking and you were screaming and . . ."

Q cuts in. "Okay, but so you saved me, right? Jamal to the rescue. And that's why you were in my room the next morning. Because you were worried about me. I wish I could remember. But I'm . . . thank you for saving my—"

"Q, I promise you, I swam as hard as I've ever swum in my life. And I was so scared because at first, I couldn't find you.

And I was afraid I was too late. But then . . . but then there you were. But you were choking on water, and I tried to keep your head up, but I wish I was stronger. Bigger. I . . . I paddled for shore, but sometimes I'd nearly lose you, and you'd go under the waves. Sometimes we both went under. But I kept swimming, Q. My legs were giving out. My arms were burning. But then it was like something inside me collapsed, and suddenly, I couldn't breathe. I tried to keep going. I swear I tried, but, but . . ."

And it's harder and harder to look at Q—to watch his face as he struggles to make sense of my story—and there's a large part of me that wants to stop right here. Tell him I was only joking. Tell him to forget the whole thing. But I know I have to finish. "We both started sinking, Q. We were sinking faster than I could swim. We just kept sinking."

"J, what are you saying?" Q asks softly, interrupting. His lips, his hands, trembling. "J, you're kinda scaring me, man . . ."

I'm scared, too, I think. And then I say it aloud. "And I'm sorry, Q. I'm so sorry, man . . . but . . . I wasn't strong enough. I wasn't fast enough. I wasn't . . . enough."

Q massages his forehead. "But I don't understand . . . so, you're saying . . . wait, you mean . . . we're . . . dead?"

"Q . . ."

"Like this is some sort of purgatory? Or heaven? Or I don't know. But we're dead, is that . . . is that what you're telling me?" He looks at his hands, at his arms, pats his stomach, his chest. Pinches himself. "Because I don't feel dead."

"Q... we didn't die..."

"Oh my God, thank goodness. You had me so fucking scared, man. You had... J, what's wrong? Why are you crying? J? J. J, talk to me. What's wrong?"

"You died, Q. Just you."

"No. It's not true." And he takes a step back, or maybe he stumbles back, and I grab his shirt, keep him righted. But he falls into the yellow grass.

"Q, I'm so, so sorry. I..."

"No. It's not possible."

"Q..."

"If I'm dead how can I be *here*? With you?"

"You were... reanimated."

"Reani—what? That's not a real thing. That's—"

"It's real, Q. They brought you back."

"No." Q's shaking his head fervently now. "No, no, no, no, no, no, no..." Tears stream down from both sets of eyes. His. Mine.

"I'm so sorry I failed you. I'm so sorry I..."

"This isn't real. This is... it's not... I'm not... dead. I'm fully alive. I'll... I'll prove it. Watch." And Q stumbles to his feet, staggering as his body and brain search for balance.

"Q, let's go home. You can talk to your mom. She can tell you."

But Q's not hearing me. "Watch me! Watch, J. I'm not dead. I'll show you right now." And he starts running out of the park, toward the busy intersection.

"No, Q! Q! Come back!"

Q keeps running, until his shoe catches, and he tumbles off the sidewalk into the road, so that if a car swerved even just a hair, he'd be . . .

I race over, grab him by both arms, and with all the strength I didn't know I had, I pull him away just enough.

He's shaking and saying something I don't understand. His body rocking back and forth, shaking and trembling.

I pull him into me. His head against mine. His face wet and soft. His tears, his cry so quiet it's as if he's behind glass.

And I stroke the back of his head because what I want to do I can't.

I want to say it's gonna be okay, you're gonna be okay. You're okay.

I want to.

"How much time do I have?" Q asks. "Tell me what happened, J. Tell me everything."

And so, I do.

I hold nothing back.

26

I keep waiting for Q to freak out again.

To flip again.

But if anything, he's even calmer than usual.

Quieter.

And every time we stop at a corner, waiting for the Walk sign, I try to engage him. Mostly just rambling on. At one point, I try to get him talking about Kendrick Fallon, but he just nods, his eyes vacant.

And maybe this is what it means to be in shock.

We roam around for a good hour, until we start back for Q's street, the neighborhood now dark, save streetlamps and the occasional headlight glow from passing cars.

Q's neighbor's backing out of his driveway, rolls down his window, points to me. "Hey, is that Jamal?"

I hold up a hand. "Hey, Mr. Richardson."

His face glows in the soft blue console lighting. He slaps his thigh. "Well, I'll be damned. The gang's back together again. Love it," he says. "I love it! Mrs. Richardson and I have missed you boys running through our backyards, haha. Guess you're probably too old for that now, though."

I smile out of politeness.

"Say Q, you think you're up to help me with some yard work next week? Finally ready to fix that shed. Oh, and I'll pay you well, of course, and Mrs. Richardson has already promised to make a huge pot of kimchi just for you."

I'm about to tell Mr. Richardson that it's not a good time for Q right now.

But to my surprise, Q says, "Sure, just call me when you're ready."

And Mr. Richardson's all teeth, all *thank you thank you*, all *you're such a good kid, Quincy*, all *it's so good to see you here, Jamal, don't be a stranger*, and then he's pulling away. We watch him pause at the corner, his taillights shriveling smaller and smaller until they vanish.

"Q! J!" Whit calls from the door. I can't read her face; her eyes are swirls of a thousand colors, like a painter's rinse cup. "Is everything . . . ?" she asks.

I nod. Overhead the sky's a ruffled deep purple: the kind of sky so dark you're not sure the sun exists. Or if it does, you can't be sure it's ever coming back.

That's how this feels.

Like the sun's just lit its last day.

We hear a car starting behind us.

And I turn to say something to Q, to make a stupid joke, to toss into this emotional cauldron a bit more levity, but Q's not there.

"Q!" Whit calls, stepping out of the house, as Q pulls his car off the front curb.

"Q!" I call, running after the car, keeping pace and waving my arms for two blocks, before the houses become a car wash, a church, a convenience store, before the speed limit leaps from twenty to forty-five.

I watch Q zip into traffic, watch him cut an entire lane of cars off, their horns slamming, Q overcompensating, the car nearly sideswiping a parked postal service van. I cup my hands over my mouth and scream his name one last time, even though he can't hear me. Even though nothing would change if he could.

I wake my phone.

I tap, tap, tap. I wait.

"Jamal?"

"Mr. Oklahoma? We . . . I need your help."

I walk back, stop at the corner four houses away from Q's house.

All around me, the world hushed and still.

Not a star in the sky.

Like we're all asleep.

Five minutes later my phone vibrates.

"I know where he is. He is safe."

Thank God. "Tell me where. I'll go get him. Take him home."

A pause. "Jamal . . . I think you better . . . it is probably best if you stayed where you are."

I bite my lip. Blink back the tears.

And I understand Ms. B—how sometimes the right thing and the best thing appear to be the same, but then you discover that jumbled cord is actually two tangled-up lines.

"Jamal. Jamal, are you there?"

No, I'm not here. Or there. I'm nowhere.

Nowhere.

When I walk back into the house, Ms. B wastes no time. "Where's Q?"

"I don't know."

"Where is he, Jamal? You're lying."

I shake my head. "If I knew, I'd tell you."

"And now Q's out there, God knows where, thinking we all lied to him. Thinking *I* lied to him. That I betrayed him. That nothing's real."

But we did.

You did.

Nothing is real.

"Ms. Barr—"

"IF I DON'T FIND MY SON, JAMAL . . ."

"I promise I'm g—"

But she's already grabbing her car keys.

She shakes her head at me, tells me this is what I was afraid of. Says I hope you're satisfied.

But I'm not.

Not by a long shot.

Because no one wins here.

Because nothing about this is remotely satisfying.

Because I can't remember the last time anything was.

Because there's nothing more explosive than a heavy secret. And keeping it inside, thinking everything will be hunky-dory, is like swallowing a live grenade, then brushing your teeth.

QUINCY

Now here you go again
you say you want your freedom
well, who am i to keep you down?
—"Dreams," Fleetwood Mac

25

I.

Two hours ago, I thought the walking dead were zombies.

Little did I know I was a card-carrying member.

Except I don't feel very undead.

I hand the woman my money.

"Good choice," she says. "Make sure you get them in water right away."

I nod.

"Need a bag?"

"No," I tell her. "I'm good."

And I *feel* good.

Which seems wild.

I feel normal—you know, betrayal and treachery from everyone I love aside.

Of course, Mom meant well, but she'd kept the most important thing that's ever happened to me a secret.

And Jamal, was this why suddenly he was Super Friend 2.0, when for the last two years he walked through me like I was invisible?

A lesson I learned from watching my dad in his final hours: when it comes to matters of life or death, people rarely tell the truth.

I pull along the slender curb.

Halfway there I accidentally scare a groundskeeper. "You sure you wanna be here at this hour, brother? Ain't you afraid of ghosts and shit?"

"Nah, I'm not worried," I tell him, already walking on. "Ghosts are my people."

He's the only blue stone in the section because he always had to be different, even in death.

Mom says the worst thing you can do to someone is forget them.

Maybe that's why he chose blue.

Make him easier to remember.

I crouch down, prop my flowers against it. Trace my fingers along the curved edge.

"Hey, man. I hope you like daffodils because that was all they had, ha.

Look, it's been a while since I've come through, not gonna lie.

It's not that you matter less now.

It's just one of those things where I knew I had to find a way to let go.

Not all the way, because I hope you know that's impossible.

Just enough to get through a day without feeling broken.

Enough to smile more than cry.

You're a hard dude to shake, though.

If you were here you'd be nodding your head like, damn straight I am.

I mean, it hurts like hell, but you do what you gotta do.

You try your best to go on. To catch up with all the life you let slip away, all the life stuff you ignored because . . . because you were too sad to care.

Otherwise the past will tie a tether to your ass, and trust me, you don't want that anchor.

You'd never have that problem, though. You were always so carefree.

Mom called you the Duck, you just let everything slip off your back.

Ha, including some shit you shouldn't have, but you heard enough of that from Mom over the years.

So, you wanna hear something wild?

I mean, HELLA wild?

Hold on to your fitted, because I'm telling you, you ain't ready for this, but.

I'm basically halfway to you. Wherever you are. If you're anywhere.

Because it turns out I'm dead.

Surprise, right?

No one was surprised more than me, trust.

You wanna know how it happened?

I was trying to be what you were.

A good person who doesn't let an opportunity to do what's good, what's right, pass by. Be a person of action, right? You beat that shit into my head real good, ha.

How am I standing in front of your grave if I'm dead, you ask?

Brilliant question, Dad!

I've been resurrected. They call it reanimation. I don't know. Whatever.

So, basically, I get a stay of execution. I'm still on my way to a pretty grave. But I get a few more days to travel there.

So.

Make room, man.

You can't be hogging space like you used to hog the couch. All spread out like nobody else wanna sit down and watch TV, haha.

I miss you.

I love you.

I'm sorry I didn't say that more.

Honestly, I don't think I ever said it.

So, I take it back, okay? Forget you heard it.

Pretty soon I'll just tell you in person.

Okay?

You'll have to show me around, show me the ropes.

They got a PlayStation there?

Maybe you'll finally give me a decent game, though I doubt it.

And I don't wanna hear no excuses neither.

None of that double-or-nothing shit you always trying to pull after I mop you.

So, you got a day or two to get ready, okay?

'Cause I'm coming, Dad.

I'm coming.

Ha, wherever you are, they aren't ready for you and me together, I know that much. There's no way.

It's not even close.

Barrantes men reunited again.

Sometimes I imagine—"

"Quincy, I am very sorry to interrupt. I waited for some time . . ."

I make a face.

"Over beyond the trees there. I could not hear anything, I assure you. I wish I could have afforded you more time, but . . . well, again, my apologies."

"Who are you? How do you know my name?"

"Oh, yes, of course." He pushes his glasses up. "My name is Mr. Oklahoma."

"I have one more stop," I tell him. "Then we can go."

I walk four rows over, two rows up, gently set the last two

333

stems on two side-by-side graves. "I love you too," I say. "And I'm sorry."

II.

Mr. Oklahoma's car is immaculate.

No surprise.

One look at him and—out of nowhere—*pristine* pops into my head.

I'm fairly confident I've never said *pristine*, ever.

Funny the randomness that hangs out in our brains just waiting for its shot.

"So, are you okay?"

I stare straight ahead. "I found out I'm dead. Everything's peachy."

"Right. I just meant . . ." He clears his throat, switches up his grip on the steering wheel. "All things considered, but you are right. Vacuous question."

"If vacuous means stupid, you have my full agreement."

Mr. Oklahoma laughs, but he immediately reins it in. "Fair," he says, his voice once more flinty.

"Ask you a question, man?"

"Certainly."

"How much time do I have before I'm fake-smiling in a box?"

"That is a question best put to your mother, Quincy."

"No one wants to give me any answers."

"You are free to ask anything."

"Yeah?" I say, glaring at him across the seat. "Would you bring your son back to life and not tell him?"

Mr. Oklahoma frowns. "That is not . . . I am uncertain, were I in her shoes, the path I would choose. But I understand why your mother chose the approach she did. It is not my place to say what is right or wrong, but . . . I do not think she was wrong. Her motivations were pure, her intention was to protect you, and I am not sure you can ask more from a person."

"And everyone knows . . . what happened to me?"

"If by everyone, you mean your mom, Jamal, Whit, and our staff at the Center."

"What about the doctors at the hospital? The nurses? The cleaning crew?"

Mr. Oklahoma shakes his head. "After we obtained permission to move your body, we transported you to our facility. No one outside of the people I mentioned knows about your reanimation."

"But why me? Why did you choose to bring me back?"

"The question you need to ask, Quincy, is why not you? You left this world a hero. You displayed courage where most would hesitate. There are plenty of adults who would not have made that sacrifice."

I laugh. "You know I wasn't trying to die, right?"

"I am aware of that fact, yes." He smiles. "But it does not change the narrative. You deserve more than what we can give, Quincy."

We ride in silence. I rest my elbow against the window. It occurs to me that I'm not sure where he's taking me. I guess I'd assumed home, but.

"You can't bring people who died a long time ago back, right?"

He shakes his head, flicks on the turn signal. "Correct. The level of decomposition renders it impossible."

"Most of your customers, they're rich, right?"

He bristles. "Our clients hail from all walks. Some of them have money, but that is not a requirement. Four of our ten reanimations were actually . . ."

"Charity cases. Like me. What's even the point? Why bring anyone back at all?"

"When Dr. Iverson first conceived of this work, Quincy . . ." He slows the car, pulls in front of a parked van, parks. "We want the Center to be a place where people find comfort. Solace. We are a long way from curing death permanently, but one day soon, grief will be no more. Death will be the last thing to die. Imagine your grandkids never having to die at all. Never experiencing that kind of loss."

I laugh before he appreciates his mistake.

"I was not . . . I did not mean to . . . I am sorry, Quincy."

"Hey, so I won't have grandkids or even . . . kids. Who cares, right?" I shrug. "I mean, there's no guarantee I would've had them even if . . . it's not a big deal." Except the truth is the thought never occurred to me until now. That I won't be able to have kids, raise a family. My mom will never be someone's grandma. Which makes me sad because she's so good with

336

kids. And the way she spoils me, I can only imagine how she'd be with my kids.

Mr. Oklahoma removes his glasses, wipes them with a cloth from his pocket. "We want the Center globalized. To be places that people can afford, places where no one's sad or in pain. Where every face inside that building is joyous and hopeful and happy. Picture this: a Center on every corner in every city."

"You want to be the crappy burger place of healthcare?"

He laughs again, this time he doesn't stop himself. "You are a funny young man, Quincy."

"Man, if I had an extra hour of reanimation for every time I heard that."

III.

I'm not sure if it's because he feels partly responsible or guilty, or because driving a dead kid around makes him feel especially sad, but when we're only two blocks away from my house, Mr. Oklahoma pulls the car over.

"Quincy, I will allow one more question. No limits."

"And I can ask anything?"

Mr. Oklahoma nods.

"Seriously, good people die every second of every day. Why did you choose me?"

Mr. O launches into some long monologue about how the eventuality all men must face is death.

"Thanks for all of that really heavy old-man . . . philosophy. But I meant why did you bring me back? Like personally?"

"Oh." Mr. Oklahoma leans back in his seat. Adjusts his glasses. "Put your seat belt back on."

"Huh? What for?"

"I promised I would answer your question. This is how that happens."

We drive for forty minutes in near silence.

Which honestly, I prefer. The chance to sort my thoughts. To sit with my feelings.

When the car finally slows, we're turning onto a long winding drive. We pass through some sort of force field of orange lights and come to a stop at the top of the hill.

"You could've just said you don't know," I tell Mr. Oklahoma.

He laughs. "Your videos do not do your humor justice, Quincy." He steps out of the car. "Follow me. Quickly now."

I have no idea where we are, only that it appears—from the outside—to have once been a factory. No clue what they made here. Or what they make here now.

I follow Mr. Oklahoma through a series of long corridors, the walls stark white with bright white lights whose source I can't track.

Each time we come to a massive door, Mr. Oklahoma presses his hand to its center—each finger pad illuminating a brilliant blue, the faintest chirp—and then within seconds the door sliding open.

We finally stop at a door unlike all the others. Mr. Oklahoma puts his hand on the knob, then turns around to me, brings his finger to his lips. *Be quiet.*

I copy his gesture.

He turns the knob.

IV.

This space is not like the rest of the facility. It is warm, inviting. There are wooden floors and elaborately woven rugs. Art adorns every wall. The air is woodsy.

We're in a massive apartment.

"Who lives here?" I ask, my eyes struggling to absorb so many details.

"The boss."

"He's not going to be upset we're in his place so late at night?"

"I think not. These days he does not sleep much."

Mr. Oklahoma removes his shoes and I follow suit. We move through the large open floor plan, hidden motion-detection lighting illuminating our path.

"There is one question you have never asked, Quincy. At least not out loud."

"What's that?"

"Why did you jump into the water?"

"Jamal said I thought I saw someone out there. A girl. But she wasn't real. She was only in my head."

"So, you believe you died for nothing?"

I shrug. "I mean, I died trying to do what I thought was right. That's not nothing."

Mr. Oklahoma taps the door in front of us and the top half of it melts away into sudden transparency. I want to reach my hand out to touch it. Is this real? Has the top half actually disintegrated, or is it just clear? I settle on the latter because that would be a lot of replacement doors otherwise.

He motions for me to come closer. To look through the door window.

It's a bedroom.

A child's room.

And in the twin daybed a little girl sleeps.

"Who is that?"

"The girl you saved," he answers, still staring into the room. "My daughter."

V.

Everything clicks into place.

Why the Center wanted to bring me back.

Who Mr. Oklahoma really is.

"So, wait, you . . . you own all this? This is your lab?"

Mr. Oklahoma nods faintly. "I am the Center's primary proprietor, yes. There are a few others that sit on a small board with me. No one should decide matters of life and death alone."

I nod. "So, you're some rich guy who wants to save the world?"

"The truth is, this began as a selfish project, Quincy. Nearly twenty years ago now. I lost someone who meant the world to me. And for a while it broke me."

340

"But you pulled out of it."

"I did." Mr. Oklahoma clears his throat. "Because as much as that death took away from me, it also gave me purpose. I'm happy to say now, the work we're doing, it's no longer just about me. About my pain."

"I guess sometimes it takes great loss to generate great gains."

"Yes, I suppose so," Mr. Oklahoma says quietly.

But there was still one question. "Why was she out there alone? In the water? In the middle of the night?"

"One of our scientists is renting a house along the lake, a few doors down from where the party you attended occurred. Our daughters are close. In age and in interests. The work I do, it requires certain sacrifices. One being that we are in constant motion. Since she was born, we've lived in twenty-one cities. These readjustments are challenging for the adults I work with, let alone our children. Even still, I was not going to let her go to the sleepover that night. She hates thunderstorms. Always has. But . . . she told me she wanted to be brave. Convinced me this would not be like all the other times, where she would grow so frightened she called me to come pick her up. This time would be different, she told me. And I wanted that for her. For her to conquer her fears. I was proud she wanted to try. So I let her go." Mr. Oklahoma sighs, rubs his temples.

"At some point during the sleepover the girls decided they would sneak out onto the beach. Pretending to be mermaids. You saw her. Swam to her. Propelled her forward, and she washed onto the shore, unconscious but alive. Her friend had run back

341

home for help, to get her father. She told me she was frozen with fear. That had you not come to her rescue, she would have . . ." He removes his glasses. Discreetly dabs around his eyes.

"I didn't imagine the whole thing. She's real."

Mr. Oklahoma nods. "Thanks to you, she is very much so."

"Sheesh. Talk about sensory overload. I may need you to hook me back up to the life machine, animate me a few more hours to process all this."

He laughs.

"And no one else knows about this?"

"No one outside of these walls, no. And now, you."

"What's her name? If it's okay to ask."

"Amarí Lillian."

"That's what I was gonna guess."

"You may be surprised to learn she has assigned you, her hero, a proper nickname."

I wag my head in disbelief. "No way! What is it?"

"Poseidon, Quincy. She calls you Poseidon."

VI.

We pull into my driveway, but Mr. Oklahoma doesn't turn off the engine.

"If you would like me to go with . . . to speak with your mother, I . . ."

"Nah, I'll take it from here." I smile, stepping out of the car. "But I owe you a thank-you."

"A thank-you?"

342

"Yeah, your slow-ass driving gave me lots of time to think."

Squinting in the headlight glare, I tap the hood, dig into my pocket for my house key as I turn for the front door.

Only the door's already open.

Mom standing in its frame, her hands on either side like she's holding up the house. Her face like I'm seeing it through a sadness filter. She looks older since I saw her this morning. "Baby," she says. "I'm so, so . . ."

But I quickly close the gap between us. "No, I'm sorry. Everyone saying I'm selfless, but I should've been thinking about you. About leaving you alone. I'm sorry, Mama. I'm so . . . I shoulda . . ."

I bury my head in her neck. "Shhhh," she whispers. "I'll be okay. You'll be okay. Everything will work . . ."

And I know she wants to say: . . . *out the way it's supposed to.*

But instead she leaves the ending wide open.

VII.

"Q," Mom says to me. We're sitting on her bed. I'm on the side where Dad used to sleep. Sometimes I forget that my parents gave me the larger bedroom. Even before I hit my first growth spurt. *We wanted you to have the room with the most sunlight,* they'd said. Sometimes I forget I have the kind of parents that worry about their kid's vitamin D levels. The kind of parents that are quick to sacrifice in ways big and small.

I shake my head. "Don't say it," I tell her. "We're not gonna cry. We're gonna be happy, okay?"

"Okay," Mom says. I wipe her face. I think, what if this is the last time I ever see this face? What if this is the last time we look each other in the eyes? "But I just want you to know that—"

"Mom. Please."

"I'm so sorry, baby."

"I know, Mom," I say. "But I don't want you to be. Not for this. Not for me. I did what I thought was right. What you would've wanted someone to do for me. And did it cost something? Yeah. It cost a lot. But . . . if I saw that little girl flailing in that water right now, knowing that if I dived in it would all happen this exact same way, I gotta dive in that water. I gotta."

"You could've called for help. You could've went for help."

I study Mom's face. What if this is the last time we're ever this close? What if the next time she kisses me, she's leaning down into my forever box? That's what we call caskets. Forever boxes. *Casket* sounds too sad. The word *casket* sounds like it belongs in a casket.

"They wouldn't have gotten there in time. She would've . . . she'd be . . . and how could I *live* with that?"

"I should've raised you to be selfish," Mom says, her voice full of holes. "Who's gonna tell me my latest meat-loaf experiment is my best creation yet, huh?"

"We both know your meat loaf is terrible," I say, smiling. "Maybe the meat-loaf experiments should die with me."

She slaps my chest. "Who's gonna take the remote from my hand when I fall asleep watching TV on the couch?"

"You can set the TV timer."

"Who's gonna do the dishes Monday, Wednesday, and Friday?"

"That's what the dishwasher's for."

"But it takes so long."

I laugh. "Because you insist on washing the dishes *before* you put them in the washer."

She shoots me a look, tosses one of her eighty thousand decorative pillows at me. Seriously, should there ever be a Great Pillow Shortage, Mom's bed could singlehandedly solve the crisis in seconds.

"I don't trust that dishwasher to clean them," she says.

"So why even use it?"

"Because it's like a second wash. Like the assurance wash."

We both laugh. "Mom, I have a confession. I *don't* wash the dishes first."

She slaps my chest again. "Quincy! You've been lying to me?"

"I mean, I wouldn't say *lying*. I rinse them. Sort of."

"I can't believe my only child would let me eat on dirty dishes all this time."

"Only Monday, Wednesday, and Friday."

"Who's gonna tell me I'm the best mom ever?"

"How many times do you think I tell you that now?"

"Well, every birthday, for sure. Yours and mine . . . certain holidays too. And then the random *just because* times. Let's see, I'd say you average about ten a year."

I do the math. "Okay, so ten a year with the average life expectancy, I still owe you at least sixty *best mom ever*s."

"So, see, you can't go. And that's just something silly. Think about . . . think about all of the other things that you're supposed to do. You've still got too much to do. All your dreams, baby. Why did you get in that water?" She pulls me into another tight hug. "You should've just turned away."

"You don't mean that."

"But I do! I do mean it!"

"No you don't," I tell her, kissing the top of her head. "It's okay to be angry at me. It's okay to be angry at this."

"I'm not angry. I'm furious. I'm sad. I'm confused. I'm hurt. I'm weak. I'm . . ."

"It's okay, Mom."

"Nothing is okay. Okay is a lie."

"You know what's not a lie?"

She doesn't answer, shaking her head *no* against my chest.

"That you're the best mom ever. Now I owe you fifty-nine."

"Quincy."

"You're the best mom ever. You're the best mom ever. Fifty-seven."

"Quincy."

"You are the best mom this world has ever seen. You are the epitome of moms. You are the zenith of momhood. Top-shelf mom-mery only. You are what God intended when he created the first mom. I could not have asked for a better mom. That's gotta count for like ten, right?"

"Why are you like this?"

"That's the easiest question you've asked all day. You."

VIII.

And later, when we've finally stopped laughing and crying, Mom sits at the kitchen table while I hunt for snacks in the cabinets and pantry. Who knew finding out that you're dead works up such an appetite?

I drop all of my goodies—chips, cookies, a six pack of soda— in front of Mom and she shakes her head. "Quincy, please, tell me you're really not going to eat all this junk?"

"Nope," I say. "I'm not."

"Good," she says.

"Because you're gonna help me."

"Quincy, this stuff is terrible for you. Do you wanna d—" She catches herself and stops.

I shrug. "Do I wanna die of a sugar- and sodium-induced brain rush? I mean, what do I have to lose, right?"

She shakes her head. "Don't talk like that."

"Like the truth?"

She crosses her arms, looks away, but not before I see the sadness in her eyes.

"I'm sorry, Mom."

"No, I'm sorry," she says, her eyes still trained on the other side of the kitchen. "I'm supposed to protect you."

I walk over to her. "You did," I say to her. "And you are."

She looks up at me and I smile. "But now you gotta do me a favor."

Her face switches to skepticism. "What favor?"

I reach across the table, rip a soda from the pack. "Soda

shotgun race me for old times' sake?"

She laughs. "Boy, we haven't done this since your dad was alive."

"He was the king, no doubt," I say, nodding. "But you were always the best."

She picks up her keys from the table, then takes the soda from my hand. She turns the can horizontally, and with the keys she punctures a hole into its side. She hands me the keys and I do the same to another can. And we pop our tabs and we're chugging, chugging—foam dripping from our mouths, I can barely drink for all the laughing. And yeah, Mom destroys me.

"Looks like I still got it," she says, punching the air in front of her like a boxer.

"Yeah, you do," I say, and I grab her arm and lift it straight into the air. "Tonight's winner and still the heavyweight shotgun champion of the worrrrrlllddd . . . Simoneeee "Mad Dog" Barrantessssss."

Mom cracks up, and I drop into the seat next to her, the tile wet and sticky.

"Hey, Mom?" I say.

Her face is still beaming. "Now what?" she asks.

"How much time do I have left?"

Jamal

24

When Whit and I get home, Autumn's on our porch steps.

"You two okay?" Whit asks, looking at us. But she doesn't stick around for the answer. She's already walking into the house. "Don't mind me, I've just gotta pee for the eight hundredth time today."

"I'm sorry," I say as soon as we're alone.

"You seem to be saying that a lot lately," Autumn shoots back.

Which, fair.

"But you know what's better than apologizing after you screw up, Jamal?"

"Not . . . screwing . . . up?"

"Okay, so if you understand that, how come we keep ending up here?"

"Because I . . . suck?"

"Jamal, this isn't funny."

"I wasn't being funny. I promise."

"Stop." She waves me off. "No more promises you can't keep."

"Autumn, if you understood everything that's been happening, you'd know that I was trying my best to do the right thing by everyone. That I'm trying and trying, but it's a lot. It's so much."

"Well, then, tell me what's going on, Jamal. We talked about this. Let me help you."

"Autumn, I want to tell you, I swear, but . . ."

She holds up her hand. "You know what? Whatever dumb excuse you're about to give me, just save it. I came over here because I wanted to fix things. Because I believed you wanted to too. But clearly, I was wrong." She steps off the porch, fishes her keys from her pocket. "Catch you later maybe."

"Autumn."

"Please, just stop."

"Autumn, wait. This isn't like before. This is something entirely different. This is something you wouldn't even believe if I told you. Damn, I barely believe it."

And she turns around, tears streaming down her cheeks. "Try me."

I wipe her face, dry her eyes. "Okay," I say. "Okay."

*   *   *

Autumn's basically a bobblehead of sheer disbelief.

"Well, damn," she says. "Damn. Like . . . *damn*."

"Fucking crazy, right?"

"So this is what you've been keeping from me?"

I nod. "I'm sorry. I didn't want to."

"And no one besides like five people even knows that he's ..."

"Yep. It's wild."

"There've been stories that they were getting close. But close in scientific terms means maybe we'll figure it out in thirty, forty years. But this ... this is ..."

"A total mindfuck."

"I know you're not lying, but also, I'm one hundred percent confident you're lying."

"I wish I was. I wish none of this were true. Like reanimation is dope, obviously. But also, it's super confusing. I mean, I'm so sad and angry that he's ... and I want to grieve him, I want to mourn my friend, but also this chance he's gotten, to say goodbye, to do whatever he wants, is like the most beautiful thing ever, and I just want him to enjoy every second of it. I want to celebrate his life with him."

"Crap, I barely know him, but I know I'm gonna miss him."

I stare at the grass. "You're not alone."

"So, in a couple days Q's just gonna ... he's just gonna, like, turn off?"

I glance at my watch as if it's the official timekeeper for Q's remaining life. "Less than two days now. Maybe only a day. He has a four-hour window."

"Four whole hours? They brought someone back to life, you'd think they'd be able to narrow the window a bit."

I shrug. "Apparently, reanimation isn't an exact science." I take her hand. "So, what have *you* been up to?"

"Nothing as cool as raising the dead."

"Underachiever."

She laughs, and we both wipe our faces, because, allergies.

23

"You sure this is cool? Your grandma isn't gonna hit me with a broom or something, is she?"

Autumn shakes her head. "She's watching Judge Keenan. She won't even notice you're here. Trust me."

We abandon Autumn's car in her driveway, and slip into the front door just in time to hear Judge Keenan deliver his trademark quip: *Nuh-uh, you better get outa my courtroom with that buuuulll-ish.*

We walk through the living room—its walls covered in family photos, its furniture zipped in protective plastic—and into the family room.

Nana's sitting in a bright blue recliner chair, her wheeled walker to the right of her, her back to us, staring ahead at the television. She doesn't even flinch as we creep behind her, start the ascent up the stairs.

"Autumn, baby."

We stop in our tracks.

"Yes, Nana?"

"I know you not bringing nobody up in my house without a greeting."

I shoot Autumn a look. She shrugs. "It's just Jamal, Nana."

"I know who it is, girl. I'm old, not dumb. And Jamal, I know you got better manners than that. Now both of you get over here and let me see you."

We walk back down into the living room, walk around to face Nana. And I'm not trying to be weird or anything, but I see where Autumn gets her looks from; Nana is old but still beautiful, regal. You can tell by the way she holds her head that she's used to mesmerizing a room.

"Hi, Nana," I say. "I'm sorry for being rude. It was Autumn's fault."

Nana holds out her hand, and for a second I wonder if I'm supposed to kiss it, but I shake it instead.

"Mm-hm. Maybe if you came 'round here more often, my granddaughter wouldn't feel the need to sneak over to your house at all hours of the night."

Damn. Nana came out swinging. I want to laugh, but also, I'm kind of scared. "Huh? Oh. Ummm...I'm s-s-sorry...I..."

"Mm-hm. What are your intentions with my granddaughter, young man?"

I smile, look over at Autumn, and then back to Nana. "I have nothing but the best intentions, I promise you."

"Yes, well, maybe you'll come over here, now, too. We'd be happy to have you. During *regular* business hours, of course. Only thing open after midnight are legs and hospitals, and neither of you are to be at either place."

"Umm, yes? I mean, no. Not going, um, there, yes ma'am. As in, no ma'am."

"Well, which is it, child?"

Autumn cuts in. "Nana, please."

But Nana's not at all vexed. "Please what? Did I say something that wasn't true? Last time I checked this was still my house."

"Yes, Nana."

"Okay, now, Judge Keenan's about to come back on. Y'all go chapsnat or play e-bingo on the dark web or whatever it is you kids do nowadays."

"Thanks, Nana," Autumn says, pulling me toward the stairs.

"It was nice to see you again," I call back. But Nana's already nodding her head at the honorable judge.

Autumn flops on her bed. "So, I don't mean to be hella forward, but, uh . . . all this heavy stuff you just dropped on me has me feeling pretty mortal right now, so . . . maybe you should come kiss me."

"Maybe I should." I fall onto the bed beside her. She flings a few decorative pillows onto the ground.

I look at her for a moment. And then I kiss her. Again and again I kiss her.

Her fingers tug at my shirt, pushing it up, up, up. "What if your nana comes up here? Legs and hospitals, remember? As in she sees your legs, I see the hospital?"

Autumn laughs. "You saw her walker, right? I think we'll hear her."

I laugh. Give her a long wink. "Or she'll hear you, you know what I'm saying? You know what I'm saying?"

"Ewww, don't do that anymore. Please."

"No? I took you back to the *Fresh Prince*."

"Well, it can stay back there, thank you very much." She smiles. "Besides, if Nana's going to hear anyone, it's gonna be your ass. I'mma have you hitting those high notes, you know what I'm saying? You know what I'm saying?"

I laugh. Pick up a pillow and throw it toward her head. She catches it and throws it back, hitting me in my chest.

"Not gonna lie, it's funnier when you say it," I tell her, sliding back over.

She's lying on her back, and the way her coily hair springs out, it's like constant motion, like fireworks erupting in every direction. How can anyone be so beautiful, I think to myself. And then I say it.

"How are you so beautiful?"

"Shut up," she says, looking away. The dimple in her right cheek is a trampoline, it goes concave, then bounces right back.

"I'm serious. I don't know if you realize how much I'm into you. I don't know if I always realize."

"Why, though?" she asks, turning her face back to me. Tears slip down both cheeks. "Why me?"

"Depends. How cheesy do you want me to get here?"

"Go full cheese."

"Okay, you asked for it." I wipe her cheeks. Take her hand. "Autumn, you're my favorite line in my favorite song. Autumn, you are the melody that never leaves me. You are the refrain that my brain can't get enough of. I see you, and it doesn't matter what mood I'm in, all I feel is happy. You're the chorus stuck in my head, and my heart. Autumn, you are the one song I add to every playlist."

"Stop," she says, wiping her eyes. "This is so terrible. So cheesy."

"I gave you a choice. You said maximum cheese."

She nods. "I did. It's all on me."

"Hey . . ."

She stares at me. "Hey, what?"

"Hey, I . . . I love you, Autumn."

"You sure? You kinda hesitated there," she says, smiling.

"I did a bit, didn't I?" I take her face in my hands. "Better try that again then." Our eyes lock. "I love you, Autumn." I kiss her forehead. "I love you, Autumn." I kiss each of her eyes. "I love you. I love you." And then her cheeks—"I love you"—brushing my lips against hers, down to her chin and the side of her neck—"I love you so much"—down the trail of black-ink hearts tattooed on the right of her stomach, down, down, down.

"I love you, too, Jamal."

So down.

22

I lean my bike against the side of the garage, walk over to the stack beside the couch, all of those photo albums still where we left them.

I pull out my phone, take a few pictures of a few pictures.

This was the last birthday we were best friends. Our fourteenth. Our arms around each other's shoulders, cheesing. Born only five days apart, we always combined our parties.

A photo of us on our bikes, age ten.

At Cedar Park for the first time, standing in front of the Gemini, age eight.

In the back seat of my mom's car, on our way to our first school dance, age twelve.

I pull up the pictures we took during Carpet Denim too.

The last one, Whit and Ms. B and Autumn and Q and me
squeezed into a selfie, the row of trees thirty yards behind us.

I tap Send.

Q: OH WOW. You know I'm already hella emotional
right. You tryna make me break all the way down huh.

Jamal: I just wanted to tell you thanks for always having
my back, even when I didn't deserve it.

Q: Friendship isn't a bandwagon you get on and off.

Jamal: damn that's deep. And hella true.

Jamal: who said that?

Q: You're texting with him right now.

Jamal: I'mma steal that.

Q: Go ahead. Not like I'll be around to call you on it.

Jamal: damn I don't even know what to say.

Q: I'm just fucking with you, man. My bad.

Jamal: fuck don't do that.

Jamal: had me sweating bullets.

Jamal: I was tryna google something to say.

Q: Yoooo I wanna know what you typed into the search.

Jamal: how to reply to your friend's uncomfortable jokes
about his impending death.

Q: lmfao

Q: you get a lot of hits?

Jamal: yeah but like zero were relevant to this situation
so thanks for nothing googs.

Q: googs???

Jamal: yeah, that's my pet name for google.

Q: what does googs call you?

Jamal: big dick j.

Q: 🤮

Jamal: lol.

Q: Hey, I'm sorry for disappearing like that.

Q: I just had to get away.

Q: like with a quickness.

Jamal: no dude I get that

Jamal: but on the real I thought your mom was gonna kick my ass!!

Jamal: I was srsly afraid for my life

Jamal: but also she has a right to hate me

Jamal: if I was her I'd hate me, what I did

Q: Nah. She wants to apologize to you, too.

Jamal: apologize? really?

Q: Yeah. She had good reason to be mad, because she's my mom, and she was doing what she hoped was best for me. But she also knows you weren't trying to hurt me. That you thought you were doing something good.

Jamal: I'm sorry for lying to you in the first place.

Jamal: Autumn was asking about you.

Q: What did you tell her?

Jamal: The truth, finally

Q: 👍 Good. She should know.

Q: I told Bri, too.

Jamal: Fr??

Q: Fr!

Q: She didn't believe me at first

Q: Tbh I'm still not sure she really believes me

Jamal: I don't blame her

Jamal: Shit's a lot to work through

Q: She said if I think telling her I'm gonna die soon means she'll hook up with me, I'm gonna be hella disappointed lol

Jamal: Damn, I like her

Q: Me too

Q: Wyd

Jamal: Honestly, I was tryna figure out what to say to you

Q: About

Jamal: 🤷🏿 I thought you were pissed at me

Q: That's what I don't get. Why would I be pissed for getting more days to live?? Lol I mean I am pissed that no one asked me first but

Jamal: Okay, well, when you put it that way lol

Q: What other way is there

Q: Lol I mean, seriously, I'm really pissed no one asked me first 🤷🏿

Jamal: You weren't exactly around . . .

Jamal: Okay, I'd rather stop joking about this. I'm happy you're coming to terms with it and you've mostly wrapped your brain around it but I hate it, I hate everything about all this

Q: YOU hate it? How you think I feel

Jamal: I didn't mean it that way

Q: I know

Jamal: Whit wanted me to tell you you're invited over for dinner tonight. Your mom, too, of course.

Q: Tell Whit thank you but I sorta think me and Mom both need some mother-son time

Jamal: Yeah, ok

Jamal: Listen, I don't quite know how to say this but like, I wanna make what I did right. Or at least make it up to you, to your mom

Q: Yeah? What are you proposing?

Jamal: I have no idea lol

Jamal: Yet! YET! I'm working on it

Jamal: but when I figure it out you're gonna love it

Q: Yeah, well, don't take too much time

Jamal: shit man I can't tell if you're being funny or introspective right now

Q: def funny

Q: lol

Jamal: ☺ ☺ ☺

Q: gotta get you back right lol

Jamal: ☹ not cool man

Q: oh you mean like lying to your friend not cool lol

Jamal: well played sir

Jamal: lol

Q: TY!

Q: But do me a favor j

Jamal: Yeah?

Q: Next time I die just tell me right away okay 🦇

Jamal: 🦇 I got you

Q: J?

Jamal: Yeah?

Q: you know what the worst thing about being dead is

Jamal: what

Q: I was just starting to live

21

I consider calling.

Or even texting.

But in the end, I know I have to fix things the same way I broke them.

Face-to-face.

Mano a mom-o.

Q lets me into the house, and we hug tighter than probably we've ever hugged.

Stay that way for longer than the last fifty hugs I've been a part of combined.

We don't even talk.

She's in the kitchen, her back to me.

I clear my throat and say her name softly—hi, Ms. Barrantes—and she pauses for a second, but she doesn't stop doing the dishes, she doesn't turn around.

"I'm sorry I went against your wishes. I know that was wrong even if I thought it was right. I know you were trying to protect Q. That you love him more than anything. That you'd do anything to keep him safe. I respect you even though it doesn't probably feel that way to you. And I don't think I ever thanked you. For the stuff you did for me and Whit when Mom and Dad . . ."

Ms. B snaps the water off.

"For the casseroles. And for the cards. And for doing our laundry. And for talking to my teachers and helping Whit figure out the tax stuff and . . . for all of it."

And she just stands there, sopping dish towel in her hand.

So I do what I would've done to my own mom.

I close the gap.

I rest my head against her shoulder.

And she rubs the side of my scalp. "You're still a knucklehead."

"I love you too."

20

"So, even though I basically bungled this whole thing..."

Whit interrupts me. "It coulda been way worse!"

"True, and thank you for your enthusiastic support, but I was just gonna say that the good news is, Q's still talking to me. And his mom doesn't want to murder me and my unborn children."

"Wow. That's a relief."

"Yeah, she's gonna spare my children. I thought that was really nice of her."

"But if you're dead..." Whit's voice trails off.

"Ohmigod, Whit, stop setting fire to my silver linings. Damn."

Whit shakes her head. "Your heart was in the right place. That counts."

I shrug. "Unfortunately, my good intentions can't seem to stop the ongoing reverberations of my initial crappiness. You think Ms. Barrantes cares that I meant well? You think Q's consoling himself with *Jamal might've ruined any peace I might've had these last few days on earth but that heart, tho*?"

"Jamal."

"If the first eighty minutes of a movie are amazing but the last twelve are a dozen pieces of shit on fire, is that movie a masterpiece? Do you excuse the ending because the beginning had so much promise, the middle was pure potential?"

Whit opens her mouth but says nothing.

"Exactly," I say. "Which is why I gotta make this right. No crappy endings allowed."

"Jamal, I applaud your exuberance, but I'm not sure this is something you can fix. Or that you should even try. Maybe the lesson from all of this is, sometimes what we see as broken, isn't. And our *fix* is the thing that breaks it."

"I just wanna atone for my mistakes. Is that so bad?"

"It's not. It's the opposite. But the best way to make things right is to ask the person how you can. And then follow through on that. You're only helpful to someone if what you do actually helps. Otherwise you're just making yourself feel better and that's what ice cream's for."

"Wow, that's kinda deep."

Whit shrugs. "Well, I'm kinda deep, so it makes sense."

And sure, we're talking about Q.

About Ms. B.

But really, we're talking about all the people who love me.

Who've put up with me.

Who did everything they could to help me, even when I refused to help myself.

When I hurt *them* in the process.

No one knew this more than the person standing in front of me.

"What's on my face?" Whit asks.

"Huh? What are you talking about?"

She wags her finger. "You're looking at me funny. What is it?"

"There's nothing on your face. Dang, can't a brother look at his sister lovingly without arousing her suspicion?"

She laughs. "I'm sure *a* brother can, yeah. But we're talking about you, right?"

"Whit, I'm so sorry. Here I am thinking about everyone else and . . ."

"Huh? Now what are *you* talking about?"

"I'm talking about how for the last two years I've been the biggest pain in your butt. I made everything about me. I lied. I broke promises. All of the stuff I've done these last few days, the stuff I'm scrambling to fix, are things I've done to you all this time. You, the only person who truly understands me. Who's been with me from the *beginning* beginning."

"Jamal, we don't have to do this . . ."

"No, we do. *I* do," I say, taking her hands. "I'll probably have to spend the rest of my life making this up to you, but however long it takes, I'll do it."

Whit shakes her head. "Don't you get it? There's *nothing* to make up to me. I *chose* this life with you. I *want* this life with you."

"I want it with you too. I'm just sorry I haven't shown that."

"Jamal, I know you love me. I feel it. You tell me. You do things that show me. But . . . sometimes you treat me like the enemy. Like you think I *enjoy* harassing you about school. Like I *live* to micromanage your life. When in reality, I just want you to be happy. And I want you to have all of the things we would've had with Mom and Dad."

I squeeze her hands. "I want you to have those things too."

"I need you to work harder. To be consistent. I need you to stop walking around like you don't care, when we both know you're the most emotional person in this whole town."

I laugh, a few tears rolling down my face. "I'm gonna work harder. And you're right, I do care. I care a lot. And I know you're only trying to help. I know that."

"But that can only happen if you let me in there," she says, letting go of my hands and tapping my chest.

I wipe my face. "You sure you want in? It can be pretty dark in there."

"Smelly too," Whit says. "But yeah, I'm still game." She leans her head into my shoulder. "Okay, between you and this kid inside me, I need ice cream and I need it now."

"Coming right up," I say. And she takes a seat at the table while I raid the freezer.

"How come they don't tell you that pregnancy makes you super vulnerable to the power of suggestion? I mention ice cream ten minutes ago and now it's all I can think about."

I laugh. "Are you really saying you're vulnerable to your own suggestions? That's like laughing at your own jokes and being like *damn I hate being so funny*."

I drop the rocky road carton in front of her and hand her a wooden serving spoon.

"Where's my bowl?"

"No bowl," I say.

"But you hate it when I eat from the carton."

"Yeah, well, we've already established I don't know anything, so."

"True," she says, and scoops what basically amounts to an entire bowl of ice cream.

"Also, what's so wrong with laughing at your own jokes? What if your jokes happen to be exceptionally funny?"

"Okay, I appreciate we just had a moment, and I don't want to ruin it, but I really hope you're not pretending like you're funny."

"Ha." She sticks out her tongue. "Face it, bro. I'm the funny one in the family. I mean, in another life, I would've been a killer comedian."

"Yeah, well, maybe you should . . . ohmigod." I stop.

"Wait, what's happening? Is this supposed to be some kind

of cliffhanger? Because I'm not all that intrigued."

I snap my fingers because that's what you do when you've got an awesome idea. "Ohmigod, that's it. Why didn't I think of that before? You're a freaking genius, Whit! Ohmigod, thank you! Thank you! If your belly wasn't so huge, I'd attempt to kiss you."

"You see I'm armed, right," she says, holding up the spoon. "You better watch yourself."

I kiss her anyway. And then I dance around the kitchen like a soulful madman because *ohmigod, that's it. That's! It!*

DAY 4

<32 Q Hours Left

19

I prepare my argument.

Try my best to predict each possible objection, prime for all of them.

I know it'll be a fight.

I know they'll resist my plan.

It's gonna be a struggle.

My only hope is that they understand why this is so important.

Why this is the only way for everyone to win.

For, most of all, Q to win.

I deliver my speech and steel myself for the missiles of rejection.

But nope. I get none of that.

I get enthusiasm.

I get jumping up and down.

I get a few sobs, but even those are joyful.

And then we're turning on music and bumping hips in Q's living room because yeah. Because this is how you love.

Because everyone gets my *I've got it.*

And I'd nearly forgotten how good it feels to make other people happy.

It's a seven-hour drive to New York City.

"Except we don't have that kind of time," Ms. Barrantes says. "Right now, every hour might as well be a bag of gold."

Whit nods.

I nod.

Q nods.

Autumn nods.

I suppose I could've said we all nodded, but I looked everyone in their eyes as they affirmed, so it felt right to acknowledge their agreement individually.

"Whit, you're thirty-six weeks?"

"Thirty-four. It'll be thirty-five in two days."

"So, you're safe to fly, but how do you feel about it?"

"Umm, under any other circumstances, it would freak me the hell out. But this, I can't miss this. Plus, I'd be traveling with an OB nurse."

"Maybe you'll deliver on the plane," Q says. "Wait, if we're flying over Pennsylvania, then would the baby still be an Ohioan?"

Autumn smiles. "You're thinking of what happens when you're born in a different country."

Q laughs. "Oh yeah."

"I'm buying the tickets now. If we hurry, we can make the red-eye."

Whit pulls out her credit card. "How much are the tickets?"

But Ms. B's face is thirty-nine levels of offended. "Never ask how much a gift costs."

"I'm not letting you pay for everyone," Whit argues. "The tickets must cost a small fortune."

But Ms. B isn't having it. Tears snagged in her eyelashes, she gets all *this is how it's gonna be*. "If I don't spend my money on this, where will I spend it after? What good is money if you don't have your loved ones to enjoy it?"

Which makes sense.

Which makes sad.

"We leave in three hours," Ms. B confirms. "Just enough time to pack and get to the airport."

And then it's like we're a basketball team coming out of a time-out, breaking our huddle and then hurrying to our respective positions on the court.

Ms. B and Q race home to get a few things.

"Nana's okay with you just picking up for NYC?" I ask Autumn, as I rifle through the dryer for clean socks.

"No. But she's okay with me spending as much time with Q as I can . . ."

I slip a sock over my hand, pinch my thumb against my index finger and say, "I'm glad you're here. Thank you." I open and close my fingers like the sock's talking.

Autumn pulls a sock over her hand. "He's lucky to have you."

I shrug. "I wish he was luckier."

18

Plane tickets, check, but we still need *Later Tonight* tickets.

"No way there are any seats left for tomorrow," I say, tapping the keyboard.

Autumn wags her head. "Paging Downer. Debbie Downer?"

I don't bother retorting *I'm a realist*. I don't bother saying what we both know, what all five of us know.

That it's likely impossible we'll get tickets to tomorrow's taping.

That, spoiler alert, Q is 100 percent *not* gonna be on *Later Tonight*.

"The point is we try," Autumn reminds me.

I scour the *Later Tonight* website for help.

There's no mention of how to meet Kendrick or even how

to audition for the comedy showcase.

But there is an email address.

For general inquiries contact us here: info@
latertonightshow.com.

Okay, a very generic address, but still it was something.

A single bread crumb on a spotless floor.

"You think our inquiry's general enough?" I ask Autumn.

"Do I think you're corny enough?"

"So is that a yes or a no?"

She reaches past me, taps the link, and an empty email opens.

I type before I can second-guess myself.

A few moments later an email pops back and my stomach
yips.

Thank you for contacting us.

No problem, thanks for being contactable.

We will make all effort to reply . . .

Okay, I like the sound of *all effort*. Most of the time we don't
even make minimal effort, so.

. . . within two weeks of receipt.

That sound you heard? Air whooshing from my sails.

We have less than thirty-two hours.

Which means, this is a good time to activate plan B.

You know, if plan B existed.

"So, what do we do now?" Autumn asks, or maybe my brain
asks—hard to say.

"If we can at least get into the audience tomorrow, I can figure out the rest."

Autumn nods. Takes the keyboard. Screens opening and closing in such rapid sequence I barely register the blinking, flitting arrow.

"So, when are you gonna admit you work for a shadowy government agency?"

She laughs. "Why is every government agency shadowy?"

"Shady?" I offer up.

She grins. "Shady works."

"Check out what I found on my dad's computer. I forgot about these."

Autumn strains to see. "What is it?"

I tap a couple of keys. "Home videos. There's, like, at least a hundred clips."

"Oh, wow, that's like a family diary or something."

"I hadn't thought of it that way, but you're right." I scroll through the list. "You think it's weird if I download them to my phone?"

"Umm, I think it's weirder if you *don't*."

I keep scrolling, looking for a good place to start.

"Let's watch one." She tilts her head. "If you're up for it."

I tap Play.

Dad: I'm just trying out my new camera. Trying to get a feel for it.

Jamal: Funny because it's giving me the same feelings as your last camera.

Dad: Hahaha, cute, Jamal. Now turn around and look at me. You too, Quincy.

Mom: Andre, would you please let these boys finish their homework.

Dad: You're right, baby. School comes first. I'll turn it off.

Jamal: Yayyy!

Dad: AFTER you two answer one question.

Jamal: Ohmigod, Dad.

Quincy: It's one question, Jamal.

Dad: See, Q's reasonable. Thank you, Q. If you ever need a place to live . . .

Whit: Dad's back at it.

Jamal: Why are you in my room, Whit? And where'd you even come from?

Whit: I could sense someone was being tormented, so I had to come see.

Jamal: Well, you've seen, now you can crawl back to your hovel.

Mom: Jamal! Apologize to your sister! And I better not hear you say something like that again, you hear me?

Jamal: Mom, she says way worse to me. And she never lets me in her room so how come I gotta let her in mine?

Mom: *Jamal.*

Jamal: Okay, I'm sorry, Whit . . . [quietly] *that you trolls live in hovels.*

Dad: Guys.

Whit: I don't let you in my room because you refuse to use deodorant.

Mom: Jamal, we talked about hygiene.

Dad: Guys.

Jamal: Mom, she's lying! Smell my pits! Smell me! Quincy, stop laughing!

Quincy: Your family's hilarious. I can't help it.

Dad: GUYS! DO YOU WANNA HEAR MY DAMN QUESTION OR NOT?

Mom: Language, Andre.

Dad: I only said *damn*, baby. That's hardly—

Mom: Andre Alexander Anderson.

Me: Awww shoot, Dad's in trouble.

Dad: What else is new? Okay, here goes: What do you want to be when you grow up? Jamal, you go first.

Jamal: Why me?

Dad: 'Cuz you're my child and because I like Q better.

Whit: Dang, Dad.

All of us: *laughing*

Dad: Okay, so whaddya gonna be?

Me: Fine. Uh. When I grow up I wanna be . . . a llama.

Dad: Boy, can't you be serious for thirty seconds?

Me: Thirty's pushing it. I can do ten, though.

Dad: Q, how about you? What do you wanna be?

Me: Oh, that's easy, Mr. Anderson. I wanna be the host of *Later Tonight*.

Dad: Wow. Now see, that's how you answer the question.
That's great, Q. I can definitely see you on that stage, mic
in your hand.

Me: Me too. I see it too.

When the video stops, Autumn looks at me, says, "Wow. That was cool."

I nod. "I can't wait to show Whit these. Our family journal."

Autumn kisses my cheek.

A handful of minutes later there are five e-tickets for tomorrow's taping on Autumn's phone. She found them on one of those buy-or-sell sites, which of course meant we paid handsomely for what are normally free tickets, but.

"Don't tell Q we paid for these," Autumn says.

"Of course not," I say. "Why would I tell him we . . ." But I manage to snag the joke before it completely sails over my head. "I hate you," I tell her.

"Couldn't if you wanted to," she sings.

She taps her phone screen and then a beat later my screen lights, chimes. "Sent everyone their ticket," she says. I pick up my phone, but she takes it from my hands, sets it back on the kitchen table.

And I won't tell you that right now the pull of Autumn's brown eyes is stronger than the stingiest black hole, or that I am instantaneously, wholly swallowed by them, or that at their center I see the entirety of our joint future, spiraling in either direction like a double helix.

That would be beyond cheesy.

She licks my bottom lip, and I kiss her. She bites my bottom lip, and pain never felt so good. I kiss her back, kiss her deeply, as if our kissing is preventing the world from nuclear destruction, and I open my eyes to see if her eyes are open and they weren't, but then they open and she catches me and she smirks. "Damn, stare much?"

I nod. "When something's worth staring."

The corner of her mouth pulls back into a smirk, like a slingshot. "Do those lines ever work?"

I grin. "You tell me."

She slips our embrace and walks out of the room.

"Hey," I call after her. But she doesn't answer. I hear the front door open and close. I walk into the front hall and she's gone. I race to the door, yank it open, and step outside. I don't see her. I move toward the driveway; her car's there.

"Hey," she calls out from behind me. "Who you looking for?"

I whirl around slowly, like I've taken ten paces and now I'm drawing my gun. I play it cool. Mad casual. "I was just getting the mail."

"Oh, that's disappointing."

"You left me."

"You asked me if that shit worked."

"So you just leave?"

"It was funnier in my head," she admits.

I smile. "Damn, I want that on my tomb."

17

Ms. B calls to say we've been warned by Mr. O that this trip shouldn't happen.

Whit puts her on speakerphone, so we can both hear. "What exactly did he say? And how'd he even know?"

Ms. B says she told him as a heads-up, asked if he had any advice on how to care for Q.

"He said that without knowing when Q will . . . this trip is too dangerous. That not only shouldn't Q go at all, but I should reconsider the hard cap. That I needed to consider Q's interests and not just my own. But I told him I didn't care what he thought, or what the Center believed. That a mom knows what's best for her son. That I want my son's last moments on this planet to be some of the best he's had."

And I know I'm the last one to object, considering I'm kinda why we're in this mess to begin with, but I have to ask. "What if . . . what if this trip *is* a bad idea? What if we're wrong?"

"Death happens when it happens, and talking about it, or planning for it, changes not a single damn thing. If our families don't know that, after all that's happened to us, then who does?"

DAY 5

<30 Q Hours Left

16

We cram ourselves and our overnight bags into Ms. Barrantes's sedan. We leave early, our departure time fully cushioned, only to watch all of our padding disintegrate in a heart-in-throat instant, Ms. Barrantes practically standing on the brake pedal to prevent us from slamming into the stopped van ahead of us.

Yo, if we were playing curse word bingo, all five of us would've been winners, waving our arms victoriously in the air, Ms. Barrantes rapid-firing words I'm not even sure are profane.

"Everyone okay?" she says, glancing at each of us. "What the hell are they even working on?"

Ahead of us, a field of orange cones and orange barrels cuts unwelcome polygons into the highway, as men wearing flashlight helmets point at the road and put their hands on their hips, the four-lane highway boa-constrictored to one pathetically skinny shoulder.

Whit opens a traffic app on her phone. "Traffic's backed up for a quarter mile."

Ms. Barrantes wags her head. "Nuh-uh" is all she says as she whips the car to the right and onto the center median, narrowly avoiding an orange cone massacre, before leaning into the gas and obstacle-coursing the fuck out of the construction zone. The construction crew's faces look horrified as they dive out of the way; but she wasn't close to hitting them. Well, not that close.

"Damn, Ms. B, you a stuntwoman in your spare time?" Autumn asks.

"That's what I'm talking about, Mom," Q yells from the back seat. "Hell yeah!"

"Who says brown people don't like NASCAR," she says, winking at us in the rearview mirror. Ten minutes later, we spill out of the car and into the airport security line, Ms. Barrantes slipping her keys and cash to the valet without a hitch in her stride. Naturally, our gate is C29, which could just as easily be renamed the Oregon Trail, it's that long of a hike.

The gate attendant tags our bags because there's no more storage on the plane, and she looks like she wants to say something when she sees Whit's belly, but instead she phones the crew we're finally here and shoos us down the jetway. We fall into our seats, Q and his mom together, Whit and Autumn, and me alone.

I took the solo seat even though Autumn argued she should.

So now I'm in the middle seat, right next to the engine so my entire body vibrates and I can't hear myself think for the relentless hum, and the cherry?

I have zero armrest real estate.

But it doesn't matter. I spot the back of Q's head, the side of his mom's as she looks at her son in a way no one has to teach you when you have *sacrifice your life* love, and I'm reminded that what I did, telling Q the truth, didn't belong to me.

That it was selfish. And holier-than-thou. And reckless.

And even if he's determined to pretend he's okay, Q shouldn't have to shuffle through his last days in fear and gloom.

He deserves peace, which is sometimes better than truth.

And yeah, if I don't tell Q the truth, we're probably not here: thirty thousand feet in the air, cruising toward his dreams, a flight so smooth it's like turbulence is officially extinct.

But that wasn't my call to make.

The truth is you can never truly make amends for the hurt you cause; you apologize, you try to atone, at best the scars lighten but they don't disappear.

You live with the pain that you pained someone.

The lady in the seat next to me elbows me in the ribs, but I don't feel a thing.

At the hotel we split into two groups.

Whit, Autumn, and me in one room. Q and his mom in another.

We have to practically lock Whit in our room to get her to

rest; the plane ride and all of the last-minute running around wiped her out, but she was determined to stay in the game. Only Ms. Barrantes's nursing expertise convinces Whit to take a nap, to get off her feet.

So we set up our plan-making committee in Q's room.

Our plan is simple.

We'll construct an assortment of handwritten signs that Kendrick will be unable to resist, let alone ignore. He'll see the signs, all singing Q's praises, along with special emphasis on Q's undying love and admiration for Kendrick, and badda-boom badda-bing!

But okay, a couple of minor obstacles to consider.

Minor obstacle number one: while assumptions are usually ill-fated, I assume that signage, even of a happy-if-slightly-solicitous nature, is probably frowned upon at the show. And understandably so; you wouldn't want a bunch of weirdos flashing signs at Kendrick while he's trying to get through his monologue.

But this, for my money, seemed to be a minor setback, easily remedied: we'd smuggle our signs into the studio under our clothes and/or bags and/or purses, then remove them from said articles at the optimal time, accompanied by a combination of jumping up and down at seats and wave-fluttering our permanent-markered pleas.

Minor obstacle number two: I seem to be the only one who understands the vital importance of these signs.

See for yourself:

Autumn:	Whit:	Ms. Barrantes:
Q LOVES YOU, KENDRICK! PLEASE LET HIM TELL A JOKE!	KENDRICK, Q CHALLENGES YOU TO A STAND-UP-OFF! MAY THE FUNNIEST HUMAN WIN!	YOU'RE A CRAZY MAN IF YOU DON'T LET MY SON ON YOUR SHOW!!

Our signs should be inspirational, yes—but also should evoke the feelings you might have as you read a ransom note instructing you what to do if you ever want to see your loved one.

Hence, my sign:

MY GOOD FRIEND QUINCY
WILL LITERALLY DIE IN
TWO DAYS UNLESS YOU LET
HIM ON YOUR SHOW.

Which I think walks the line brilliantly: it's in good taste, the tone is spot-on, but also it's just direct enough that its message is unmistakable.

"But J, I'm going to die no matter what," Quincy had argued

when I'd proudly held up my work. "That feels sorta . . . manipulative."

"I stand by my sign, Q."

"But it's essentially a lie."

"I said *what I said*." I reach over to his work space. "Let me see yours."

He holds it up.

> KENDRICK,
> YOU ARE THE REASON I LOVE COMEDY.
> SO MANY TIMES YOU MADE ME LAUGH
> THROUGH MY TEARS. YOU ARE NOT
> JUST MY COMIC INSPIRATION. YOU ARE
> UNDENIABLY HILARIOUS OFC, BUT I THINK
> YOUR GREATEST TALENT IS YOUR
> ABILITY TO TRULY SEE PEOPLE. YOU
> UNDERSTAND WHAT IT MEANS TO BE
> HUMAN. TO UPLIFT AND UPBUILD EACH
> OTHER. YOU ARE WHAT IT LOOKS LIKE
> WHEN AMAZING WORDS COLLIDE WITH
> ACTION. THANK YOU FOR EVERYTHING.

"I mean, it's okay," I say. "But you don't list your demands. Like, I think it's lacking that *oomph*."

"I think it's great," Autumn says. "If someone held up this sign for me, I'd melt where I stood."

"Except the idea isn't to melt him. We're trying to get Q on the show. Besides, how is Kendrick supposed to read all of that from the stage? It's like Handwriting font size ten."

Q coughs. Then coughs more.

"You okay, man?" Autumn asks.

"I just feel a little dizzy. And my throat's itchy. I think maybe a cold's coming." Q coughs again, this time semiviolently, then finally clears his throat. "I didn't want to say anything before, J, because I can tell how much this means to you."

"What are you talking about?"

"We all know I'm *not* gonna be on *Later Tonight*, right?"

"We *don't* know that. He's brought audience members on stage before. There's dozens of clips on TuberOne."

Q shakes his head. "Yeah, but what are the odds he does that *this* show, and even if he does, that he chooses *me*? But it's okay. That's not what this trip is about for me. I just wanted to be there in the same space as my comedic hero. I wanted to see him work, feel his energy, laugh at his jokes in real time."

"Which will all happen, but . . ."

"But you know what the absolute best part of all this is?" Q asks.

"The prospect of Kendrick melting on live TV?"

"Being here with you guys. Spending my last few hours on this planet surrounded by the people I love, who are sacrificing to help me do this thing that I love. Honestly, I could die right now and be happy."

And if it had been up to me, this might've dissolved into some tearful exchange where we discussed the purpose of life or whatever.

But instead Autumn throws her arms around us both. "Aww, the love in this place is fucking humid. I love it."

And we group-hug like nobody's business.

And we make it our business to group-hug.

Ten minutes later Ms. Barrantes bursts into the room holding a brown paper bag with grease ovals on either side, like armpit stains.

"Someone order *pad kee mao*?"

And I guess Whit hears our enthusiastic affirmation in our adjacent room because she's knocking at the door a minute later, looking less tired but more hungry.

"Angeles sends his love," Whit says, taking a seat in the desk chair.

Q smiles. "Is there a better guy than that dude?"

"No way," Whit says, slightly swiveling her chair toward Q, then to me. "But I can think of a couple guys who are just as good."

And we pass the containers around, dishing noodles and chicken and crispy duck and lots and lots of veggies, and it's nice. To not be planning anything for a few minutes.

To be quiet.

To let things settle where they fall.

15

EMILIO HAS ARRIVED.

I get a notification our car's in front of the hotel.

Turns out *Later Tonight* is taped at one in the afternoon, go figure.

"You got the tickets, right," Whit asks me not for the first time since we've gotten into the car.

"I got them. Sheesh. A little trust maybe?"

Q goes on another one of his coughing jags, but then finally manages a big laugh, which I feel all of, each laughter vibration, because we're squished together in the back seat, he, Ms. Barrantes, Autumn, and me. My pregnant sister nice and comfy in the front passenger seat.

And sometimes this is how life works. You're in a car with

people you love, you're happy, you're singing—you can't imagine anything different. You'll never run out of gas. All your favorite songs will play one after another. You're smiling, waving at the cars you pass and the cars that pass you. You don't know if the sun is truly shining or if it's just the way you feel inside. Either way, you're warm. You're full.

We get to the studio where they film *Later Tonight* and there's a door marked Studio Audience Guests Enter Here.

"That's us," I say, holding open the door for everyone.

Autumn claps her hands together. "I'm getting excited."

"Me too," Q says. "Not gonna lie, this is pretty cool."

"Just everybody stick to the plan."

We all nod our agreement.

"Should we huddle up and do that thing where we each put a hand in the middle and then in unison say something semi-inspirational before throwing our respective hands in the air?" I ask.

"Well, yeah, but I think it would've been better if we'd just done it, rather than you breaking down each step," Autumn says.

"Yeah, I agree," Whit says. "I like this girl."

"I third that," Q says. "Organic huddles are the best huddles."

"I think it's fine if we still do it, Jamal. I don't think you ruined anything," Ms. Barrantes says with a wink.

"Hmph, thank you. At least someone gets me."

"Wah wah," Whit says, pretending to cry. "Is that whining coming from inside my stomach?"

I roll my eyes. Stick my hand out. "You guys in?"

"In," everyone says, stacking their hands on top.

"Okay, Get Q on Stage on three," I direct. "One . . . two . . . three . . ."

"Get Q on Stage," we all shout with conviction, our hands lifting into the air.

Tickets scanned, we take our seats. The lights dim and the audience claps as if our lives depend on our enthusiasm. And out skips Kendrick. Each time he smiles, it's like he's yanking a sheet off a blanketed object and revealing something special. Each locced dread falling away from his face like the frozen trajectories of so many skipped stones. Black skin so smooth if you ran your fingers across his arm left and then right, it would change texture like velvet. Okay, maybe that's not true, but what *is* true is Kendrick's got mad gravitational pull. Before he said one word, you already *wanted* to like him.

Soon as he launches into his three-minute monologue, I give the team the signal and we work on removing our signs from their hiding places.

But there's something we hadn't anticipated.

How dark it is.

We wave the signs, even make them flutter, but if Kendrick (or anyone other than the people seated behind us) notices, no one says anything. Kendrick doesn't bat an eye.

Eventually, everyone drops their signs to their laps. I keep trying though. Waiting for the lights to change. Waiting for our luck to change.

But nothing.

I stand up, and Whit tugs on my shirt. "What are you doing?"

"I'm trying to get his attention."

"Sit down."

"Yeah, sit down, kid," a man behind us says. "You're not supposed to have posters, anyway."

"Excuse me, sir, but I don't see how this is any of your business. I'm trying to do something important for my friend here and if you'd . . ."

"Sir, sir, we need you to come with us," a man says, who has materialized at the end of our row. As he aims his flashlight at my face, I catch the word SECURITY embroidered on his shirt and hat.

"What did I do wrong?"

"You're causing a disturbance. Other guests are complaining."

"We're all together. If he goes, we all go," Autumn chimes.

But the security guard shrugs. Waves his flashlight at all of us. "Fine, let's go, all of you."

"No, wait," I say. "Wait. Just take me. They didn't do anything. It was all me."

"Listen, I don't care if it's just you or the whole lot."

I turn back to the others. "I don't want Q to miss the show. He has to see the show."

"I don't wanna see it without you," Q says. "This was your idea."

I shrug, because there's no way I'm letting Q down today.

"Nah, I'm actually more partial to *Much Later Tonight* anyway."

"Jason, what's going on up there?" says a voice I've heard so many times on TV but never in person. I look down at the stage and there's Kendrick cupping his hand above his eyes, squinting, as he fights off the spotlights.

The security guard—Jason, apparently—shakes his head. "Sorry, boss. We'll be out of the way in a moment."

In a moment.

And it dawns on me, why can't this be the moment?

Kendrick nods and is about to turn around when I yell out:

"Kendrick, sir, I'm so incredibly sorry to interrupt your show! You're brilliant and funny and you seem like an awesome human, which is why we're here! Why we came here to see you because . . ."

Kendrick offers the faintest wave—he's unmoved. This is a speech he's heard before, can recite from memory, only he'd write it better. "Thank you for coming," he says, walking toward the stage wings.

"Wait, Kendrick! My friend is sick! He's gonna die in a couple of days and all he wanted, the only thing, was to come see you! Please, please, just give him a second of your time. Please. I'm begging you."

Kendrick pauses, turns his head back to us. "What's your friend's name?"

"Q! Quincy!"

"Quincy, you up there?"

Quincy nods but doesn't move—if Q were a cartoon his pupils would be two black spirals spinning, like when someone's hypnotized.

"Feel free to talk, Quincy," Kendrick says, laughing.

"You're my comedic hero."

"Thank you, Quincy. And thank you for using your last . . . thank you for coming all this way from . . ."

"Ohio," Ms. Barrantes pipes up.

"Ohio," Kendrick repeats. "I wish you and your family peace and solace."

"I've watched *Purple Tape* a hundred times," Quincy blurts.

Kendrick's brow lifts. "My mom hasn't even watched *Purple Tape*. There are probably only four people who even know it exists."

"I bought it online. It's not the best copy, and there's a couple spots where the video goes out for a second, but it's all there. I saved up for it for a long time. But it was so worth it. Your jokes are like a freaking master class in writing. Most of the time they don't even feel like jokes. Just like awesome stories that make you laugh."

Kendrick nods. "Well, thank you, Quincy. That's one of the nicest things anyone's ever said." He takes a step toward the wing. Looks back again. "Take care, man."

And then he's gone, presumably to change clothes for another bit, or grab a beer, or whatever hosts do in between segments.

Q trash-compacts his cheeks with both hands. "Ohmigod!

Did that just . . . did Kendrick stop and talk . . . did . . . ?"

And I'm laughing because this is what it's all about. This is why we've come. To see Q's face look like this. To witness Q's tongue make these sounds. To see Q's eyes stretch this wide.

The guard pokes my back, pops my thought bubble. "All right, you've had your fun. Let's go, kid."

"Is there like a phrase book all you security people use?" I ask.

"Hardy-har, now get moving," he barks.

Whit tries to push herself up from her bucket seat. "You aren't taking my brother anywhere. I'm his guardian and he didn't do anything wrong."

The guard holds up his hands. "Look, we're just headed for the lobby, ma'am. There's a TV in there, he can watch. Bagels, too, if he behaves."

I step into the aisle. "See, I'll be fine. I'll see you guys after, okay?" But I'm already walking down the stairs toward the exit before they can protest anymore.

It's not the worst thing, watching in the lobby. Chairs are comfortable enough, and there's free coffee. I sit on the edge of my seat for most of the taping, fingers crossed, hoping by some miracle Q finds his way onto the stage. But then the television monitor dims and the screen falls black, flipping the switch on the last of my optimism. But I don't move. I know it's not happening, but I can't accept we've failed. *I* failed.

Maybe I could run onto the stage.

Or slip behind it and find Kendrick's dressing room and do that action-movie thing where I get some momentum and then lead with my shoulder into the heart of the door, ripping the bolt from its lock.

Or find his car. I find his car and wait there for him to come out. There are probably pictures of his car online, shouldn't be that hard to find, and if the other guards are anything like this one, how hard could it be to sneak through undetected?

"Don't even think about it," the security guard says, reading my mind. "Here, have another bagel."

I look at the door behind him, the door from whence we came. No way he's fast enough to stop me. I stand up and fall into a track-meet stance.

The security guard laughs. "Kid, I've been second runner-up at five amateur wrestling tournaments. I'll suplex you so hard your kids'll come out dizzy."

I laugh because that was funny. I drop the track pose and stand up out of respect for my unborn children.

There must be another way, which is when the security guard starts grinning.

"What's so cute?" I ask.

He nods toward the monitor. "Looks like your friend didn't need you after all."

My knees feel buzzy, wobbly. Or maybe that's my head.

I can't believe my eyes. This can't be happening.

Q, a chrome mic in his hand, smiles and gazes into the camera like he was made for TV. No, like TV was made for him.

"So, I flew in from Ohio and it got me thinking about the first ever commercial flight. Can you imagine how that must've gone?

Your dad trying to convince you it was safe?

Now, son, I promise it'll be okay. What's the worst that could happen?

Dad, it's a giant sardine can with flimsy wings flying thirty thousand feet in the air? Mom was right. You really do lack imagination.

You know what I hate most about flying?

The half can of pop they serve you. What, the seven thousand dollars I paid for this flight won't cover a couple more swigs of lemon-lime? And to make sure you have even less to drink, they jam-pack your cup with ice. I'm sorry, are we still cooling my soda? Or should I grab my pick-ax and start climbing?

And this is no regular ice. No. This ice instantly melts on contact. Soon as she pours the capful of soda, boom, the top layer of your drink is pure tap water. You down half of your cup before you can even remember what you ordered, that's how watered down that thing is.

You take two more slurps and it's gone and now you've still got a bag of mini pretzels you can't tear open to save your life. And who came up with mini pretzels anyway? Were pretzels really so big we needed to shrink them?"

I couldn't tell you how long Q's set is.

Only that he kills, slays, murders.

When he's finished, he takes the deepest, most expressive bow ever.

And then he drops the mic.

Except it doesn't hit the ground because he's still hanging on to the cord.

He pulls it up back by the cord and laughs. "Just playing, I know this costs more than this entire audience makes in a year. This thing heavy as hell. What's this made of? Gold bullion? I didn't wanna break it because soon as I walk off this stage, I'm stuffing it my pants, taking it back to Ohio."

And it doesn't matter if I now remember just how hilarious Q is.

It doesn't matter if all of America falls in love with his charm, with his humility.

I hope they appreciate what they've just experienced.

I hope his words pop into their brains in the middle of a random Tuesday and they start laughing seemingly out of nowhere.

Because Quincy Michael Barrantes isn't just comedy gold.

He's just gold, period.

13

We hit up this Italian spot for our celebratory dinner because Q's got a hankering for pasta and Whit says she'll murder someone for a slice of tiramisu—which, satisfying a craving *and* preventing homicide, no-brainer.

My phone rings midway through dessert.

"How was your evening in studio prison?" Mr. Oklahoma asks.

"I'm not gonna lie, man. You knowing the intimate details of our lives is kinda scary. Anyway, Q brought the house down. Even you would've laughed."

"Suppose he'd collapsed on that stage," he says. "Then what?"

"That's no way to live, Mr. O."

A beat.

"I am glad it worked out for Quincy."

"Me too." And maybe it's rude to say, but. "Mr. Oklahoma, I didn't like you when I first met you."

"I'm not here to be liked."

"I said when I *first* met you."

"I know what you said."

This guy. "So, is that it? You just called to talk about how well Operation Get Q on *Later Tonight* worked?"

"No, Jamal." A long pause. "I just called to say *good job*. So, good job, Jamal."

Before I can reply, he's gone.

12

Whit orders a car, and we stand in a huddle outside the bistro.

"Where to next?" Ms. Barrantes asks.

I smile. "I mean, only one of us got dessert." Whit shoots me a death look.

Autumn taps *best dessert in NYC*, reads us a list of choices.

"Q, you choose," I say.

But he shakes his head. "Damn, word? A brother should die more often."

Except when the car comes, I take Autumn's hand, stop Q from getting inside.

"Let's walk," I say. "It's only a few blocks."

Q smiles. "Uh-oh, you got that look in your eyes."

"Look? What look?" I laugh. "I don't know what you're talking about."

II

What I finally understand about Q's Comedy Hour, about Jauncy, is that it wasn't *just* about being funny.

It was about two kids finding their voices.

Learning to believe in themselves.

And maybe, most of all, it was a way to bring people together.

And, sometimes, reunite them.

10

That night, before we fall asleep, Autumn already snoring lightly, I turn to Whit, a nightstand between our beds, and I ask her—

"How did I get so lucky?"

And at first, I can't be sure she's awake—the room dark save for the slant of city lights stretching across the top of the pulled curtains—so I ask her again.

"Hey, you awake? 'Cuz I'm serious, Whit. I haven't felt this happy since . . . thank you for being the coolest sister ever, and I'm not even just saying that because I'm in a good mood."

Still no answer. No movement. I listen for her breathing, but between Autumn's and the outside rattle of passing cars, I don't hear anything over there.

"Whit?" I ask the darkness.

And I think I hear a small but sharp sniffle, the beginnings of a light sob, but no matter how quiet I am, how much I slow my own breathing, I don't hear it again.

"Don't you hate people who use big words just to prove they're not hebetudinous?" I ask, hoping if she is awake, she'll laugh.

But she doesn't laugh.

So I pop in my earbuds and listen to the latest Mighty Moat album, *Sad Songs Make Me Happy*, until I drift drift drift.

DAY 6

<7 Q Hours Left

9

Our flight's set for dawn's ass crack, which means when we crowd into the hotel shuttle it's still dark.

I feel bad for our driver because everyone's snoring combined, it's basically a snore-a-palooza for the ages, but hey, it's been a crazy couple days, give us a break, right.

When we finally make it back to Ohio, it's that weird feeling as we walk through the airport parking garage to Ms. B's car. That feeling when you've just had a profound, intimate moment with a group of people and you're not ready to go your separate ways.

And everything feels like deep feels, if that makes sense.

Like everything is super cold or super hot or super tiring or super frustrating or super funny because we've lost all of our filters and barriers and cushions and buffers and we're just straight feelings, no chaser.

And it doesn't help that I can't stop checking my watch.

That even as we load our luggage into the car, I catch everyone doing the same, although we all try to do it undetected. Glancing at our phone screens like we're checking for a message or an alert or whatever.

But we're all looking at the same thing:

How much time Q has left.

And I wasn't gonna tell you because I don't want that to be the focus.

But I know it's the room-elephant.

So here it is, for your countdowning pleasure:

We're T minus two hours from Q's four-hour departure window.

Happy now?

8

We squeeze the last bag back into Ms. B's sedan and close the trunk.

And it's a question we've been avoiding.

Dodging.

Doing our best to tap-dance and tiptoe around, but it's something we have to address. Q sees to this.

"So, uh, aren't you guys gonna ask me where I wanna be when I kick the bucket?"

And the car is silent.

Q laughs. "Guys, it's gonna happen. I mean, that's what this whole thing is about, right?"

And he's right. So I try to be brave. "So where do you wanna be when . . . ?"

Q doesn't hesitate.

Fires back as if he's been waiting to answer this question all his life.

Maybe he has.

All his second life.

"You sure?" Ms. B asks from the driver's seat. "Isn't that kinda..."

"Masochistic," Whit chimes.

"I think it's fitting." Q nods. "Circle of life and all that."

Ms. B shakes her head. "Well, it's your decision, Quincy," she says. "And we're gonna support you whatever you want, baby."

They smile at each other through the rearview mirror. "Thanks, Mama," he says.

"We probably should drive straight over, right?" Autumn suggests. "Maximize the time."

We all agree.

So, yeah, you guessed it.

The last four hours of Quincy Michael Barrantes's life are spent at...

...the beach.

Which, not gonna lie, is eerie as hell.

But hey, it's his funeral.

Damn, that was awful.

Okay, the only person who gets to crack jokes about Q's death is Q.

Ms. Barrantes starts tearing up before we even get to the

actual sand. "I'm not crying," she says. "I think I'm allergic to something out here."

Q laughs. "To sand? Water?" He wraps her in a hug.

And when they start walking along the water, Whit, Autumn, and I hang back. But apparently, crying's an infectious disease, because Whit breaks out in tears. And then I'm next. And Autumn joins in on the fun.

And I promise you haven't lived until you've had an ugly-cry party.

When Q comes back, he looks us all over, like a drill sergeant examining his cadets. "Look at you all. This is supposed to be a party, remember? This is pathetic. You can do better than this. Pull yourselves together, you hear me?"

"Yes sir," we say, our hands raised to our foreheads in salute.

"Now, turn the music on and let's have an ugly dance-off." He turns to me. "Don't worry. I'm not gonna make you start because you'd destroy us all."

I push him away. "I couldn't ugly dance if I tried."

"Ha!" With his toes, Q draws a line in the sand. "Well, then, let's do this, my friend."

The music starts and our battle is barely underway—Q already with a sizable lead because his *normal* dancing is already ugly. He's basically starting this race at the finish line. But whatever—when I see someone walking toward us down the beach.

I stop dancing and Q gives me a look. I nod, and he turns around.

"Bri," he says softly. And then loudly, "Bri!"

He tears down the beach and they're hugging and he's lifting her off the ground. And I know what Q said. That we're pathetic. That this is a party.

But a guy can only take so much.

And there's no way this is possible, but I feel like Bri's a ringer.

Within seconds of the music resuming, it's clear this is not her first ugly-dancing tournament.

Nope. She's a pro among amateurs.

Wouldn't surprise me at all to find out she's an ugly-dancing hustler who roams from city to city, town to town, baiting the unsuspecting into challenging her to a dance duel, fooling them into upping their wager, only to dance them down in the dusty street, the sheriff, the townspeople, helplessly looking on.

Which is to say, Bri's ugly-dance annihilates every last one of us.

She is the ugly-dancing champion of . . . Elytown beach.

Q keeps calling her his dancing queen, which is only more proof he was born in the wrong century, but what do I know?

We all take turns spending a few minutes alone with Q. And every time he walks away with someone, I'm not gonna lie, I get nervous.

Afraid that we won't get to talk before he goes away.

But then with about forty-five minutes left, Q motions for me to follow him down the beach.

"Don't go too far," Ms. Barrantes. "Or be too long."

Q shakes his head. "We'll be right over there, and we'll be right back. Just gotta have a word with my friend."

We walk about thirty yards toward the water and stop, our backs to everyone. The waves are less sloshy than when we first arrived. The sun lower in the sky.

"Yo, we're cutting it close," I say.

"Haha, you know I like to take my time, do things right."

I smile. "This I know, yes. Among the many other things I know about you. Some of which I wish I didn't know."

Q laughs. "I gotta say, that worries me. You don't exactly have the best track record for keeping secrets lately."

"Wow," I say, covering my mouth with my hand, in exaggerated disbelief. "Did you really just say that? Wow. You went there."

Q shrugs, still laughing, and I can't help but join in.

"So, listen, I had this whole speech written out last night. I wanted to be witty and clever when we talked. I wanted my final, private words to you to be the kind that stick with you forever, but . . ."

"Everything about you is gonna stick with me forever, Q."

He forces out a smile. But his face's heavier now. "I'm just gonna freestyle, if that's cool? Yeah?"

He waits for me to nod before continuing. "So, you know how you spend most of your time compiling in your brain things that you one day want to do? How you often bound from one great idea to the next one without even starting, or at least finishing, the first idea because you figure, hey why not, I'll get back to it eventually? Yeah, don't do that anymore. Don't wait for those days to come to you, Jamal. Make those days happen. Because as it turns out, we do not have all the time in the world. We only get a finite amount. Don't waste it being sad, or angry, or frustrated. Don't waste it with regrets. Don't waste a second. Live each day like it's your last four hours. Live each hour like the seconds matter. And most of all, don't be afraid to be you, Jamal. Because you're awesome—no matter what other people say. You're the best, man. And you've got the whole world right in front of you. So, live like it, okay? LIVE LIKE IT!"

And I nod like my head's on fire. "You know I love you, right?"

"I do," he says. "But it's always nice to hear you say it."

"I'm sorry I didn't swim better. That I didn't save you."

"What? Get outa here." He punches me in the chest. "I'm sorry I put you in that situation."

"You were just being heroic."

"Ha. Who woulda thunk it? Quincy Michael Barrantes, a hero?"

"You," I say, jabbing his chest with my finger. "A goddamn hero."

A mob of seagulls squawks farther down the shore. A

golden retriever rushes past us, a woman in shorts and a base-ball cap jogging behind, a black leash wrapped around her hand. She waves at us as she zooms by.

"Remember when you tried to get me to believe my middle name was actually pronounced *Michelle*? You swore my mom had shown you my birth certificate and that there was an accent mark over the *a*."

"What do you mean I tried to get you? I absolutely got you to believe it. The only reason I told you the truth was because you said you weren't gonna give me back my officially authorized behind-the-scenes Mighty Moat: The Last First Tour poster."

"Yo, you were fanatical about that poster."

"I stood in line for seven hours for that poster. And every-one in the band signed it, so the fact that I even let you borrow it showed how much I trusted you."

"That is true. You didn't even let Brenda Williams hold it, and she offered to kiss you."

"Q," I say, putting my hand on his shoulder, which is always much higher than it looks, and squeezing it. "I will always, always put you ahead of making out with Brenda Williams . . ."

"Thanks, J."

". . . *but* just behind my officially authorized behind-the-scenes Mighty Moat: The Last First Tour poster."

"That's real cold, man." Q chuckles, strokes his chin like he's deliberating. "But also, I respect the honesty. Thanks for keep-ing it real."

And we hug. And not the cool, nonchalant bro hug we normally do. I'm talking a full-on, both-arms-wrapped, sweaty-chest-to-sweaty-chest, nearly-fall-onto-the-sand HUG.

And boy, it feels good.

And man, I don't want to let go.

But I guess that's sorta the crux. Everything ends at some point.

Q drops his arms, steps back. "You be good to our girls, okay? And to your amazing sister. And to your sister's kid, who hopefully looks nothing like you. And most of all, to my mom, because one, I'm biased, and because two, she's gonna need you. She's gonna need you and you've gotta step up. You hear me?"

"I hear you. And I will." I grin. "Especially your mom. I'll be sure to keep her *real* safe, you know what I'm saying? You know what I'm saying?" I hit him with a few pelvic thrusts just in case he doesn't know what I'm saying.

Q groans. "Bro, really? My mom? That's just over-the-top nasty."

"Yeah? That bad?"

"Yep. And I thought we agreed that you were done with that whole *Fresh Prince* bit."

"I'm telling you, one day it's gonna make someone laugh."

Q smiles his trademark smile, the one that's been lighting up rooms for seventeen years. "I wouldn't hold your breath."

"Uh-oh, speaking of breath holding . . ." I clear my throat, nod toward the waves. A cluster of small fishing boats dot the horizon. "You wanna play one last round of Mercy?"

430

Q scratches his head. "You really want the last thing you remember about me to be me kicking your ass for the millionth time?"

"Nah, I'm feeling magical tonight."

Q laughs. "That's what you always say. Right before you lose."

"Well, you've got bigger lungs, so genetic advantage."

Q smirks. "Just working with what I was given, shorty. Plus, you got them gargantuan chipmunk cheeks. You oughta be able to hold four times as much air in there as me."

He grabs my cheek, and I slap his hand away. I smile. "Yeah, well, I'm going for the record this time."

"Good," he says. "And don't even think about letting me win. I want the final L I give you to be undeniably a loss you earned."

"Whatever."

"Plus, you know you like to mope. I don't want you walking around thinking you coulda won if you wanted to."

"Get outta here. Man, you've always been like this. I'd win like forty-seven times in a row, but then the second you finally won you never wanted to play again. The game was barely over and your happy ass was already running down my driveway headed back home. Remember that one time you finally beat me at *Raiders and Warriors 2*? And you were so afraid you'd never win again that you broke your own controller?"

We both crack up.

And he holds up his hand, offers me a high-five palm, which I happily meet with my own. "Hey, even back then I knew, you should always go out on top."

And you know how these four-hour windows go.

They tell you they're gonna make the delivery between ten and two.

That they'll call you when they're on their way.

But of course, they never call.

And without fail they always show up at 1:59.

This time I'm thankful it's last-minute.

Instinctively, I take Q's hand, Ms. Barrantes takes his other. Whit takes mine, Autumn hers, Bri closing our circle. We stay that way until . . .

"So, can I just say this whole dying-in-a-few-minutes thing has me thoroughly bummed out?"

I nod my head. "Umm, I'm pretty sure you get to say whatever you want, Q."

"Okay, cool. I'm gonna make this quick." Q hops up in the middle of our circle, dusts the sand off his butt. "Now you guys are gonna think I'm crazy, but don't laugh, okay, because this is real."

"Baby, I don't mean to rush you, but . . ." Ms. Barrantes makes that open-hand circular-wave gesture that says *come on, get to it, please.*

"Right, right, my bad," Q says. "But first y'all all gotta promise not to laugh."

"Ohmigod, Q, who cares if we laugh, man?" I groan.

"Mm-hm. Everything you say is sorta hilarious, so that's a tough ask," Bri agrees.

"Damn, y'all not even gonna try to honor a dying man's final request?"

"Okay, okay, we swear we won't laugh," we all say in almost freaky unison.

We all laugh, Q the hardest.

"Okay, here's the thing I'm mad about." He shakes his head in disgust. "That I won't get to be a grandpa. You know, the kind that makes up stories and expressions that seem really wise and enlightened even though most of the time you have no idea what they mean? Like, I want that so bad, y'all don't even know. I always imagined my grandkids walking around saying to their friends, to their teachers, to their stylists, "well, it's like my grandpa used to say." But nope. Not gonna happen. Definitely in the 'bummer' column."

Q sits back down, between Bri and his mom, so he's directly across from me.

We're quiet for a moment as a plane flies by.

"I'll make sure my kids know all of the wise and funny things you've said. And maybe they won't go around saying 'my grandpa said,' but would you settle for 'uncle' or, I don't know, maybe 'my dad's best friend who incidentally was by far the most charming, funny, and awesome person he's ever known'?"

Q cracks up. "Well, damn. Maybe it doesn't quite have the same ring to it as 'my grandpa said,' but I feel like it could work."

"I got you, man." We bump fists. "*We* all got you."

"And I got y'all. Always."

7

Listen, I'm not going to give you any more play-by-play.

If you came for death porn, you're gonna be disappointed.

Because there are things in life (and death) that just shouldn't be shared. And after all that's happened, Q deserves some privacy, finally.

That said, I'm no monster, I appreciate we all need as much closure as we can squeeze from the closure lemon, so let's leave it at this:

At seven minutes past seven, surrounded by his friends and family, Q cosmically exited this world for the mysterious beyond.

I say cosmically because those who know him best know that Q is always the last person to leave a party.

"I hate the idea of missing something," he'd say.

And trust me, not even dying can change Q.

6

"Do you want me to call Mr. Oklahoma?" I ask Ms. B.

I didn't know how I'd feel, how I'd be when it actually happened. Now that it has, I feel surprisingly calm. Ms. B appears the same.

Like when gravity hasn't hit you yet.

She nods.

I make the call.

Two men in black Center jumpsuits lift Q from the beach blanket.

We walk with them as they carry him to the lot.

Watch as they lower him into his forever box.

Mr. O and Ms. B off to the side, talking furtively, until finally he pats her softly on her arm and sad-smiles.

And I know it's a weird thing to think about right now, but I wonder if they play music when they're driving someone's loved one away?

Are they old school, listening to whatever random thing is on the radio?

Do they have a music app?

And if so, a playlist?

Does Mr. O have a special compilation he plays for someone's Final Last Day?

Does he make a playlist for each case, for each person?

What songs would he choose for Q?

"Jamal," he says, walking over to me. I half expect him to put a hand on my shoulder, say something adultish like: *Hey, it's gonna be all right. You'll get through.* Except his face, it starts making this weird sound and—

"Are you crying?" I ask him. "You're crying."

"No. Something is in my eye," he says, looking away.

Mr. Oklahoma shakes his head, removes his glasses, wipes his cheeks.

"Those are called tears, my friend. Welcome to Earth. You may grow to love it here."

He chuckles. "It was nice to meet you, Jamal," he says. "Perhaps we will bump into each other another time."

"Hopefully not too soon," I say. "And under much different circumstances."

"Agreed," he says. He tips his head, then walks over to the side of the van.

"Hey, wait," I call out. I hold up both hands, like I'm directing traffic. "There's something I gotta ask you and I need you to tell me the truth. The real truth."

He doesn't nod, or frown, or move, his face already resuming its normal neutral state. He waits for me to speak, but I stare at him for a good while, wanting him to understand how important this next moment is to me.

"Why do this? And please, don't give me any more of your *the dominos of death come crashing down* speeches. We both know there's no cure for death. Not really. So, why do any of this?"

He pushes up his glasses. Tilts his head. "Because it's hard to let go even when you know it's coming."

"One day I'll get you to talk straight with me."

He smiles, opens the van door.

And the door motor hums, begins to close, but while there's still enough daylight to slide my arm through and touch his shoulder, take his hand, I say, "Take care."

To Q.

Take care.

To Ms. B.

Take care.

To Mr. O.

Take care.

To all of us.

Please, take care.

From the front passenger seat, he gives us a small wave, the kind where your arm stays tight against your body, when maybe you don't want to say goodbye.

And even when the van's driven so far down the road that it looks like a toy vehicle, even after it turns down another road and there's no way we can see it, we stay right there.

We move for nothing.

5

And I suppose the story moral is:
    You can die and still live on.
    You can be alive but be consumed by death.
    The difference between living and being alive is:
    Everything.

4

We walk Bri to her car.

She and Autumn confirm their plans to meet up this weekend.

"Don't be a stranger," Ms. B tells her.

"Are you a hugger?" I ask her. And she answers with a hug.

She wipes her nose with her sleeve. "We only just met, but I feel like we're supposed to know each other, you know? Like we're here for a reason."

And I don't know if that's true.

If there's some grand purpose behind all of this.

Honestly, I doubt it.

But it doesn't change what's happened.

Doesn't make the journey of these last few days any less real.

"Take care of yourself," I say as she closes her door, starts the engine.

We drop off Ms. B at home because she just wants to be alone for a bit, if that's okay with everyone.

I lean my seat back as far as it'll go, slide the moonroof cover open.

Overhead, stars puncture the night, and then we're driving faster, and they're no longer perfect glowing orbs; they're streamers, fluttering, burning.

What if we become stars when we die?

Q would be easy to spot; the brightest, glossiest.

The funniest star the constellation has ever seen.

I look for him up there.

And then I close my eyes.

Autumn hugs me in our driveway.

"He left feeling loved," she says. "That's a lot."

"I love you, Autumn. And that's everything."

She kisses me, long and hard, before hopping into her own car, her grandma calling her home for dinner.

Funny how life just goes, man.

It just fucking goes.

I cue up a video from my phone, beam it to the TV.

"What you doing?" Autumn asks.

"Figured maybe we should reset our memories," I say.

She slides onto the couch beside me. Slides her arm around me.

And I push Play and let it wash over us.

Let them wash over us.

Every last wave.

"Andre, Andre, you're too big for that thing! I thought you said that was for the kids!" Mom yells across the yard, her eyes squinting against the brightening sun. She's on our back deck; I forgot it used to be red. Dad complained the entire time he painted it—*I just don't see it. A red deck, Jada?*—until it was finished and he and Mom and me and Whit stood back a ways from the house and Dad just put his arm around Mom's shoulders and squeezed her and she said *not even gonna tell you I told you so.*

"Babe, you think I'm gonna let our boys get in this thing without me first making sure it's safe?" Dad calls back.

"Andre!"

But it's too late—"Cannonball!"—Dad tries to tuck his knees but slips and dives face-first, plummeting into the red and yellow and blue and green balls. He sinks immediately, completely.

Until suddenly his hand juts through the plastic-sphere surface and we hear a garbled "I'm okay. Don't call 911 . . . yet."

And Mom shakes her head, but she's laughing. Ohmigod, she's laughing so hard. And so am I. And so is . . . Q. Our twelve-year-old selves, our shirts off, our swim trunks sagging from belly flopping down the Slip 'N Slide Ms. Barrantes brought over. Whit and Ms. Barrantes come running out the sliding patio door.

"What's going on out here?" Ms. Barrantes asks.

And we all just point to the bouncy house, because we're laughing too hard to talk.

Q's laughing harder than anyone, which explains the shaky refraction.

"Hey J," Q says, his voice so soft and more than a little squeaky.

I reach out to touch him, my hand piercing his bird chest, but he doesn't notice, he's too busy filming young me.

"Yeah," young me says, turning toward him.

He slowly zooms in on my face. "What are you gonna wish for?"

"I can't tell you, man. You trying to sabotage my wish or something?"

Q laughs more. "Never."

"Happy birthday, Q."

"Happy birthday, J."

"Friends always," I said.

"More than always," Q said.

Because for us, *always* meant something different.

Because we held forever in our bird chests, felt it in our peach fuzz.

We were time travelers, see.

We knew the future.

There would be no surprises.

We saw everything coming.

14 DAYS
POSTREANIMATION

3

Whit and I are hanging out on the porch when it happens.

Her face squeezed in discomfort.

"Oh my God, Jamal!"

"What's wrong?"

"Jamal!"

"Tell me what's happening."

"We need to get to the hospital, Jamal. We need to get there right now!"

I grab the packed overnight bags just inside the front door. "Can you walk? Can you make it to the car?"

She grits her teeth. Nods.

"I'll get the car!"

I pull the car up through the grass as close to the front door as I can manage. But Whit doesn't move. Her entire body is shuddering, her face a tight knot of agony.

"Whit, what's wrong? Are you okay? What's happening? Whit! Whit!"

I see her face relax just a bit. "Umm, I'm having a baby, Jamal. That's what's happening!"

I help her into the car, throw the car in reverse, and zoom down the street.

And every light on the way to the hospital—every last one—is a brilliant green. Nothing can stop us.

I pull as close to the OB entrance as possible.

I'm confident we're in a fire lane, but you know, prioritizing. I look over at Whit.

"Do you think you can walk?"

Her head bobs. "I can walk."

I jump out, run around to her side just as another contraction strikes. She groans, pulverizing my hand in her own with the sudden strength of the Incredible Hulk. I choke down a yelp.

We wait for her pain to subside and then carefully get her on her feet. Her hand immediately goes to her back, the other to her belly, that tropey pregnancy pose. "You're doing so good, Whit."

"Don't lie to me," she says.

"I wouldn't."

"I'm really glad you're here." Except the way she says it feels like she's omitted *still*. I'm glad you're *still* here. A side effect of losing so much.

"What? You think I'd miss this?"

448

We take a few steps, but another wave comes raining down, and she leans into me, her face a clenched fist. "I think I may need that wheelchair."

"Yeah? Okay, sure. No problem." Except there are no wheelchairs in sight. Probably a few at the main entrance. But I can't exactly leave her.

The glass door flies open, a wheelchair barreling toward us. It's squeaky AF but easily the best thing all day.

Well, second thing.

The first is the person steering.

"Whit, come on. Sit down. I'm gonna get you up there," Ms. Barrantes says, putting the brakes on.

"Oh my God, I'm so happy to see you," Whit says, as we help her sit, lifting her feet onto the shiny foot pedestals. "I think the baby's coming right now, Ms. B."

"What are you doing back at work already?" I ask her as I unlock the brakes.

Ms. Barrantes spins the chair around. "Just trying to keep busy." She laughs. "Plus, when I stay home, a certain someone thinks he has to keep me company all day."

I shrug. "He doesn't think he has to. He just wants to."

I run ahead, prop open the glass door, move my feet out of the way as she steers Whit straight in. Ms. Barrantes slaps the elevator button.

Whit groans, her hands squeezing the chair handles, her back slightly arched.

The doors open and we all climb/roll in.

449

"Whit, I know it's hard, baby. But try not to push, okay? We're almost to triage. Just hold on. You're doing great, Whit. You and your baby are gonna be just fine."

The elevator chimes, the doors part. Two other nurses waiting on the other side. Whit's OB, Dr. Stokes, behind them, shaking his hands like pom-poms.

"Let's go have a baby," he sings.

I'm not allowed in the delivery room. Well, I guess *not allowed* isn't right. More like *it's probably weird to be in the room when your sister is having a baby.* I stand beside the door, though.

I hear Whit bringing life into this world.

I hear a baby cry out.

I hear Whit gasp.

I've never heard anything more amazing.

Not even close.

2

Whit's beaming when I enter the room.

"Look who's heeerrre. It's your Uncle Jamal."

With every step toward the bed, fear and joy battle for my brain.

But I see her face and it's an immediate KO, joy's hand raised in victory.

It's true, brown eyes are a dime a dozen, but hers are devastating, like twelve photon torpedoes simultaneously crashing into my heart at close range.

"She's a girl," I say. "Called it."

"You did."

"She's the most beautiful human alive, Whit. You did so good. Look what you made. Like, wow. Nothing you do from here on out will ever top this, you know that, right?" I say, laughing.

Whit cracks up. "I wanna argue with you but you're probably right."

"Am I allowed to know her name now, or is it still a secret?"

"Actually, I think I might've just changed it, but I wanted to know what you thought."

"So, let's hear it."

"Jada Quinn Anderson."

And it's perfect.

"You think Dad would feel left out?"

Whit shrugs. "Next kid's his."

"Next kid," I say, but before I can press her for details, someone's knocking at the door. And then Ms. B's walking in, out of her scrubs and in street clothes.

"Hey," Whit says. "Look, Jada, it's our favorite nurse."

Ms. B smiles. Her eyes red, maybe for crying, maybe from exhaustion, I'd put my money on both. "You up for a little company?"

Whit nods. "Jada's been waiting for her godmother to come back and see her."

Ms. B's really cheesing now, and I carefully transfer Jada into her arms. "Jada Quinnnnnnn," she coos. "Jada Quinnnnn . . ."

And okay, I know it's not possible for a newborn, but I swear Jada grins.

A familiar voice at the door. "Heard there was a party in here," Autumn says, flowers and a string of balloons in one hand, two gift bags squeezed together in her other.

I hurry over, take the balloons and flower bouquet.

Kiss her face and feel the rush I always get when she kisses me back.

"Hey, baby," I say.

"Hey, baby," she sings back.

"Eww, get a room, you two," Whit yells, waving her hands like we physically stink.

"But not a room *here* anytime soon," Ms. B pipes up, giving us her patented stare. "You hear me, you two?"

And we crack up, even though we know she's serious as hell.

Because we know she's serious as hell.

She's already told us she's gonna use the time she has on her hands to make sure we all stay in line. She's already talking about painting a room for Jada, when she watches her when Whit starts back up school in the fall.

I wonder if it'll be Q's room.

Part of me hopes not.

But also, I think Q would like that.

Would want that.

And then just when I think this room can't possibly be full of more joy.

Three rapid taps on the door, and standing there with more shiny foil balloons in one hand, a vase of yellow flowers clutched against his chest, and tears in his eyes is . . .

"Whit, ohmigod, ohmigod, I can't believe . . . I'm so sorry I wasn't here, baby. But wow." He moves quickly to the bed. "You look so beautiful. Radiant."

"Liar." Whit wipes her eyes. Smooths her hair, which she'd thrown up in a messy bun. "I look terrible."

He kisses Whit's forehead, gently, like she might break. "You've never looked terrible a second in your whole life."

I clear my throat extra loud. Wave at my sister, at Angeles.

"My bad, I'm so rude," Angeles says, pulling me into a hug. "How's my ace?"

"Making it," I say.

"Dang, either you been lifting or you really trying to crack my ribs right now," Angeles says, squeezing my bicep. He rubs the top of my head and then takes in the rest of the room. "Autumn! Did you get that article link I emailed you?"

"The one about renewable energy? Umm, yeah. I read it like three times."

He laughs. "Figured you'd be all over it. How are you?"

"Making it," she echoes.

Whit tugs at Angeles's shirt. "Angeles, there's someone else I want you to meet. This is . . . this is my mama . . . what should I call you?"

"That's Mama B," I chime in.

"Has a nice ring to it," Mama B says. And she turns to Angeles. "Do you want to hold your daughter?"

Angeles grins, his hands shaking. "I'd love to."

He reaches down, and Mama B holds up Jada. "Say good morning, Daddy. We're so happy to see you."

My niece in a room full of people who love her.

Who'll protect her.

And okay, even when you do your best to keep the people you love safe, things still happen. But you still try.

You still love them with your whole self.

Love them forever.

Even if their forever turns out to be not nearly long enough.

"She has your eyes, Jamal," Angeles says.

And I don't know if it's true or not, but it feels good to hear.

"But she has her mama's mouth. Look! Already pouty."

And we all laugh, Whit loudest of all.

"I do *not* have a pouty mouth. *Potty* sometimes, but not pouty."

Angeles nods. "I can already tell she's a heartbreaker."

Jada swaying in Angeles's arms, Jada's tiny eyes fluttering, exhausted.

We all are.

So, how do you know when it's time to stop grieving?

When it's time for our hearts to move on?

I thought it was when the loss stopped hurting so bad.

When breathing stopped being so hard.

But the hurt-intensity isn't letting up.

My heart isn't ready to ease up.

I guess it's like having a physical injury and asking, *how does your body know when to stop hurting?*

We don't get to decide.

We wait.

And while we wait, we maximize our time.

I look toward the window, the sun pushing its way through the closed blinds.

A few tears roll down my face, but I laugh them away.

"She hails from a family of heartbreakers," I say.

We laugh some more.

Because comedy rule number one, jokes are always funnier when they're true.

Dear Q,

Yesterday in therapy, Dr. Ocean suggested that when I miss you so bad it hurts, I should write to you. Which, to be honest, I'm not sure how I feel about this. It's weird, but man, Q, I really wish you were here right now. So here I am.

And I won't lie to you. Since you left, there are days when I really struggle. When I want to do nothing more than stay in bed for the rest of my life, cocooned in a thousand blankets.

I can't tell you how many times a funny thought crosses my mind and I reach for my phone to call you. Every now and then, I do call you—just to hear you say *Wait, are you really contemplating leaving me a voice mail? Listen to me. Texting is your friend.*

Sometimes I scroll through our text chain and just crack up—I did this yesterday while waiting for Dr. Ocean to finish up with a patient, and the receptionist glared at me like I just cut her off in traffic, which I blame you for.

But mainly, I see this as a true testament to your gift.

You're so funny, I *read* your jokes and laugh my ass off.

I guess your jokes are kinda timeless. But don't get a big head or anything, okay? I'm still funnier. Ha!

Speaking of funny, Jada is hilarious. Like, she makes these faces where her entire face scrunches and her little mouth turns up in this awesome smirk. Whit says she's just gassy, but Angeles and I disagree. She's sassy, and we love it. Also, I've pretty much realized I'm never gonna be able to say no to her, so cool, cool.

Your mom is doing okay. A few times a week, we eat dinner together. She's teaching me to cook! Last week, we made enchiladas. And okay, mine tasted a little weird but still! I want you to know I'm going to live up to my promise. She's in good hands, don't worry.

Okay, well, Autumn just got here. I hear her downstairs laughing. She's actually using the front door these days, haha. I guess, eventually everything changes.

That's it for now.

I love you, Q.

Sincerely your favorite co-host,

Jamal

I walk downstairs and into the kitchen. Whit's standing at the island, an empty blender box on the counter, next to what is apparently a new blender. She looks up at me and smiles. "Hey, have a good nap? I didn't wake you up with the noise, did I?"

"Your sister's making her own baby food now," Angeles says, bouncing Jada on his knee. "And we get to be her taste testers for her very first batch. Yay."

Whit shoots Angeles a look, but he's too busy lifting Jada up to sniff her butt. He makes a disgusted face and motions for me. "Hey, favorite uncle, your niece wants you."

I wave him off, and kiss Whit's cheek.

"Nice try, man. But Uncle Jamal doesn't do poop, sorry." I peek into the living room. "Autumn's not here? I thought I heard her."

But before they can answer, someone yells "BOO" behind me, and I nearly jump out of my shoes. I clutch my chest. "Ohmigod, you could've killed me."

Autumn laughs. "You're so easy to scare, I couldn't resist," she says with a shrug.

"Yeah, yeah," I say, pretending to be upset.

"Don't be mad," she says, draping her arms around my neck and pulling me into a kiss. "There, did that help?"

I frown. "A little, but I'm still pretty shaken up."

She laughs, kisses me again. "Now?"

"We're getting there," I say.

"Ohmigod, groan," Whit exclaims. "I thought you guys were going out."

"We are," I say. I turn back to Autumn. "Except Autumn

won't tell me what we're doing."

"We're gonna have fun," Autumn says. "Trust me."

And by fun she meant . . . a bike ride.

"Bike riding is good for the soul," she says.

You should see us, decked out in elbow pads, helmets—the ones with the blinking light *and* the little rearview mirror thingy that extends like an antenna out in front of you—because safety, right?

Whit's alternating between taking pictures and laughing her ass off, although I'd say the ratio is more like thirty to seventy in favor of the laughs. Angeles is pumping Jada's arms up and down, like she's cheerleading. And I swear she's smirking at me.

"You guys look *so* cute," Whit says.

Autumn's one of these people who keeps her bike attached to her car at all times. A hood-rack-having, waterproof-match-carrying human. One of those *nature over Netflix* types who walk around insisting *a little fresh air* is the solution to all our problems.

That being said, I love the heck outa her.

And I gotta admit, she's not wrong. Being outdoors is already making me feel calmer. You know, except for the one-woman paparazzi.

"See you guys soon," Whit calls out after us.

"Remember to use your hand signals," Angeles yells, and I wave goodbye to him with my middle finger.

The wind is howling something fierce; with each gust I jump, the way you do when you're nice and toasty and someone comes in from the cold and rubs their icy feet on you.

"Deadman's hill," Autumn shouts over the breeze.

"Thought you said a nice leisurely ride?"

"Are you down?"

I give her a thumbs-up and we pedal faster, with purpose. Leaves, no match for our rubber-burning, crumble beneath our wheels.

Cars slow down to honk at us and encourage us along. Or maybe to tell us to get out of their way. But either way, people are taking notice.

Autumn pulls up first, straddling her bike with both feet firmly on the ground. "You sure you're up for this?" she asks.

Deadman's Hill is not named ironically. With its steepness, its skid-prone asphalt, to even walk down it feels like you may be unnecessarily putting your life in jeopardy. So to bike down, it is probably not the sanest thing we could do.

But life is nothing if not a series of risks.

Taking chances.

Rolling the dice.

I unsnap and resnap my chin strap, pulling it tighter. I glance over either shoulder; no traffic as far as I can see.

"The only thing I'm worried about is whether you'll be able to keep up," I say.

Autumn laughs. "Oh, please, for the sake of your lungs, I'll try to keep my dust to a minimum."

"Haha, you're hilarious. I hope you're a fan of participation trophies because that's all you're gonna—"

But I don't get to finish my boasts because Autumn is a madwoman.

Autumn starts pedaling feverishly down the slope, before lifting her feet and letting gravity do the rest.

"Hey, you're cheating, man," I yell after her.

She laughs into the wind, howls with excitement, and I push off after her, a little scared, yes, but feeling all sorts of alive.

At the bottom, Autumn throws her arms into the air and laughs.

I'm smiling, laughing. This is what it feels like to find something you've lost: happiness.

Hey guys!

This is gonna be a really, really short video, but also a really cool video—

Becaaauuusee I have a very, very special guest rejoining me!

Jamal! That's right! The gang's back together!

Jamal: Reunited and it feels soooo good. Yep, do not adjust your screen, you aren't seeing things. Q and J, your favorite comedy duo you never knew you needed, is baaaaack.

Q and J: It's Jauunnncccyyyyyyy!

J: Wuuuuut up, guys?!

Q: As you can see he's very excited to be here!

Jamal: The excitedest!

Q: He's even making up words, that's how pumped this man is. So some of you are probably like, why a guest, you've never done a guest before, Q—

And you're right!

KIND OF!

Because this guy—not only has he been one of my best friends since diaper days, he was also one half of Jauncy, a comedy duo-ship we had back in the day . . . then we had a bit of a hiatus—

J: Because I suck

Q: You don't suck, man.

J: C'mon, bro, I sucked.

Q: Okay, you sucked. But you're not sucking anymore.

J: I'm doing my best to not suck. How am I doing, man?

Q: Not bad, not bad. You've got a bright future.

J: That means a lot.

Q: Now look who's getting all emotional. You told me not to get all emotional and now it's you.

J: I'm not being all emotional.

Q: Mm-hmm. It's okay, man. Let it out.

J: Can I just . . . I just wanna say something . . .

Q: The stage is yours, my friend.

J: Life is short. Sometimes more than we know. And you can't prepare for that shit. Even if you could you still wouldn't be prepared. So . . . listen, the best thing you can do is get

464

yourself a good-ass friend. Like this man right here. He's not just my friend. He's my brother.

Q: J.

J: So, yeah, that's all I gotta say about that. Should we . . . let's do what we set out to do.

Q: We got something for y'all.

J: Get ready.

Q: Spoiler alert, it's a . . .

J: No, don't tell 'em.

Q: Can I just say what it's not? I feel like they may think it's an epic poem or a three-act play if we don't at least do that.

J: Okay, fine.

Q: Guys, it's a . . .

J: Wait, you said you were gonna say what it wasn't.

Q: . . . special edition of JAUNNNNCCCYYYYY!

J: Damn, you told 'em.

Q: I mean, they were about to find out in like ten seconds, so.

CUT TO: busy metropolitan sidewalk

Q: Guys, boy, do we have an awesome treat for you today! Because this episode of Jauncy is coming at you from the mean streets of . . .

Camera zooms out to include Jamal in the frame, standing to Q's right

J: New. York. City.

Q: That's right! Jauncy's international!

J: I mean, we're still in the US so technically . . .

Zoom in on Q's face, mad embarrassed

Q: True, true, but you know, NYC's got that melting-pot flavor going on.

Zoom in on Jamal's face, rubbing his chin, eyebrows raised

Q: Damn, you know what? I actually meant to say intercontinental . . .

Zoom in closer on Jamal's face, rubbing his chin and arching his eyebrows even more vigorously

Q: Intercontinental is the same thing as international, isn't it?

J: I think this might be a good time to shout out our lovely camera person, who, incidentally, is also this guy's girlfriend. Say hi to the people, babe.

Camera turns around and is far too close to Autumn's face

A: Hey, everybody. In case you were confused. My name is actually Autumn, not babe, so cool.

Q: Well, okay, now that I've thoroughly embarrassed myself and Autumn's been introduced, I think it's time Jauncy . . .

Q and J: TAKE IT TO THE STREEEEEEETS!

CUT TO: the subway train platform

Q: Yep, you can ask one of us, or all three of us, any one question and we have to answer it truthfully, no matter what.

Lady in Pajamas: I wanna know, who was your first kiss?

Q: Okay, who are you asking?

Lady in Pajamas: All three.

Q: Okay, let's see. Molly Robinson.

J: Ohmigod, what the hell?! Molly Robinson!?

Autumn: Who's Molly Robinson?

J : One of the cafeteria ladies!

Q (shrugging): She was like nineteen.

Jamal: Whatever. I guess purple meat loaf wasn't the only thing they were serving.

Jamal winks hard at the camera

CUT TO: the sidewalk in front of a pharmacy

Quincy: What do you think of the legislation passed earlier this month preventing people over the age of eighty from purchasing prescription medications?

Dude with Huge Beard: I mean . . . it sucks, for sure . . . but uh . . . frankly, there's a lot of people in this country and, like, would it be that bad if, like, you know . . .

Q: I'm not sure I follow.

Huge Beard (shrugging): If you're eighty, I mean, you've lived a pretty long life already . . .

Q: So you're suggesting we let old people . . . die?

Huge Beard: We're not going to physically kill them or anything like that.

Q: Just, like, take their life-saving medications away?

Huge Beard (snapping his fingers): Exactly. Like, how many rent-controlled apartments you think are gonna open up now?

Q: I . . . I don't even know what to say.

Huge Beard: You know what they say, time's up!

Q: That's not at all what that phrase is referring to . . .

Huge Beard (rubbing his chin): It's a good time to be an estate lawyer, damn.

Man Pushing Stroller: When I heard about it, I just shook my head. That's the world we live in, though.

Q: How do you think this is gonna affect people eighty years old and up?

Man Pushing Stroller: Honestly? They'll find a way to get the medicine. Probably buy it off the streets.

Q: People sell blood pressure pills on the street?

Man Pushing Stroller: Man, this is New York City, people sell actual blood on the street.

A chime plays and CORRECT flashes on the screen

CUT TO: promenade along the river

Jamal: Which of the three of us is cuter?

Jamal smiles brightly

Lady in Beret: The girl holding the camera.

Turtleneck Teen: Her. Definitely. Those eyes, ohmigod. She single?

Jogger 1: She's cute. But I gotta go with this dude. How tall are you?

Quincy: Six two.

Jogger 1: Bet you've screwed in lots of bulbs.

Zoom in on Q's face, perplexed

Jogger 2: I think she and the tall kid are tied.

Jamal (winking to the camera): For second place?

Jogger 2: No, that's you.

Jamal: I think it's the lighting where I'm standing. It doesn't really accentuate my best features.

A buzzer sounds and WRONG flashes on the screen

CUT TO: a park bench

Chess Player: Okay, umm, would you rather live forever and be liked but never loved or live for a short time but be really, truly loved?

Whit: Hella love, easy.

Mama B: Better to have love, even for a short while.

Autumn: Love, hands down.

Jamal: I mean, love is always the answer.

Zoom in slowly on Q's face

Q: Yo, if I got the choice to lead the life I've led, or start over and live forever but even slightly differently? Honestly? I'd choose this. Knowing everything I know now, I'd still choose this life. Exactly the same. Every time.

Chess Player: You must have an awesome life, young man.

A chime plays and CORRECT flashes on the screen

Q: Well, that's our time, guys.

J: It's been hella fun.

Q: A wild ride.

J: Super rad.

Q: You forgot how we wrap the episode, didn't you?

J: Umm, nooo.

Q: Yeah, you did.

J: Yeah, I did.

Jamal cracks up

Q (also laughing): You're supposed to say we hope you enjoyed this special edition of . . .

J: Then we say Jauncy in the Streets, right?

Q applauds, both Jamal and Q laughing into the camera

Q: There he is, ladies and gentlemen. The Jamal we know and kinda love sometimes. Welcome back, man. So, you got it now? You ready to finish this thing?

J: I got it, man. I'm ready.

Q: Okay, let's try it again. This time together.

J: Again, but this time together. I got you.

Fade to black

Acknowledgments

Writing is often a solitary endeavor, but truly this book isn't in your hands without an abundance of contributors, most of whom I addressed in OOA's hella long acknowledgements. So, this time we'll keep it short and sweet—

Educators, librarians, teachers, I can't thank you enough for your enthusiastic support. Growing up in an educator-librarian household, I understand the power of placing the right book in the right hands. Thank you for helping my stories find great new homes.

Thank you to my incredible family, near and far, but especially Kennedy, Brooklyn, Pam, Mama, Ally, Pops, and Grey. Thank you for forever holding me down, especially in the ways I don't always see, but most definitely feel. I love you all.

Thank you to a few of my oldest and wisest friends and family: Scales, Ariana, Aunt Sheila, Aunt Dana, TJ, Tosha, Michael and Melanie G., Pam H., Tanya W., Carolyn Z., Esther H., Joyce S., Terry K., Rob B., Drew O., Amma O., Jesse M., Khadijah J., Karen M., Becky L., Michelle S., Alechia P., Bailey C., and Jillian G. You are some of the rock-steadiest people I have the privilege of knowing.

A special shout-out goes to my creative family: Ashley W., Tiffany J., Angie T., Nic S., Dhonielle C., Mark O., Jalissa C., Saraciea F., Patrice C., Kwame M., Dana D., Bri C., and Natasha D.—I can't begin to thank you all enough for accepting me as I am, showing me the ropes, and making me believe I have the chops to keep pulling this off.

Thank you to my exceptional agent, Beth, for your unwavering confidence, hella jokes, and ridiculous hustle; and to my amazing editor, Ben, for rolling up your sleeves and helping me excavate the best version of these stories.

Thank you to my beyond awesome US publisher, Katherine, and her imprint Katherine Tegen Books, my great UK editor, Rachel, and UK publisher Macmillan, the outstanding cover designer, David, and gifted artist, Stephanie, my stellar publicist, Aubrey, all of the brilliant marketing minds, every diligent assistant (Tanu!), and the entire hardworking, uber-dedicated team. I'm so very fortunate to have each of you by my side on this dream of a journey.

Thank you to the great people at Gallt and Zacker, who are as good of humans as they are agents. The same goes for Gemma and Victoria at Bent; thanks for being the best advocates.

Thank you to the Beoples. To Mojo's for the best coffee and better vibes. And to Cleveland, my home no matter where I live, for still rocking.

Truly, the list of people deserving of my gratitude is easily longer than this book's first draft, ha.

So, to YOU I say:

I hope WE live forever, but if not, I want YOU to know I'd travel back in time to save YOU, or dive headfirst into any situation were there the slightest chance to pull YOU out.

Thank YOU for your encouragement, for your kicks-in-the-butt, for the laughs, for the caffeine, for the chocolate, for the supportive texts and savage emails, for rolling your eyes, for your unreserved smile, for loaning me your belief, for bugging me, for reminding me, for your ear, for giving me space, for your honesty, and for your love, always.

YOU are the heartbeat within these pages. I hope you hear it.

All my love,
justin